THE DAYS OF GUNS AND ROSES

BY NATHANIEL WEBB

Published by Vulpine Press in the United Kingdom in 2019

Cover by Claire Wood

ISBN: 978-1-83919-296-8

www.vulpine-press.com

Rose of all Roses, Rose of all the world!
You, too, have come where the dim tides are hurled
Upon the wharves of sorrow, and heard ring
The bell that calls us on; the sweet far thing.
Beauty grown sad with its eternity
Made you of us, and of the dim grey sea.

W.B. Yeats, *The Rose of Battle*

PROLOGUE

21 DAYS

Seventy-nine nights ago, the door opened for the first time.

The door stood upright and alone at the back of the great hall, not a part of any wall. It was a plain wooden door of the sort found throughout the Castle Forlorn, and despite its strange solitude, it had maintained its place for as long as even the old Marcher Lord could remember. It had always been ignored; now it was a symbol of terror.

The great hall was an old place, originally built as a feasting hall in a time when the Marcher Lords of Finalhaven hosted warriors by the hundreds. The Castle Forlorn grew erratically around it, absorbed it, changed it from a lone building to one room of many. In those days, whole armies sat alongside the Irregulars and the castle guard, spilling from low benches set before tables laden with steaming food. Now the long, flickering shadows thrown by the hearth fire outnumbered the people.

In the council chamber of the Marcher Lord, one floor up and across the castle from the great hall, the senior staff were drawing up plans for the defense of the Castle Forlorn against an invasion of unknown strength by an unknown foe. Guardsmen paced the walls and corridors, anticipating danger in the shadows more keenly than they had in a generation. But in the great hall, the Irregulars, who trusted that their foe would not appear for twenty-one days, threw a party.

The door watched as the Irregulars drank and laughed.

1

Jack Twelve-Fingers played a seven-stringed guitar. He sat on a long, pitted table covered with half-empty wine bottles that jostled as his foot beat time on a bench. His left hand moved lazily across the strings, forming chords that glimmered momentarily before collapsing, like the embers smoldering beneath the great fire. His right hand strummed and slapped in magnificent flamenco flourishes and rhythmic strikes.

Michael Fletcher sat down the bench from Jack, patiently folding roses from fragile white paper, following a secret mathematics. As he finished each rose, he held it close to his mouth and whispered a word that was lost beneath the riot of Jack's guitar. Each paper flower softened and curled and became real as, smiling, he placed it gently on a growing pile at his feet.

By the great hearth, Ernest Graves leaned forward in his high-backed leather chair. The firelight glinted in his eyes as he spun an epic poem for Daniel and Flora, two squires from Albion. The knights to whom they swore service were in council above, and the squires sat childlike on the flagstones at Ernest's feet with their knees hugged to their chests. Nearby, their fellows Merry and Luke played chess with yellowed bone pieces and a board carved into the floor. Merry sacrificed her knight to protect her queen, and Luke wondered if he stood any chance at all.

Uther and Wulf Blodring stood watching the game. Uther, the older brother, had his hands clasped behind his back and occasionally murmured or clucked his tongue at a surprising or unsatisfactory move. Wulf, the younger, nodded at the boldness of Merry's sacrifice, but his nervous eyes flickered towards the door.

From an archway in a shadowed corner Julian de Luna, the head of the kitchen, emerged bearing an overloaded tray on one hand, sweeping the other in a dramatic gesture as he showed his best grin. Behind him followed Wentworth, his assistant, his hands full with more wine bottles. Julian deposited his offering on the nearest long table, turning the motion into a theatrical bow. The Irregulars raised a ragged cheer, the next course driving thoughts of death momentarily from their minds.

Seventy-nine days ago a servant found the door slightly ajar, with the corpse of Alexander Cho sprawled out before it. He had a dagger in his back and his right hand outstretched, with "100 days" written in his cold blood on the stone floor. The servant ran shouting to the Marcher Lord. The senior staff was woken, the blood scrubbed away, the corpse carried off, and the door shut, but it couldn't be moved. Nobody had dared reopen it.

Jack glanced over his shoulder at the door and struck a wrong note. The noise startled the room. Michael tore the paper in his hands and became completely still. Ernest repeated himself. Luke put himself into check; Merry didn't see his mistake. Uther and Wulf caught each other's eyes then looked away. Julian disappeared back down the stairs, his moment past, a mouse among men.

The castle cats stole scraps from forgotten plates.

By a great arched window, Bronwyn Queen, captain of the Irregulars, looked westward out over the ocean, where a heavy fog was rolling in from the deep darkness. Night reached around the torchlight to touch her, and she zipped her sweater up to her throat. She should have been upstairs with the senior staff, but tonight she was with her Irregulars. Tonight, her hopes rested with a glass bottle that bobbed tight-corked in the gray sea.

It carried a message that might never be read, if read might not be understood, and if understood might never be acted upon, for all the good that action might do. It carried their last prayer against a force that for seventy-nine days had been pressing down on them from all sides, walling them in, until she gave the order that they eat and drink and dance and laugh and for one night, at least, ignore the helplessness that had seized all their throats.

Her message had twenty-one days to be found before an unknown enemy opened the door at the top of the hall and turned their weapons on everyone in the Castle Forlorn, the way they'd done for Alexander Cho.

CHAPTER 1

13 DAYS

There was just one photograph left taped to the stone wall of Emily Sledge's quarters at Harkness Academy. She'd left it for last, but now, with the walls bare, her clothes folded and packed away into a duffel bag, and her weapons and exercise equipment boxed up, the photo had to come down.

Emily tugged at a corner of the photo, and it resisted for a second, then came free with a sudden snap of broken tape. Looking up at her from the picture were four laughing faces framed by furry hoods, one of them her own, the others her three best friends across all four years at Harkness. They stood in the snow, giving various signs of victory above the corpse of a long toothy purple worm.

Chris McLeod had a fist raised in triumph. He was a Mental, a genius; he'd spent four years building fighting robots and had left school a month early to join a team in the wilderness of Madawaska trying to cut their way through the Veil between dimensions. Kayo Jackson, making vees with the fingers on both hands, was an Arcane—even in the photo there was a hint of purple fire in her eyes—and she was going back to her parents' farm for the summer before starting a job as a junior defender in Cascadia. Andrea Butcher was a Combat like Emily; the two girls stood shaking hands in the picture. Emily had always thought that they shared

4

the same dream job, but just yesterday Andy had announced that she'd been asked to stay on at Harkness as a teachers' assistant and had said yes.

The alarm clock buzzed, making Emily jump. She'd already been up for half an hour, packing. With a sigh, Emily placed the photo at the bottom of a small wooden box she had reserved for her prized possessions. She gently shut off the alarm and turned to her dresser, where a few last mementos waited to be packed away.

Emily picked up a long, serrated fang from the dresser and twisted it nervously between her finger and thumb. It was ridiculous, really, how anxious she was. They'd been through a lot in their time at Harkness. Her freshman year, Emily had almost been expelled for breaking a teacher's femur with an illegal leg lock. Sophomore year, she and Andrea had ventured into the caverns below campus on a field trip that got lost for almost two weeks, surviving on cave moss until a foul-smelling lizardman had led them back above ground. Last year all four of them had contrived to share a semester abroad in Trolldom, driving off lindworms that still threatened rural communities. The first worm they'd killed was memorialized in the photo from Emily's wall; the last one had left this fang in Emily's shoulder as a farewell present.

None of those things had scared her, not really. If there was one thing Emily Sledge knew, it was that she was tough. Like every student at Harkness, Emily had a Gift, and hers was for fighting. She was faster than a normal person, and a lot stronger, but more than anything she could take a ton of punishment and stand up again with a smile on her face.

None of which was any help on Career Day.

Emily set the lindworm fang on the photo in the wooden box. It felt as though everybody had a job lined up but her, like she was going to be fumbling from interview to interview alone while all the other seniors were saying their goodbyes, swapping addresses, getting in one last hookup or game of splinty. The worst was that there was only one job she really wanted, and it wasn't with any of the Gifted Nations or Shadow Academies looking for junior defenders and teachers' assistants that she was meeting today.

Emily took a pair of trophies off the dresser and stowed them next to the fang, flipped one upside down, then flipped it back. The Sabre & Torch Society, that was the group for her. It was a recruitment year for them, and Emily knew as well as anyone that every once in a blue moon they took a student fresh out of Harkness, Killoke, Great Plains, Starling, or one of the other Shadow Academies. It didn't happen often, but it happened.

Turning away from the dresser, Emily grabbed a suit jacket off a pile of boxes and pulled it on. Though it had been custom tailored to her broad-shouldered, six-foot frame, Emily was used to the loose cotton trousers and unrestrictive tank tops of the fighting ring. Even body armor—hell, even old-school metal armor—felt better than her interview suit. At least armor was supposed to be heavy. The suit was tight in weird places, too stiff to bend her elbows easily, and would probably tear if she rotated her shoulders fully. And the shoes—well, at least the heels made her a bit taller, though they'd be impossible to run in.

Emily glanced at her alarm clock. She was almost an hour early, but there was no point waiting around in her old room. All the adventures, all the medals and trophies and awards—and she was eighteen years old and off to interview for jobs like she wasn't even Gifted at all.

"Okay, fighters, settle!" barked Montrose to the dozen or so Combat students assembled outside the doors to the gym. The head of the Combat school at Harkness, Montrose looked every inch the fighter. He seemed as wide as he was tall, and his blocky head was grizzled and gray. His scarred face, his broken nose, his cauliflower ears, all told stories of a life's experience fighting before he retired to an easy life of whipping new fighters into shape. Emily adored him—all the Combat students did.

Montrose smiled at them. "We've had some times in this gym, fighters. You fought each other. You took apart whatever junk the Mentals could throw at you. Some of you even had the guts to step into the ring with me for one or two throws." The students laughed; getting your ass kicked by Montrose was a rite of passage for Combat students. "Now I know you're nervous about this Career Day, and I'm here to tell you, you got nothin' to be afraid of. The folks in there are lookin' for fighters, and that's what you lot are. So just get in there, give 'em a big smile—except you, Trout—and you'll get snapped up." The fighters laughed again, and Trout grinned, showing black gaps where about half his teeth should have been.

As Montrose continued his pep talk, Emily tried to peer past him into the gym. The school staff had set up a series of card tables out on the concrete, and representatives from a number of Gifted Nations, Shadow Academies, and independent groups were waiting behind them.

Hoping against hope, Emily looked for the massive form of Durgan dun Raven, the Sabre & Torch warrior who had come by Harkness once or twice a year to confer on some sticky problem with his friends among the teachers. Dun Raven was a hard man to miss, and there was no sign of him. With sinking hopes, Emily wondered if maybe the S&T had sent someone else.

Dun Raven hadn't always been their man at Harkness. Freshman year, Emily had gone to see a presentation by a fighter named Alexei Laredo just a week before he'd been eaten by an ogre in Minnesota. A long, lanky knife-fighter, he'd sat with his boots up on an expensive conference table, picking his teeth with a dagger while he told them stories of his adventures in a nearly incomprehensible drawl. When he was done talking about the Sabre & Torch's mission he'd tipped his hat and winked right at Emily. She'd fallen in love that day, not with Alexei, but with the S&T. They operated outside of the bounds of the Gifted Nations, crossed borders with impunity, and went wherever they were needed, whenever something unexpected fell through a tear in the Veil.

"Sledge! You listening back there?" Montrose's battlefield bark cut through into Emily's memories.

"Yes, sir," Emily replied instantly.

"All right, then," rumbled Montrose. "You're mine until graduation, don't forget. I'm about to let you loose, but let me give you a last bit of advice. If you want to go for an opponent's head but his guard's too good, you gotta change your strategy or you're gonna waste yourself punchin' his hands. Same thing here. You probably got a job you're gunnin' for, and that's fine, but don't let that make you blind." The fighters nodded nervously. "Okay, fighters, move out!"

Emily shuffled towards the doors with her fellow seniors, but Montrose put a plate-sized hand on her shoulder.

"Not you, Sledge. Got a word for you."

Montrose and Emily watched her classmates enter the gym. As they passed through the high double doors, each of them leapt to slap the lintel some twenty feet above. It was an old good-luck tradition, and the concrete wall was worn thin from generations of Combat students hoping for a little good fortune in whatever danger they were headed towards.

"Listen, Sledge," Montrose said. "You know I was talking to you a second ago."

"I know, sir. I just want to find a job."

Montrose shook his gray head. "Don't lie to me. We've spilled blood together. You got your eye set on the Sabre & Torch, but they ain't here. Durgan was thinking of coming down, but he's dealing with some witch up in Nova Scotia callin' herself the Ice Queen."

"Thanks for telling me, sir." Emily looked away to hide her disappointment.

"This ain't the end. You'll get another chance, you know."

"Yeah, when I'm twenty-five," Emily said. "You know the S&T only recruits every seven years. What if I get soft? What if I get comfortable where I am?"

"Emily Sledge, in four years of throwing down with you the one thing I never figured was that you'd get soft. Ask Bozer—it's been years and his leg still aches when it rains. Every one of my students has the Gift, but they ain't all born fighters. You are, and that ain't what I'm worried about."

Emily frowned. "Then what, sir?"

"You remember what I told you after you busted Bozer's leg, when you were a freshman?"

"Honestly…?"

Montrose laughed. "No, didn't think you would. You were too busy pissin' your pants that I was gonna expel you. Bet you were surprised when Bozer retired and you got to stick around, huh? Anyway—I told you you had to start thinkin' *before* you hit, not after. Look, around here you were queen bee for a few years, but when you're a student all that matters is how you fight. Out there it ain't so simple. You can't just bust your way through all your problems. And you gotta listen to your boss." His eyes narrowed. "You hear me?"

Emily shook her head. "Sir, you taught us to trust our instincts. That's true even if I'm the new kid at some job, right? And besides, a lot of people have power they didn't earn. They were born in the right place at the right time, or their parents were. Am I supposed to trust them over myself?"

"You think you shouldn't have trusted Bozer when he was trying to tap out of your leg lock, Sledge?"

"Sir…" Emily paused, then remembered she was about to graduate and plunged ahead. "Mr. Bozer was a jerk and we both know it."

Montrose gave a great bark of laughter. "Well, no one can say I didn't try, dammit. Go get 'em, Sledge."

"So, Miss…Sledge, is it?" The Albian woman looked up from the short list of experience and accomplishments Emily had handed her, giving her a dry gaze over horn-rimmed glasses. She had introduced herself as Miss Scrivener, and although her pants suit was more or less indistinguishable from Emily's, she wore it with the certainty of a woman born to middle management. She had long blonde hair pulled back into the tightest, sleekest ponytail Emily had ever seen and bland brown eyes behind her thick glasses. Her English accent seemed to resonate in her long, straight nose.

"Yup, Sledge like the hammer," Emily replied. That usually got a chuckle, but as far as Emily could tell Miss Scrivener hadn't even heard her. She was back in Emily's resume, running a manicured fingernail down the sheet.

"Now, Miss Sledge. It says here you won the Harkness Combat School tournament both last year and this year, is that so?"

"I did!" Emily replied. "Hammer the first time, knives the second. A senior pretty much always wins, so a lot of underclassmen don't even enter, but I went for it junior year and I ended up taking it."

"I imagine you were very pleased," said Miss Scrivener without looking up.

"Well, yeah, wouldn't you be?"

"I shouldn't think so, no. I'm not a fighter, Miss Sledge; in fact, I find displays of the Gift of Combat somewhat distasteful." She sighed and looked Emily right in the eye. "Nevertheless, your sort is quite useful for fighting back the dimensional riff-raff that comes through the Veil, and heaven knows Albion is no less prone than any of the Gifted Nations to such incursions."

She paused as though waiting for a reply, but Emily wasn't really sure what to say. A few seconds passed, then Miss Scrivener sighed again.

"Very well, let's get on with it. Miss Sledge, why would you like to work for the Gifted Nation of Albion?"

This question, at least, Emily had prepared for. "Well, Miss Scrivener, I'd like the opportunity to improve my skills while defending innocent people, Gifted and regular alike." She'd practiced that one in front of the mirror more than once. It was true, as far as it went, in the way that saying "That's so nice of you!" about a present you don't like was true.

"I see." Miss Scrivener frowned slightly. "And what has that got to do with Albion?"

Emily shifted in her chair. "I'm sorry?"

"I said, what has that got to do with Albion? Why would you like to 'improve your skills' serving Arthur the Thirtieth in particular?"

"Oh, well…" Emily thought furiously. She wasn't ready for this one. When she'd imagined her interviews, after she gave her perfectly prepared answer, her interviewer would nod sagely at her wisdom. Then her imagination would fail her, so the middle bits were always hazy, but the day-dreams always ended with the interviewer shaking her hand and saying, "We're lucky to have you, Emily!"

"Miss Sledge? If I'm not terribly mistaken, I asked you a question." Miss Scrivener was still there, tapping her fingernails on the table. So this was what the middle part of the interview was like.

"Well…well, I guess I just want to be a part of such a long tradition of, um, tradition." *Where did that come from?* Unlike her last answer, that one was a total lie. Emily didn't care about tradition, especially not the way the Albians did it. They'd had thirty kings in a row, and all of them were named Arthur. Emily always had to stifle a giggle when she thought of the current young king, Arthur XXX.

"I see. Our tradition of tradition." Miss Scrivener jotted something down on the edge of Emily's resume. Emily imagined what it probably said: "disrespectful." The thought of this fancy Albian woman, who had probably never been in danger a moment in her life, thinking Emily was disrespectful made her suddenly feel very disrespectful indeed.

"Is it true Arthur the Twenty-Ninth had a secret daughter?" Emily asked.

Miss Scrivener's eyes widened for a moment, then her mouth tight-ened into a straight line and her nostrils flared. She gave Emily a cold, appraising stare.

"Where did you hear that?" she asked quietly.

"Oh, here and there," replied Emily airily. "You know how it is with rumors."

"Well, I can assure you that it is most certainly not true. As I'm sure you've heard here and there, the Albian kings only have sons. The Line of Arthur extends back over a millennium."

"I'm not a Mental or anything, I'm just saying it seems unlikely. Statistically speaking, you know?"

"Miss Sledge." Miss Scrivener took off her reading glasses and folded them with finality. "Thank you for your time."

At the next interview table, Emily took her seat across from a tiny white-haired man. As if she hadn't had enough of stuffy old Albians, this interview was with the Lancers. They were an order of dragon hunters, originally from Albion, which had probably been pretty cool five hundred years ago when dragons still existed. Apparently they'd been really good at their jobs, though, because all the dragons had been hunted. Emily wasn't totally clear on what the Lancers did nowadays.

The relic across the table wore an old-fashioned tweed suit with a red pocket square; his oversized jacket was threadbare at the elbows and had a few moth holes on one lapel. He peered at her blearily from under bushy eyebrows, his mouth moving quietly in his lined face. Emily stared back, feeling grouchy and not inclined to make the first move. Eventually, the old Lancer seemed to have seen what he wanted to see, and he spoke in a quavering voice.

"Hello there, young man. And what can I do for you?"

His name was Corporal Rupert Brimble and he had a memory like a leaking boat. Emily spent twenty minutes trying to bail him out, but she never did discover what Lancers did now that all the dragons were gone.

Failure followed failure as the morning wore on. After Brimble, Emily interviewed with Irina Glukhov, a dour, stocky woman from Korporatsiya who made Emily demonstrate fighting stances for nearly an hour as she snapped photos and took notes in a big manila file. Herbert

Ailes was a small, twitchy academic in a rumpled corduroy jacket, representing a "consortium of interested parties" obsessed with corporate espionage and hiring Gifted security for what he assured Emily would be a dull six months. Last was Professor Wygand, the head of the Combat school at Great Plains. When he suggested for the third time that perhaps he and Emily ought to fight to test her skills, she no longer felt any surprise that he hadn't just hired one of his own students.

And that, unfortunately, was it.

It was nearly midnight, and Emily couldn't sleep. Thinking about graduation the next day was bad enough, all her friends' families asking what she would be doing, but such an epic run of disastrous interviews—she just couldn't put it aside, however much she'd laughed with Kayo and Andrea about it at dinner. She lay on her bed staring up at the bare stone ceiling, visions of calamity running through her mind. Not only was she not joining the Sabre & Torch this year, if her instincts were anything to go by, she was about to be unleashed on the world with no way to get by.

She couldn't go back to living with her dad. He could barely afford to feed himself, let alone another fighter with their massive appetite. Maybe she could strike out into the non-Gifted world, turn her back on fighting monsters and defending innocents and get rich as a pro wrestler, or whatever really athletic normal people did.

Emily wasn't totally sure. She'd grown up in the Gifted World, which hid beneath the mundane world like a message written in invisible ink: easy to spot if you knew how, but something most people would never think to look for. Her whole life, she'd been prepared for the moment of her graduation, when she'd take a job defending the vast mass of unknowing billions that made up the mundane world against incursions through the Veil. She'd been raised by Gifted parents, had gone to school with nothing but Gifted classmates. If she couldn't find a place in the secret machinery of Gifted society, she had no place at all.

She swung her legs off the bed, sat for a moment, then stood up decisively. Zipping up a hoodie over her T-shirt, Emily headed out into the hallway of her dorm. Moving silently on the heavy rugs that covered the cold floor, not wanting to wake any of her classmates the night before graduation, she followed a familiar path outside. In the moonlight she crossed the empty quad, heading for the gym, but at the last moment she took a side path towards the great, tottering tower that housed the offices of the Combat teachers.

The Tower of Trials, or as the students called it, the Fighthouse, was famously climbable. Irregular and half-broken stones jutting out at odd angles made perfect hand- and foot-holds, and its gentle curve, always suggesting that it might collapse at any moment, was easy on one side and challenging on the other.

Standing in the tower's long shadow, Emily spat into her hands and began to climb. She was going up the hard way, beneath the curve of the upper floors, so if tonight were the night of its collapse the Fighthouse would fall directly on top of her. The moon was completely hidden behind the tower's black bulk, so that she moved upwards in near-darkness, trusting her instincts and experience to lead her.

A dozen yards up there was a particularly sharp outward angle to the curve of the tower. This spot was known as the Backbreaker, both for the contortions it demanded of anyone who climbed it and the handful of students who had been sent home on stretchers after falling from this point.

Sweating, Emily dug her fingers into a gap where mortar had crumbled away, then swung one leg up to catch a jutting rock. She began to gently ease her weight back onto that leg, when a light snapped on unexpectedly in an open window a foot above her head. Surprised and blinded, Emily tried to pull herself in to hug the wall.

There was a sharp crack as the rock beneath her foot snapped. Suddenly she was swinging free, dangling from her fingertips thirty or forty feet above cobblestones.

"You hear something?" A low voice rumbled from the window above—Montrose's voice.

"No," came the reply, another warrior's bass, but with impatience where Montrose's had kindness. It was familiar, but Emily couldn't place it, especially with her mind on not getting killed. She could pull herself straight up by her fingers, but that would put the top of her head over the windowsill.

"Drank too much, I guess," replied Montrose.

"Always do, end of the year comes 'round," was the familiar stranger's reply.

"You bring out the worst in me, Durgan," Montrose said with a laugh. Durgan—dun Raven from the Sabre & Torch! His was the voice Emily couldn't place. He was here, when Montrose had told her just that morning that he was up north. Dammit, maybe she should just pull herself up and say hello. Despite her strength, Emily was starting to get tired, her fingers feeling the strain of supporting her entire weight.

"I'm for bed, though," came dun Raven's voice. "Had quite a swim today. Expect I'll be gone early tomorrow."

"Night, Durgan," Montrose said. "Think about what I told you. You might be surprised."

"We'll see," dun Raven rumbled, and Emily heard his footsteps heading back down the spiral staircase that ran the inside wall of the tower. She hung there for another moment, indecisive, then made up her mind as Montrose's footsteps headed upstairs. With a grunt, she hauled herself upward until her chin cleared the windowsill, then threw an arm over the stone and pulled herself inside.

She collapsed onto a stone landing, panting in relief beneath a wrought-iron chandelier. The stairs curved away above and below her, so she figured she'd give Montrose and dun Raven a minute to get wherever they were going before she headed back to the dorm.

After she caught her breath, Emily stood and turned downstairs. She was about to head back down the tower when she heard Montrose's voice behind her.

"Sledge? What're you doin' here?"

Emily turned in surprise. Montrose was quiet for such a big guy. What on earth could she say...?

"Um—what are *you* doing here?"

"Forgot to put out the light, Sledge." He looked at her workout clothes and the open window behind her, then laughed. "One last climb, huh?"

"Something like that, sir," replied Emily.

"Can't sleep?"

"Nope."

"I'll be honest, Sledge. You didn't do too great today."

Emily's mouth quirked in a half-smile. "I know."

"Yeah, I figured." Montrose gave her a long, appraising look. "Well, listen. I shouldn't tell you, but it might make you sleep easier. You've got one more interview."

CHAPTER 2

12 DAYS

Stentorious Knowles had been headmaster at Harkness Academy for as long as anyone could remember. Nobody Emily had ever asked knew how old he was, but as his voice had vanished almost completely over the last quarter-century, he was no longer up to the task of delivering welcoming addresses, commencement speeches, or any other of a headmaster's usual oratory duties.

Emily stood sweating in her graduation robes in the bright New Hampshire sunshine, thinking for the hundredth time how, in a way, it was kind of a blessing that Knowles was so far past his useful years. It meant that throughout the school year, various luminaries from the Gifted world came to lecture and exhort the students to greatness in the headmaster's place. Most of them came from the other Shadow Academies, Harkness's sister schools around the world, and they tended to have interesting things to say about the stuff they'd studied or fought.

During Emily's time she'd also heard representatives from many of the Gifted Nations: Cascadia, Trolldom, Korporatsiya, Albion, and of course the Secret Commonwealth, where Harkness was located and where Emily had lived her whole life. In contrast to the academics, she hadn't really liked the politicians; their speeches had seemed nearly identical, all about how great their home Nations were.

Now the commencement speaker at her graduation was the First Baron Wasteland of Deseret, and she expected to dislike him just as much—or even more, if his title was anything to go by. A few years ago Deseret hadn't even been a Nation, just a bunch of scattered weirdos doing what they wanted in the sands of the American southwest with nobody bothering them. Then a spellcaster calling himself Baron Wasteland had come out of nowhere, healed some people and made some friends, and a new Gifted Nation was born.

Headmaster Knowles was making what Emily guessed was an introduction of Baron Wasteland from a small stage set before the graduates, who all stood in neat rows seeming just as uncomfortable as Emily under the beating sun. Listening to the Headmaster was like listening to a dying air conditioner. After what seemed to be the ultimate powdery gasp, Emily felt the students and families assembled on the quad collectively hold their breath: was the headmaster dead, or just done? But then Knowles shakily indicated to stage right and shuffled away to make space for the Baron to a smattering of awkward applause.

The Baron looked stupid. He was younger than Emily had expected, tan and fit with a huge white-toothed grin, but the colored beads woven into his long blonde hair made him look like a surfer who'd gone Rasta on a trip to Jamaica, then insisted on sticking with it back at his day job. He wore a long white robe stitched with gold, obviously expensive and not at all subtle.

This wouldn't play in the Secret Commonwealth, Emily thought. Northeasterners were a bit more discerning. It was sort of disappointing to think that the people of Deseret could be taken in so easily.

"Hello, Harkness," the Baron said. "For anyone who doesn't know me, I'm the First Baron Wasteland, First Father, Layer-On of Hands, Beloved Giver of Laws, Bringer of Miracles, and Wise Administrator of the Gifted Nation of Deseret." He gave a brief smirk as though it wasn't his fault he had to recite all those titles. "For your graduation speech, I want to talk to you about the history of the Gifted. I'm sure you've heard it

18

before. Hundreds of times, for some of you." That smirk again. "But try to listen anyway, because it's all about you and your place in the universe, which I'm sure you've been thinking a lot about recently. Plus my speechwriter did a really good job on it, and we wouldn't want to hurt his feelings."

Emily shifted uncomfortably in her heavy robe. The Baron seemed charming enough, but he was clearly about to give the traditional graduation speech, which explained the three Gifts and laid out the rules of Gifted society. It was dull stuff, necessary to drill into kids and parents from mundane families but beyond redundant to those who, like Emily, had been raised in the Gifted world.

The Baron cleared his throat and squared his shoulders, looking somehow more formal and respectable than he had a moment ago. "For as long as mankind has existed," he began, "there have been Gifted. Whether these lucky few are called by Heaven or just the result of a fortunate arrangement of molecules, nobody knows. But we do know that since the beginning, the same rules have governed our society. The exploits of the earliest Gifted have come down to us as legends, and if we know how to read them, they have a lot to teach us.

"Think of brave Achilles, standing proud before the walls of Troy. He's soaked in the blood of his enemies, but there isn't a scratch on him. He's just won eternal fame as one of history's great warriors…but he's about to die. Why? Because he turned from his calling. He used his Gift to change the fate of the mundane world.

"Beside him is Odysseus, clever beyond words. He also played mundane politics, and he'll be punished, too. Rather than death, he faces exile, a decade spent wandering the seas in search of home. He spends the time fighting incursions from the worlds beyond the Veil: Scylla, Polyphemus, the Sirens. As a reward for these services, he's eventually returned to his family.

"Circe, the witch, snares Odysseus for a year during his journey. On her island, she's stayed far away from the mundane world; instead she's

19

learned all the Arcane dangers that sailors will face on the sea. She tries to trap Odysseus, but eventually sees the error of her ways and becomes his advisor instead."

Emily blinked, realizing that she'd been listening to the Baron, actually listening. It was obvious he'd memorized a prepared speech, but he made it seem like he was speaking off the cuff despite the formal language.

"Three paragons, one with each gift. So, what do they teach us? Achilles, the legendary fighter—if he were eighteen years old he might be standing with you Combat students right now. But rather than use his Gift to hold back the dangers that come through the Veil, he squandered it fighting the little wars of kings. He teaches us that no matter how great we are, as Gifted it's our duty to ignore the struggles of the mundane world. We could fight their wars for them, even rule them if we wanted, but we don't.

"Why? For that, we look to Odysseus, the genius. He would sit with those of you with the Gift of the Mind. He's an example of a Gifted who did his duty, struggling with the creatures of the worlds beyond the Veil, what we call monsters. That's the calling of the Gifted: to guard the doors between realities and send back whatever comes through. We protect the mundane world without ever letting them know we exist.

"Finally, Circe, given the Arcane Gift. She lived far from the mundane world, studying the creatures that came through the Veil. When first she met Odysseus and his men, she tried to enslave them, but in the end she made a gift of her knowledge. She teaches us that we can't isolate ourselves or hoard our Gifts. Instead we live together, in our Gifted communities, and call each other sibling.

"Harkness Academy is one such community. My own Deseret is another. The Shadow Academies, the Gifted Nations, give structure to our world. They give us support and guidance in our times of need, and we fight for them when they call us up. We rely on them, and they rely on us. And that's my charge to you, Harkness: shun the mundane world.

Forget it. Dedicate yourself to your community, and to each other. This is the calling of the Gifted."

The Baron nodded once, gave a final little smile, and returned to his seat behind the lectern. Emily shook her head, blinking. At least it was over; all that was left was the diplomas.

Magister Tate, the head of the School of Arcana, stepped forward. He was a barrel-chested man with a shining bald head, and he spoke in a commanding voice as he began reading out the names of his students.

As the Arcanes received their diplomas, most of them performed little tricks of magic to the laughter of friends and family. One boy conjured a booming fireball; another turned his graduation cap into a dove. Kayo, Emily's friend, accepted her diploma wearing a dress of purple lightning.

The School of Combat was next. Emily wished that she'd been able to stand next to Andrea Butcher, but of course they'd been lined up alphabetically. Andy was second, and she hugged Montrose after he said her name, earning cheers from the rest of the fighters.

Finally, Emily's turn came. As she took her diploma, Montrose shook her hand vigorously, and whispered, "Stick around after the ceremony." He gave her a wink as she headed for the other side of the stage.

Emily's heart thrilled with excitement, just as it had done the night before. Durgan dun Raven was at Harkness, and Montrose was hinting pretty heavily that she was going to meet him, maybe even get a proper interview. What was it that Montrose had told dun Raven in the Fighthouse the night before? "You might be surprised." It sure sounded like an old teacher telling a friend to take a chance on his favorite pupil.

The rest of the graduation passed in a blur. Emily couldn't stay focused, and almost forgot to clap when Credenza Limn, head of the School of the Mind, announced Chris McLeod as receiving his diploma in absentia. She was imagining Durgan dun Raven saying, "We're lucky to have you,

Emily!" in his animal rumble. It was sort of hard to put those words in that mouth, but she tried.

After a few closing wheezes from Headmaster Knowles, graduation was over. Unlike her friends, Emily had no family to greet, so she set out immediately to find Montrose. It took her a while to get his attention, as he was surrounded by new graduates saying goodbye and old Combat alumni greeting him with firm handclasps and pats on the back. At last she caught his eye.

"Ah, Sledge! C'mere!" He waved her over. "Someone I want you to meet." He reached a big hand into the crowd of people around him like a stage magician reaching for a rabbit in a hat, and as if from nowhere, pulled out Emily's least favorite person in the world.

"Emily? Emily Sledge? Emily, it is you! What a treat!" Suddenly she was coming in for a hug like a gabardine whirlwind: Clea Coates. Looking at Clea in her perfect power suit, Emily felt strangely ashamed of her graduation robes, despite the fact that Clea was the one who stuck out. Clea's ability to make you feel bad about yourself was like a Gift all its own. "What a treat! What a surprise!"

"How could it possibly be a surprise, Clea?" Emily snapped. "The entire senior class is standing right here. Where else would I be, sitting behind my dad's desk?"

"Now now, that's not fair." Clea wore a theatrical pout. "I was still a girl when Daddy lost his last election. I got my job at the Commonwealth fair and square."

"I was even younger," Emily snapped. "And when your daddy lost his election it cost my parents their jobs. Montrose, sir, is this—" But Montrose was gone, swallowed up in the crowd of students, parents, and friends. Emily suddenly felt very alone and very stupid. This was who Montrose had been hinting about? Clea Coates was just a bureaucrat in the government of the Secret Commonwealth. She didn't even have a Gift.

"Well, Em, putting your rudeness aside for a moment," Clea sniffed.

"Your dear Montrose told me about your bad day yesterday. Hard luck, darling, hard luck. But trust Clea to make it right! I've gotten you just the best interview down in Boston."

"Thanks but no thanks," Emily said with a confidence she didn't feel. "I'm still planning to join the Sabre & Torch."

Clea looked dramatically horrified. "Really! A bunch of murderous vagabonds, if you ask me, wandering from place to place doing massive property damage, causing more problems than they solve. Much better that you come work for us at the Commonwealth."

"You can't be serious."

"Very serious, darling Emily. You know the walls of reality are a little thinner here in the northeast. I think it's all the cold." She gave a little mock shiver, ridiculous in the summer heat. "But we always need good fighters."

"You think you're such a big fish, just because your dad was prime minister for a while." Emily shook her head. "But you're nothing now, just somebody's assistant. After the way your dad treated my parents, I would die before working for the Secret Commonwealth. And even after I'm dead I'll never work for you."

"Oh, Sledge, we used to be like sisters!" Clea's pout was back. "And now you're so angry all the time. Well, a word of advice, just between sisters: never say never."

All that was left of Emily's four years at Harkness Academy was one meal. The school pulled out all the stops for the graduation feast, producing the best food a school cafeteria was capable of and serving it on circular tables arrayed on the lawn where graduation had been held.

Still trying to shake off the funk that the surprise appearance of Clea Coates had put her into, Emily headed across the grass. She passed a group of undergrad fighters playing splinty, the incredibly dangerous game be-loved of all Combat students. Their huge swords flashed in the summer sun as they batted a heavy stone ball around the lawn with the flats of their blades. One girl who had to be a freshman—Emily didn't recognize her—mistimed a swing and shattered the ball with the edge of her blade, sending wicked splinters flying to the laughter of the other players. As they paused to catch their breath, a few of them spotted Emily and yelled for her to come join them. She returned their waves but kept moving.

Soon she found the table where Andrea and Kayo sat with their families. Kayo's parents, Kim and Trevor Jackson, were among the rare people who had a Gifted child despite having never even heard of the Gifted world. They ran a dairy farm in Vermont, where Emily and her friends had spent a few glorious summers goofing off with Kayo's three non-Gifted brothers. Andrea was the exact opposite, the only child of Kevin and Melanie Butcher, two fighters from respected Gifted families in New York City. Both sets of parents greeted Emily with hugs and smiles, then Andrea pointed to a laptop sitting on the table.

"Look who's here!" Emily grinned when she recognized the black hair and missing eyebrow of Chris McLeod on the monitor, and she gave him a wave.

"How's Madawaska? Traveling across dimensions yet?"

"That's next week," Chris replied from the screen. "We're still arguing about the best design for our new power plant. I drew up some plans for a sort of cold fission thing, but then—"

"Okay, okay, genius!" Emily waved her hands in defeat. "Don't get going. I'm sure your thing is right and they'll all figure it out eventually."

Andrea pulled out a chair, and Emily sat between her and Kayo's mom. Mrs. Jackson was a slender Japanese woman with laugh lines baked into her face and more gray than black in her thick hair. It was strange to see her in a dress and heels; Emily had almost thought a work shirt, jeans, and Wellingtons were part of the woman's body.

Leaning in, Mrs. Jackson said in a half-whisper, "So, Emily, Kayo tells me Career Day didn't go so well."

24

It was precisely the last thing Emily wanted to talk about, but Mrs. Jackson was about as close as it got to family for her, so she sighed and said, "I don't think I'm job material."

"What do you mean, sweetie?"

"She means," interjected Andy, who had of course been listening, "that's she's no good at taking orders."

"That's not true!" said Emily indignantly, and the whole table laughed. "I'm serious! I just don't like taking orders from people who, I don't know…shouldn't be giving them."

"Oh, wine!" interjected Kayo's dad, a large, bald man with an easy grin that flashed brightly against his dark skin. An underclassman holding a tray of plastic cups stood at his shoulder. Sticking his fingers into the cups, Mr. Jackson lifted four off with each hand.

"Here we go, here we go," he said happily as he deposited the wine in the center of their table. "Waiter, might I ask the vintage?"

"Um, I think it's Vino Piggio, sir," said the underclassman shyly.

"Ah!" Mr. Jackson laughed. "From the vineyards of Gruspiggio, a fine, cheap vintage for a large, well-attended party. Now then, ladies, Kevin, let us drink. Chris, I'll have yours in your honor."

Andrea downed her cup of wine in a heartbeat, making Emily smile as she recalled how much experience her friend had at secretly sneaking drinks when they had been the awkward underclassmen serving at these parties. Kayo gave her mom a questioning look, received a shrug in return, and took a sip. It was weird to get handed a drink instead of stealing it, and they were probably breaking some mundane law, but as far as the Gifted world was concerned she was an adult. Emily tasted the wine, found it was perfectly cool and bright for a hot day in early summer, and drank half of it before a thought struck her.

"We should toast," she said. Everyone around the table turned to look at her. "We should! This is the last time the four of us will be together until…until who knows when?"

"I agree!" said Andrea. She grabbed the cup that Mr. Jackson had said he'd drink for Chris, and stood up. "Here's to us! Who's like us?"

"Damn few," chorused Emily, Kayo, and Chris, "and they're all dead!"

They drank. Next, Kayo stood.

"You three"—she looked at her friends—"are as much a part of my family as my parents and my brothers. You got me through some really tough times. Thank you."

They drank again, and Emily noticed Mrs. Jackson wiping away a tear.

"I can't really stand up," said Chris from his laptop screen, "but thank you all for listening to me, keeping me grounded, and only sometimes destroying my robots. I love you guys."

They drank. There was only a tiny bit of wine left at the bottom of Emily's cup, but she stood. It was suddenly very hard to meet her friends' eyes, so she stared at her little splash of wine as she swirled it.

"You guys...you know how it is with my family. And you know how it is with me. I don't know what's gonna happen tomorrow, or after that, but—"

"Emily," Andrea interrupted.

"No, hush, I'm toasting!" replied Emily.

"*Emily*," Kayo said, more forcefully, and pointed over Emily's shoulder.

"What?" Emily turned around, and almost dropped her wine.

It was Durgan dun Raven, looming like an iceberg in the anxious sea of teenagers and parents. The top of his shaggy blonde head broke the seven-foot mark, and his shoulders were permanently hunched from leaning down to listen to people smaller than him. A ragged scar down the left side of his face forced his mouth into a permanent half-frown. Draped in animal skins, a huge sword hanging from his belt, Durgan dun Raven was the Gift of Combat personified.

Emily was transfixed, and stood there stupidly, holding her cup in toasting position, until dun Raven reached her.

"Emily Sledge?" he asked, his voice a low animal rumble. Emily looked up at him. She was a full six feet and she wasn't used to people towering over her.

"Mister—Mister Raven," she stammered. "I guess the Ice Queen didn't keep you too long?"

"No. I melted the ice with my piss and pulled my chains free, then strangled her with them." Dun Raven picked a louse out of his furs and flicked it away.

"Oh, uh, cool."

"Swam back across the Bay of Fundy yesterday."

"Wow," said Emily. She knew conversation wasn't really her thing, but somehow she hadn't imagined a chat with Durgan dun Raven would be so awkward. It was hard to think with him looming in front of you.

"I found something while I was swimming." He reached beneath his fur cloak—*it must be incredibly hot*, Emily thought suddenly—and pulled out a bottle, which he handed to Emily. It was heavy, made from a thick green glass, and crusted with sea salt. It was stoppered with a cork that had been dipped in red wax, but the wax was broken; clearly the bottle had already been opened. She could see some sort of paper rolled up inside.

Emily's mind swam. What was happening right now? What was she supposed to do? The emotional whiplash was stunning; dun Raven wasn't at Harkness, then he was, then she was going to interview with him, then it turned out to be Clea Coates, now he was here with a glass bottle for her.

"Open it," he said.

She opened it, pulling the heavy cork out. Bits of red wax flaked away and fell to the ground. Reaching a finger in, she caught the paper against the side of the bottle and dragged it out. It was a heavy parchment of the

27

sort Emily associated with spellcasters, with a feel of age and pent-up power. She pinched one edge of the parchment between two fingers of the hand holding the bottle and unrolled it carefully.

A multicolored symbol of breathtaking complexity and beauty took up almost the entire sheet of parchment. Its heart was a small circle of golden paint that glimmered in the summer sun. Jagged lines of red ink stabbed into the gold circle from a series of black runes that ringed it, as forest-green whorls played in and out of them. The whole sigil was contained within a larger blue circle made up of writing in a flowing script.

"It's incredible," breathed Kayo from over Emily's shoulder. She'd been so lost in the image that she hadn't heard her friend come up from the table. "What is it?"

Emily, still lost for words, looked up at dun Raven.

He shrugged. "Dunno."

"Give it here," said Kayo, gently pulling the parchment from between Emily's unresisting fingers. "It's obviously a magical sigil of some kind. Though I don't really recognize it…" Kayo trailed off, lost in the swirls and lines of the symbol.

"You just found this floating in the ocean?" Emily asked dun Raven, who nodded.

"Be surprised if it were a coincidence," he replied. "Someone wanted it found."

"Did you—has the Sabre & Torch seen this yet?"

Dun Raven nodded again. "Just another mystery to them. Don't have men to spare on it."

Emily could feel her heart quickening again as understanding dawned. "But I could look into it for you," she said quietly.

"That's the idea," said dun Raven. "I've got a thing in Belize or I'd do it. Figured I'd hand it off to one of you Harkness kids, let you chase after it for a while."

"And the S&T is okay with that?"

28

"Like I said, they don't think it's important. Probably right. Wanted me to give it to a Mental or a wizard or somebody as a test sort of thing."

Emily's heart sped up again. "You know, I'd love a chance to show the S&T what I can do."

"That's what Montrose said."

The next time Emily saw that man, he was getting the biggest damn hug.

"So what should I do if—when I figure it out?"

"Just find anybody from the S&T, let them know. I'll be around for a day or two before I head south, you get it sorted by then." Dun Raven paused, squinted, and raised his head like a hunting dog sniffing the air. "Gotta go. See you."

"Uh, bye," said Emily. Dun Raven was already walking away, students and parents parting around his massive frame. When she turned around, Andrea, Kayo, and their parents were all staring at her expectantly. Even Chris looked transfixed from his monitor. There was a moment's pause, and then everyone started talking at once.

"That guy is huge—"

"Did he say 'test?'"

"What does he—"

"Are you gonna join—"

"Whoah, whoah!" Emily said with a laugh, patting at the air to slow them all down. "One at a time. Actually, no, shut up, just me explain. He doesn't know what it is. The S&T apparently don't think it's that big a deal, so they told him to give it to a Harkness student to figure out. Yes, he said 'test,' and I'm gonna pass it. Whatever it is. I think Montrose convinced him to give it to me rather than a Mental or an Arcane so I'm not gonna let him down. I'm gonna figure out what this thing means and why somebody put it in a bottle in the ocean and I'm gonna impress the shit out of Dugan dun Raven." Emily paused to catch her breath. "Now then, does anybody have any clue how the hell I do that?"

"Well, let's all have a look," said Mr. Butcher.

Andrea rolled her eyes. "Dad, we're fighters. Mystic symbols aren't really our thing."

"Just let me see it before you scoff, Andy," her father replied as Kayo handed him the parchment. He glared at it with a look of intense concentration for a minute before announcing, "Nope, no clue."

"Pass it over, Kevin," said Mr. Jackson, and before Kayo could even begin rolling her eyes, laughed, "I've read a book or two, you know!" Mr. Jackson gave the painted symbol even less time than Mr. Butcher had before declaring that he also had no idea what it was.

From him it went to his wife, and while Mrs. Jackson was certain that it was a work of beauty and skill, she had no insight into its meaning. Mrs. Butcher waved it off with a fork in the midst of cutting her third steak; she still fought for the Secret Commonwealth fairly often, and so possessed the monstrous appetite of fighters in their prime.

Andrea gave the symbol little more than a glance, then finally handed it back to Kayo.

"Okay, Miss Magic, tell all. This is your wheelhouse, isn't it?"

"Well," Kayo began, "well, I'm not sure. It's real, that's for sure. I can feel the power tied up in it, so it's not just some random painting. It's old. And…I don't know quite how to explain it, but it feels like it's describing something, not doing something. It's a noun, not a verb, if that makes any sense."

"Like…" Emily waved her hands in the air, trying to grab inspiration. "Like a name?"

"Yeah, like a name. Sort of. I don't know." Kayo shrugged anticlimactically and sat down.

"Hey, guys," said Chris from the laptop. "Forgetting about someone?"

"Chris, I'm so sorry!" Emily laughed. "I totally forgot you were there! It's your fault for moving to the Canadian wilderness."

"Well, wherever I am I'm smarter than the rest of you—don't make that face, Kayo, it's a fact. So how about letting me take a look?"

Pushing aside plates and glasses, Emily unrolled the parchment on the table and pinned it down with salt and pepper shakers. She picked up the laptop and tilted it so the camera pointed down at the symbol.

"Bit too close—lift me up a little—little more—ah, thanks," came Chris's disembodied voice. "Huh."

Emily waited, but she was getting impatient. "'Huh' what? 'Huh, I've seen this before?' 'Huh, I have no idea what this is?' 'Huh, I have something to say but I'm doing a dramatic pause because I'm a big show-off?'"

"The last one," said Chris.

"So?"

"I think you should take this to Professor Graves."

CHAPTER 3

11 Days

Chris had described Professor Rutherford Graves as "something of a recluse," but Emily thought the teacher was taking it a bit far. The old Mental lived in a small, tumbledown brick house set far back in the tangled forest that surrounded the Harkness grounds. Apparently it was something of a rite of passage for Mind students to trek through the woods to Graves Cottage, sent by another professor to retrieve some obscure tome or bit of knowledge, armed only with a quick rundown on the paths to follow, where to turn clockwise or counterclockwise to disarm various fairy charms, and what treats to bribe which of the forest guardians with.

Chris had summed up the department's attitude nicely: "If you're not smart enough to follow instructions, you probably shouldn't be at Harkness anyway." Apparently it was pretty rare for a student to disappear while seeking Graves Cottage, and the few who did tended to turn up eventually, though "eventually" often meant thirty or forty years later.

Luckily for Emily, she'd been wandering these woods looking for trouble since she was a freshman. The various creatures that dwelled in knotholes and hid amongst ferns, waiting for inattentive students to wander off the carefully marked paths, knew from long experience that she was tougher than they were. So as she tromped in a straight line directly for Graves Cottage, the sprites and spirits of the forest contemplated the times they'd met her before and left well enough alone.

Half an hour of walking brought Emily within view of Graves Cottage. It was worse than Chris had described. The house squatted more than sat in a small clearing, ivy covering all but a few hints of brick. Birds flitted in and out of a chimney that leaned threateningly to one side out of a roof that was noticeably lower in the middle. The windows were all blocked up from the inside, and in some cases broken or lacking glass entirely.

Shaking her head, Emily approached the cottage and knocked solidly on the door. There was a groaning as the roof settled another inch, then silence. Emily waited for a moment, then peered in one of the broken windows. It was impossible to see inside; the view was completely blocked by books and papers stacked in precarious piles. Some of the books were yellowed or even rotted with age, while others had bright white pages and sharp corners. There was no apparent logic to their order, or even relationship between their topics, which covered everything from sixteenth-century torture methods to reptile anatomy to the dialects of the American South in the one pile Emily could see.

Emily sighed and knocked again, harder. The door swung open an inch, revealing near-darkness within the house. Emily knew an invitation when she saw one, so she slowly stepped inside. The interior was just as she'd expected; piles of books and papers covered every surface and much of the floor. Paths from the front door to the other rooms of the house suggested that someone did indeed live here, but it was someone beyond the usual levels of obsession and strangeness that you found among people with the Gift of the Mind.

She'd heard a rumor once that Professor Graves had disowned his own son for being a distraction from his work, and she was more ready than ever to believe it. But as Chris had put it, while most Mentals made it their business to master one or two complex fields of study, Professor Graves's life's work was to know absolutely everything.

"Hello?" Emily called. There was a brief creaking, like floorboards, above her head, then silence. Emily waited a few more seconds, heard nothing, and let out her breath. She wasn't scared, not really. There was nothing in an old professor's house that could hurt her, and now that she'd graduated she couldn't exactly get into trouble. But something about the house made her nervous, a feeling that there was bad news hidden here somewhere, on a random page of a forgotten book, waiting to be found.

Moving around a particularly large outcropping of old newspapers, Emily found the stairs. No matter how carefully she placed her feet, she always seemed to find the creakiest spot on each step. The stairs turned ninety degrees at a small landing; above was darkness. She took a breath and continued up.

At the top of the stairs was a hallway in near-total blackness. The windows had been papered over and the ever-present books were here, too, so that the only light came from the door Emily had left ajar downstairs. Luckily there was a clear path among the stacks, leading from the stairs to a single door. Emily walked slowly, her fingers brushing the books on either side of her for guidance.

At last she reached the door. She held her breath, listening, but heard nothing. Taking a deep breath, Emily tried the doorknob. It turned, and she pushed gently.

Emily blinked in the sudden light. As her eyes adjusted, she saw a small, tidy office brightly lit by a large skylight in the ceiling and a few open windows, all revealing the blue summer sky outside. Set between two windows were a large writing desk and a tall leather chair with its back to her. The stacks of paper that dominated the rest of the house were missing here; aside from the desk and chair there was only a handsome silver tea service on a small cart.

Emily caught her breath as a cat jumped off the leather chair and ran past her into the hallway. She opened her mouth, but before she could speak, a voice came from the chair.

"Come in, come in! And shut the door, you're letting all the light out!"

"Professor Graves?" Emily asked as she did as she was ordered. When she turned back from shutting the door, she found a man standing before her in the center of the room. He was small, with the compact frame of an Iberian fencer, wearing neatly pressed khakis and a sharp white Oxford shirt. Dark, mischievous eyes twinkled deep in a lined face, but Emily was surprised to see that the professor's hair and mustache were still a thick, rich black. She'd been expecting a wild-haired old relic in musty robes; the real Professor Graves hardly looked older than fifty.

"The same," replied Graves. "And you must be Emily Sledge."

"How did you know?" asked Emily, taken aback. She hadn't had any reason to mention her visit to anyone after Chris had suggested it. Graves gave her an impish smile.

"How did I know? Emily, when you know everything, there's not much that you don't know. Now please, come to my desk and let's see if I can't help you out."

Still a bit stunned, Emily followed the professor to his desk.

"Professor, do you mind if I ask—"

"The house? The books? Not what you expected, I take it. I'm sure you can imagine how much fun it is for me, though, watching you muddle your way through. And I'm sure you can imagine how often students will bother a professor who is famous for knowing everything. A few sinister touches go a long way toward keeping your visits to a manageable level." As he spoke, Graves tidied up the few papers on his desk, stacking them into neat piles that he squared off against one corner. "Though I'll admit, it's not every day I have a Combat come knocking. As a matter of fact, that's why I let you in. I imagine your question will be either much easier or somewhat more interesting than the ones I usually suffer from the other Mentals."

Emily laughed to hear a professor in the School of the Mind use the slang term for people with his Gift. It was hard not to feel at ease around Graves, she realized; he had a sly energy that was infectious.

"Well, I hope I can live up to that," she said. "I was hoping you could help me identify something that—that I was given. It's a sort of magic symbol, I think. I asked some friends, a Mental and an Arcane, and they didn't know."

"Who?"

"Who? Oh, Chris McLeod and Kayo Jackson."

"McLeod. Great mind, shame he wastes it on death machines and theoretical physics. Not enough of us recognize how much work is still to be done with the knowledge we have. They insist on inventing new facts almost as fast as I can learn them. It's infuriating."

"Oh, um, I'm sorry," replied Emily. "Anyway…" She pulled the crusted glass bottle from her bag, uncorked it, and carefully removed the parchment. Storing it in the bottle had just seemed like the right thing to do.

"Yes, of course," said Graves, settling himself in his chair. "Let's see what you've brought me. This should be interesting. Go ahead, you unroll it."

She did.

Instantly, Graves's twinkling eyes widened in shock and horror, showing his black pupils fully. His smile disappeared as his mouth opened in a silent gape. He sat completely still for a moment, and Emily mimicked him, frozen, leaning over the desk in the act of unrolling the parchment.

Then Graves took a deep, ragged breath and the moment broke.

"Good god, Emily, where did you get this?" he gasped. "No, don't tell me. I don't care. I don't want to know—good lord, I don't even want to know!" White beneath his swarthy complexion, he pushed his chair away from the desk and stood up as if to flee from the paper that still lay open before him.

36

Emily stood as well, and let the parchment roll itself back up.

"Professor, I'm so sorry—I didn't—but what is it?" Clearly the professor had recognized it, could tell her what she needed to know, could help her help the Sabre & Torch.

"Emily, please, promise me. Promise me you won't follow wherever this is leading you." He stared up at her with wide eyes.

"Professor, sir, I can't. I can't! Please just tell me what it is!"

"Emily, the less you know about this symbol, the safer you will be. Please believe me. Please just trust me. Now go. Out, out, out!" He began physically shooing her towards the door. It would have been a funny sight, this little man trying to push away a fighter six inches taller than he was, except for his obvious terror.

Emily could feel the answers she needed slipping away. Desperately she tried to grab them and pull them back. "Professor, please, I'll go. Just give me something!"

"I'll tell you this, and only to show you how serious I am. Emily Sledge, do not—do not—get involved in the affairs of dragons!"

10 Days

At the entrance to the Harkness Academy grounds, a tall brick gate opened onto a cobblestone drive that wound up a long, gentle hill to the Academy's buildings on its flat top. The woods that Emily knew so well surrounded the hilltop on three sides like hair on a balding head. The cobblestone was old, rutted, and unreliable, so cars rarely made it beyond the great gate where Emily now sat on her luggage, trying to figure out what to do next.

The tension inside her was unbearable. She had gotten so close to touching the mystery of the parchment, only to be denied answers. She'd taken the parchment with her—Professor Graves hadn't wanted anything to do with it—but it had stayed in its bottle since she left the cottage in the woods.

Emily stood up and began pacing, walking back and forth through the gate, onto and off of the Harkness campus. She knew exactly what she wanted, but she was at a dead end about how to achieve it. In the meantime, hunting mysteries didn't put food on the table if nobody was paying you to do it, and as a fighter Emily needed a lot of food. Her dreams were in reach but untouchable, the real world was staring her in the face, and the only job lead she had was...

"Darling Emily!"

"Clea." Emily wasn't even surprised to see her there at the gate, with her arms crossed and a look of irritation on her face.

"How long were you planning on sitting on your luggage?" Clea asked. She grabbed the handle of a duffle bag and pulled, but the bag stayed where it was. "Good heavens, who taught you to pack?"

"It's packed fine, thanks," said Emily, snatching up the bag and slinging it over her shoulder. It would be heavy to a non-fighter, she supposed.

"Well," said Clea huffily. "I've been looking for you just everywhere. I thought you'd be saying goodbye to your barbells or something. Instead I find you sitting here waiting for a bus that doesn't exist." Emily shrugged. "All the other students have gone, you know, and their families, too. How sad that your father couldn't come to graduation."

Emily dropped the duffle bag, which landed with a heavy thud and sank an inch into the dirt at her feet, and started advancing towards Clea. "You know perfectly well why he couldn't be here—"

"Okay, okay, I'm sorry! That was a low blow." Clea patted the air with her hands, trying to ward Emily off. "Look, I'm here to offer you a truce. No, just listen. I know you hate me, though I can't even begin to fathom why, and I want to show you I still love you. Emily, we grew up together, let me do something nice for you."

"I don't need your help, Clea," Emily said, still moving forward. "I have a plan, thanks."

"That parchment thing? Yes, I heard all about it, you know how these things get around. Emily, it's a no-go. A non-starter. It's probably nothing. The job interview I got you is the real deal. You'd be bodyguard to the Prime Minister of the Secret Commonwealth herself!"

Emily stopped. "You can't be serious."

"Well, all right, a junior member of Minister Stein's retinue. But it's a steady job with a lot of room for advancement. And, to be perfectly honest…it pays very well."

Emily looked back through the gate, back up the long cobblestone drive to the school that she was leaving behind. Then she looked at her pile of luggage, everything she owned, which was looking very small and battered. She sighed.

"Can I at least get a ride to Boston?"

9 Days

The Guild Hall of the Most Excellent Brotherhood of Lancers, New World Chapter was an old brownstone townhouse on a narrow, sloping lane in Boston's ritzy Beacon Hill neighborhood. Nestled amongst the homes of well-heeled businessmen and legislators, the headquarters for dragon-hunting operations in the Americas hid neatly in plain sight.

Emily paused for a moment before pushing open the door, which had recently been given a fresh coat of bright red paint. The front hall was just how she remembered it: narrow, dimly lit, with faded paintings hung on the walls over hundred-year-old wallpaper. To her right sat a low table with a basket for calling cards; ahead of her was a staircase leading steeply up to a closed door.

Emily climbed the stairs slowly. Every step felt like it took more effort than the last, as the nervous ball in the pit of her stomach grew. She made it to the top step and reached for the doorknob in front of her, but the door suddenly swung open, forcing her back down a few steps.

It was her dad.

"Oh, 'scuse me, I—Emily? Emily! What are you doing here? Are you—come in! Here, just squeeze past me—there you go—Emily, I'm so glad you came by!" They stood in the room at the top of the stairs, a large drawing room that took up nearly the whole footprint of the townhouse. A few overstuffed chairs sat empty near low tables, and the walls were lined with bookshelves.

Above the bookshelves, mounted in the shadows between flickering gas lamps, the stuffed heads of long-dead dragons glowered down with glass eyes set in tattooed faces. From what Emily had heard, American dragons were sad little things compared to their European cousins, but the heads in the Lancers' drawing room had always seemed big enough to her. Far from seeming smaller now that she was grown, they were even more intimidating after Professor Graves's warning. The shifting gaslight made their ancient tattoos waver and bend hypnotically...

Realizing she was looking at everything in the room except the man she'd come to see, Emily took in her father for the first time in a year. Robert Sledge was still a head taller than Emily, but the mighty warrior of her youth was now far too skinny. The eyes that gazed down at her with love seemed too big, and his cheeks looked hollow. In fact his entire head seemed oversized atop a long, frail body that was hidden in baggy black slacks and a bright white work shirt, also too big, with its right arm pinned up at the shoulder.

Robert pulled her into a tight one-armed hug.

"Hey, kiddo," he said with a warmth that immediately made Emily feel terrible for never visiting.

"Hi, Dad," she said, squirming out of the hug. It was too easy to get away—when she'd been a kid, they'd spent hours wrestling, Emily shrieking with laughter as she tried to wriggle out of her father's powerful grasp.

Was she so much stronger now after years at school? Or was he really that much weaker?

"So, let me look at you!" Robert squared her off, his left hand on her shoulder, and gave her an appraising look up and down. "They feed you enough? Food still as bad as ever?" Emily nodded. "Not bad—look at those triceps, damn! Hey, I heard you won the tournament again this year. Good for you, kid."

"Yeah, thanks. Hey Dad, can I talk to you about something?"

"Of course! Let's take a walk, huh? I'll give you the grand tour."

He led her out of the drawing room, through a polished oak door into a narrow hallway that looked like it made three sides of a square around the drawing room. There was a plush red carpet on the floor and the walls were lined with paintings of old men with the pale, jug-eared look of Albian nobility.

Robert narrated as they walked: "These guys are all old Lancers who did important stuff. Oh, you'll like this one—that's Lieutenant Sir Cecil Howe, he was a cartographer, mapped more dragon's lairs than anyone in history. Commodore Sir Trevor Leslie-Yost cleared out a nest of sea snakes in the English Channel…who else—oh, yeah, here's a good one! General Sir Marshall Alder. He killed the last dragon in America, not even that long ago. Sir Daniel Hendrix, he was bursar for about a million years, that one's not really that exciting."

"Dad. Dad!" Emily stopped halfway down the portrait-lined hall, and Robert stopped when he realized she wasn't following him. "Can we just talk, please?"

"Oh, yeah. Of course, sweetie. Look, if you need some money, I'm really sorry—"

"It's not about money, Dad. Not exactly. I just wanted to ask you—would you work for the Prime Minister again, if you could?"

Robert looked down at his missing right arm with a smile. "I'm not sure they'd want me, kiddo."

"You know what I mean. I've got this job interview this afternoon, that Clea got me, to be part of the PM's bodyguard. I guess the pay is good, but I just feel weird."

"Oh, I'm glad Clea is looking out for you. She was a good kid." Emily raised an eyebrow, and Robert chuckled. "Okay, I know she's kind of snooty, but—"

"Dad, you're avoiding the question."

"Okay, okay, sorry! Yes, I would, in a heartbeat. Look, I know you blame Clea's dad for me and your mom losing our jobs. But it's not his fault he lost that election, and once he wasn't PM anymore there was no way he could afford to keep us on."

"Dad, they threw us out on the street! We lived in a shelter for a month before Mom found work, and then—"

All at once, Robert deflated, his relentless positivity escaping in a heavy sigh. "I know, kid. And then she was gone. It was a dangerous job and she shouldn't have taken it, no argument there. But you need to understand how bad we needed the money. Trying to raise you in a shelter would have killed your mom the same as that monster did, just slower."

"Dad…"

Robert snorted. "Having a fighter for a parent is bad luck…" His eyes flickered toward his missing arm. "Worse if it's both parents. But you can't blame Minister Coates for losing the election any more than you can blame Minister Stein for winning it. It's just politics."

Emily stepped forward suddenly and hugged her dad. "I was afraid you'd say that."

Behind them, a door opened. A tall, skinny man in a well-cut pinstripe suit stepped out, immersed in some papers, then looked up to see Emily and Robert in the middle of the hallway. He paused, cleared his throat, then said loudly, "Robert, the gold in the trophy room is in need of a polish."

"At once, Mr. Treat," said Robert with a smile and a nod of his head.

"Sorry about Emily, sir, she knows the way out." He pulled a rag from the pocket of his slacks and brandished it at Emily. "Duty calls."

Where the Lancer's Guild Hall had been rich, warm, and stuffed full of tradition, the office of the Prime Minister of the Secret Commonwealth was as blankly modern as any office building in the non-Gifted world. Emily shifted uncomfortably on a black vinyl chair that sat along one wall of a long bright room with white marble floors and huge glass windows for three of its walls. Despite the sun spilling in through all that glass, it was chilly, though Emily couldn't see or hear an air conditioner anywhere.

The identical chairs that made a long row to either side of her were all empty, and Emily wondered if that weren't because they'd been specially designed to discourage anybody from actually waiting around for their appointment. She was wearing her interview suit again, still just a bit constricting in all the most irritating places; for the hundredth time she plucked at her armpit as the jacket pinched her shoulder.

This wasn't the life she'd been looking forward to: waiting on a hard chair in a cold office, wearing a suit, hoping for a job. She was meant for action, built for it physically, trained for it mentally, utterly bored by sitting still.

Emily stood and walked to one of the huge windows that showed an impressive view of Boston beneath a wide blue sky, boxy buildings of red and gray and glass peppered with old-fashioned landmarks whose names and histories were probably common knowledge in the mundane world. She laid her hand on the glass, which was cold. Closing her eyes, she could see the many threats of adulthood looming above her like dragons' heads in flickering lamplight. Where would she live? What would she eat? How would she pay for it all? And how would she change the world by making sure some politician didn't get killed?

The Lancers weren't politicians; at least they had that going for them. Old-fashioned, sure. Out of touch, out of date. But at some point they'd been like the Sabre & Torch, travelling the world fighting dangerous fights against ancient monsters who had stepped through the Veil to lair on Earth. The dragon heads were proof of it. A dragon was a terrible thing, a real challenge: as skilled and powerful a fighter as it was a magician, as its mystical tattoos attested.

Instinctively, Emily put a hand on her shoulder bag, where the mysterious parchment sat safely rolled up in its bottle. Thinking of dragons had of course made her think of the symbol that had so frightened Professor Graves. But there was something else scratching at the back of her mind...

She returned to her chair, pondering. The tattoos. It had been hard to tell in the gaslight, but those ancient whorls and runes, blue-gray on mottled white skin, red on black, gold on green—hadn't they looked something like the symbol on the parchment? Of course they had; they were all magical symbols, dragon magic even.

But it was more than that. One of those mounted heads, the biggest one, a great gray face with broken teeth jutting from a snarling mouth...its pattern of circles, curves, red lines, black runes.

Emily jumped up. She was sure of it now. Whoever that dragon was, whoever it had been, it had worn the symbol she'd been given, or something close to it.

Emily grabbed her bag and slung it over her shoulder. Her jacket, confronted with a motion it had never anticipated, popped a seam with a satisfying rip. Emily threw her bag off again, tore off the jacket, crumpled it into a little ball and jammed it in beside the bottle. She untucked her shirt and pulled off her heels.

At the far end of the blank white room, a door opened, and an aide poked his head out.

"Miss Sledge? We're ready for you now."

But Emily was already gone, out the door, down the stairs, on the street, running barefoot in the summer sun.

CHAPTER 4

"Dad? Dad!" Emily called from at the top of the first-floor stairs in the Lancers' Guild Hall. She hopped from foot to foot on the creaky stair: only a locked door stood between her and the drawing room where the dragon head hung.

The door opened, making Emily step back, and not for the first time she wondered why on earth this door opened out onto the narrow stairs.

Standing between her and the drawing room was Mr. Treat, who straightened his tie and coughed.

"Young lady, I'm sure your father will have time for you once his duties are completed for the day," he said in his clipped English accent.

"Oh, Mr. Treat! I was actually just wondering if I could take a peek in the drawing room."

"I don't think so," replied Treat, already closing the door. "Run along home now."

"But—"

The door closed shut with a very final click.

Emily stood still for a moment, stunned. This wasn't at all how she'd imagined things going when she'd thrown her high heels in a trash can out on the street.

"Okay, Sledge, think," she murmured. She couldn't start yelling again; she'd gotten her dad in plenty of trouble for one day, and she knew how much he needed this job. And whoever Mr. Treat was, he certainly didn't seem to be in a forgiving mood.

Emily found herself wishing she'd been a bit worse of a student. She hadn't really been friends with any of them, but she'd had classmates at Harkness who spent their free time sneaking around the school, hiding from teachers and getting through locked doors, rather than studying or practicing. It had seemed like a big waste of time only a few days ago, but now a bit of lockpicking would really come in handy.

But still—it wasn't like she was without skills. She had neither the tools nor the knowledge to pick a lock, but there were other ways to get through a door. It opened out towards her, which meant—yes, the hinges were on her side.

Silently thanking whatever lazy architect or contractor had put the door on backwards a hundred years ago, Emily examined the upper hinge, which was just above her eye level when she stood on the top step. Luck was with her. It was an old door, and while the half of the hinge that attached to the doorjamb was hidden, the other half was screwed into the face of the door with a large, ornate plate.

Emily took a moment to listen at the door and heard nothing. Treat must have left the drawing room—either that or he was just really, really quiet, in which case she was about to get in serious trouble. She took a deep breath, then gripped the entire hinge plate with her fingers on the top and her thumb on the bottom. It was only a fraction of an inch in height, just barely standing out from the door, but she dug her fingertips into it and squeezed.

This wasn't the sort of thing she normally had to do in a fight; things were usually big enough for her to punch them. And the damn plate had to be made of a tougher material than it looked like. Emily began to sweat. Steel? Titanium? Some magic shit that wouldn't just give up and break already?

With a terrible shriek, the plate bent in half like a closing book, popping screws in all directions as it tore away from the wooden door. Emily gave it a tentative push, and it swung away from the door silently.

"Okay then," Emily said.

The lower hinge was, impossibly, even more unwilling to break loose. When it finally did, it was the door itself that gave way, and a jagged chunk of wood came off along with the hinge. Gingerly, Emily laid her hands on the door, then put one foot at its base and pushed. The door tilted out over her head, revealing a sliver of the drawing room beyond. She took the stairs backwards one by one, lowering the door as she went until it lay flat over the top five or six steps.

There was the click of a handle turning—the door from the drawing room to the portrait hall.

"Shit shit shit shit—" As quickly as she dared, Emily lifted the door off the staircase and pushed it towards its open frame, stepping up the stairs behind it. It bumped the jamb and stopped, with an inch-wide line of open space on the left side where she hadn't fitted it back in quite right.

Through this space, she saw Mr. Treat enter the drawing room.

Emily didn't dare move the door, which for all it had wanted to stay attached to its hinges now seemed to really want to tumble down the stairs with her beneath it. So she held her breath and watched in panic as Treat moved around the drawing room slowly, checking for dust beneath the bases of a few lamps, rearranging the cushions on one chair, straightening a line of books on their shelf across the room from Emily.

He turned towards the broken door—and turned back to the books, apparently unhappy with the position of one of them, which he nudged gently with a single finger. Satisfied, he appreciated his work for a moment, coughed quietly, and left, closing the hallway door behind him.

Emily let out her breath. She waited for a few minutes, then, deciding that Treat wasn't coming back, lowered the door back down to her feet and wedged it against a bannister post so it wouldn't slide down the stairs.

Entering the drawing room, Emily realized that the great gray dragon's head she was looking for had pride of place on the wall, directly across from the stairway door with empty space on either side of it. Her eyes were drawn to its toothy sneer and blade-like horns, which seemed to glow in the dim light of the gas lamps.

Moving slowly closer, Emily could make out the faded tattoos on the dragon's cruel face. Laid over the ridges and wrinkles of the ancient head, they seemed misshapen and warped, but there was no doubt now: they were a match for the symbols painted on the parchment rolled up and tucked away in her bag.

Emily realized she was holding her breath again but she couldn't bring herself to let it out. She could feel answers waiting for her behind the dragon's hypnotic eyes. She took another step closer, drawn in. It would be so easy to scale the bookshelf, pull the head down from the wall—

"Emily? What are you—what happened to the door?"

Emily spun around, the spell broken, to see her dad standing in shock in the entrance from the hallway.

"What are you doing here? What about your interview? Did you—did you pull the door off its hinges?"

"Dad, I can explain! Just—shut the door, would you?"

Robert did, but he didn't look very happy about it. Emily knew she had to talk fast if she had any chance of making it out of this one—so she talked. She told her father about her dream of joining the Sabre & Torch, about Durgan dun Raven and his message, about the chance she was being given. She told him about the interview at the prime minister's office and the revelation she'd had there, apologizing for tearing her expensive jacket. And finally, she pulled out the parchment and showed him, showed him how it was the symbol from the dragon's head.

When she was done, Robert was silent for a minute that felt like a year.

Finally, he said, "Why didn't you just tell me all this before you went tearing a door down?"

"Dad, I tried," Emily said. "That Treat guy answered the door, and he was a jerk, and I just thought—I don't know, it just seemed like the fastest way to get in."

Robert sighed. "Well, like mother like daughter, I guess. C'mon, kid, help me with the door."

So she did, and together they got the hinges screwed back into the wood. It was painfully obvious where they had torn away, and Emily had to bend the upper hinge back into a roughly flat plane before they could reattach it, but the door fitted back into its frame well enough that you couldn't tell from inside the drawing room that some pretty massive damage had been done.

When they were done, Robert smiled in relief and gripped Emily's arm tightly.

"Okay, kiddo, I told you you should have talked to me before you did something stupid, so talk to me. How can I help? Anything you need."

Emily nodded. "Okay, well, I want to ask someone about this symbol. Someone who will actually answer my questions, and not just shoo me away. I figure since it's up on the wall there, one of these Lancers can tell me. Is there, like, a head Lancer? Can I talk to him?"

Robert ran a hand over his face wearily. "Oh, Em. I wish I hadn't just said 'anything.'"

"What's the big deal?" Emily asked. "I know you're just a janitor or whatever but surely you can ask somebody if they can meet with me. Or if there's somebody here who likes you, ask them to ask for me."

"You don't get it, Em." Robert shook his head. "The only somebodies here are me and Mr. Treat."

"That's it?" Emily's eyebrows shot up.

"That's it. As far as the American headquarters goes, we're it. Kinda sad, when you think about it."

"What about all those guys in the hallway?"

"Dead, most of them. General Alder is up in Maine somewhere, I think." Robert shrugged. "Anyway, that's not the point. You want to talk to the head Lancer? Mr. Treat is it. And I don't think he likes you."

"How do you know? Maybe he secretly thinks I'm charming."

"Well, he told me he didn't like you."

"That's not what I said, Robert," said Mr. Treat from the open door to the portrait hall. "I told you she was disrespectful of her elders and incapable of understanding when she ought not be underfoot, and I intimated that perhaps it was due to a flaw in her upbringing."

"Mr. Treat!" Robert spun around. "Ah, Emily was just leaving, sir—
"

"Perhaps you should be leaving as well, Robert. I'm sure I can find a replacement for you easily enough. One with both arms, even."

"Sir, please—" said Robert at the same moment that Emily said, "Okay, that does it!"

Robert turned back to her and put a hand on her shoulder, which she brushed off as she pushed past him towards Treat, standing in the doorway with arms crossed and lips pursed smugly.

Jabbing a finger at Treat's chest, Emily began, "Listen, old man—" His right hand whipped up and grabbed her wrist; he twisted sharply, and she dropped to her knees, facing away from him, her hand pinned behind her back. Instinctively Emily tried to break the hold, but the sensation of her wrist bones grinding against each other warned her to stop before something was crushed. Damn, he was strong!

"I'm listening," said Treat.

"Let her go, Treat!" Robert's face showed open fear, but he seemed frozen to the carpet.

"You saw her advance upon me. Now, Miss Sledge, what was it you wanted to say?"

Emily forced herself to relax. Treat had gotten the jump on her—she had never expected the skinny Lancer to be a fighter, but he must be all steel wire under the pinstripe suit—but he was strong enough to make the advantage stick. She wasn't fighting her way out of this one.

She took a deep breath, and began. "Look around you, Mr. Treat. If you fire my dad, you'll be alone in here. With—with what? Taxidermy, and—and paintings, and old books. Nobody comes here. Nobody is going to replace you when you retire. I mean, what do you even do all day? The dragons are dead, and the Lancers are dying."

"You're not helping your cause," Treat said quietly, but some of the venom had drained from his voice.

"Well—well, what if I told you I have something that could help?"

"Em, what are you talking about?" said Robert, unfrozen by his surprise.

"Yes, Miss Sledge, what are you talking about?" echoed Treat.

Emily twisted her head around to look Treat in the eye. "Don't fire my dad and I'll tell you."

"Miss Sledge, you're in no position to negotiate. With your father's release from our service, you are both trespassing on Lancer property."

"Fine," Emily replied. "Then let me up and we'll go. You'll never hear from me again."

Treat was silent. Emily could feel his cruel grip loosening; she thought she could break out now, if she wanted to, but something inside her told her to wait. The silence stretched on for another long moment, until Treat broke it by suddenly drawing a sharp breath.

"Very well. Let us go to my office, Miss Sledge. If what you have to say is as meaningful as you promise, Robert may yet have employment here."

Mr. Treat's office seemed almost as packed with old junk as Professor Graves's house had been. Emily rubbed her sore wrist as she took it all in from her seat in an old leather chair that faced Treat's huge oak desk, and behind it, Treat himself in a matching leather chair before an imposing wall of books.

The wall on Emily's left was given over entirely to weaponry. Swords and daggers, spears, axes, polearms, and one long spiked chain hung in rows, polished and honed to a killing edge, no doubt by Robert Sledge. Opposite the weapons was a wall of shields, as dirty and battle-scarred as the weapons were gleaming. One was scorched almost solid black; another showed two intersecting sets of deep parallel gouges. A third was split straight down the middle and hung almost in two parts. The emblems and coats of arms on them were all faded and illegible, with the exception of one, which bore a phoenix in flames and the motto "RESURGAM." The shield was in remarkably good condition.

"I shall rise again," said Treat, following her eye. There was a note of something in his voice that seemed alien to the cruel, sneering man she'd met so far. It was almost…wistful? "That shield was borne by Marshall Alder when he slayed the last dragon in North America. The creature never so much as landed a blow, from what I understand." Treat sighed. "He left it behind when he took command of the castle at Finalhaven."

"I see," said Emily politely. It seemed like a good idea to get Treat in a chatty mood before she started asking about the parchment, still waiting in its bottle. "And, um, is that dragon around here somewhere?"

"Hm? Oh, yes, indeed. In the drawing room, as a matter of fact. The great big gray right in the middle."

Emily nearly jumped. She could feel the presence of the parchment in her bag, as though it were calling her name. She firmly reminded herself that the dragon was dead, then plunged ahead.

"Did it have a name?"

"A name, Miss Sledge? For a dragon? Oh, we men had names for it, certainly. We needed something for our curses and our funeral songs. One may as well name a storm or a star for all the good it does. But then, we name everything we fear, in the hopes that we might gain some small measure of control over it."

"Oh," said Emily, stunned. "I just thought maybe dragons were like the elves, like they had names for themselves that we couldn't pronounce or didn't know."

"And we named the elves, too, didn't we?" Treat leaned forward, resting his elbows on his desk and fixing Emily with a cutting stare. "Alpha, Beta, all the way down to Omega in an attempt to understand their hierarchy. But they didn't abandon the Earth because we gave them mean nicknames."

Emily looked away from Treat's piercing eyes. Getting him talking was one thing, but this conversation was taking a dark turn. Time to try to get back on track.

"Well, about our deal. What I have to show you actually has to do with that dragon, whatever it was called."

Treat immediately came out of whatever mood had taken him, sitting up straight as he regained his composure, all professionalism again.

"Yes, tell me, what do you have to show me?"

Emily reached into her bag and found the glass bottle tucked into her torn suit jacket. As soon as her hand closed around it, she hesitated, overcome with doubt. Treat had given her no reason to trust him. But she'd followed a fragile chain of chance and luck to get here, and now the chain had run out. Maybe this time she'd actually get some answers—plus, her dad's job was on the line.

She pulled out the bottle, uncorked it, and drew out the parchment. Treat watched her with hungry eyes. Emily forced herself to hand it over without another telling pause.

Treat also exercised obvious restraint when he took the rolled-up parchment from her hand carefully, rather than snatching it away as he so clearly wanted to. With a quiet sigh, he unrolled it on his desk, weighting it down with an inkpot on one corner and a small gold-capped fang on another.

Treat moved. It was a tiny motion, probably imperceptible to the average person, but just barely visible to the fighter's senses Emily had honed over four years of grueling practice. The Albian's face never lost its impassive mask, but the fingers of his right hand flickered momentarily, the first tiny step in an aborted motion. He had clearly been about to do something, reach for something, before getting himself under control.

But what? As Treat stared blank-faced at the sigil painted before his eyes, Emily catalogued everything at Treat's right hand. The weapons on the wall were too far away. A few quill pens were within reach, but why would he want to write on the symbol? Nothing else on his desk seemed relevant: a small stack of papers, a matching paperweight made from a fang, an old book.

No, not on the desk, Emily realized. In it. There must be a drawer in the desk at Treat's right hand. And there in the drawer was something he wanted—to use, to look at, to hide even deeper? She couldn't guess.

"Miss Sledge," said Treat.

"Yes?" she replied, forcing her voice to sound as though she'd been politely waiting for his opinion.

"Allow me to make you an offer. I'll take this…painting off your hands. And in return, your father remains in the employ of the Lancers."

"Ah—"

"Let me finish, please. You must also vow that your investigation into this paper ends here. I don't need to know where you acquired this, nor who sent you here to bother me. I ask only that you let it rest, and I promise your father will be treated well. If I hear otherwise, I will have no compunctions about throwing him out on the street."

He was already lifting his paperweights off the parchment, beginning to roll it up. Emily's eyes flickered to Treat's desk, where the drawer must be.

"You've got a deal."

CHAPTER 5

8 DAYS

Six hours later, as a church bell rang midnight in the darkness, Emily clung to the bricks of the Lancers' Guild Hall three stories above the pavement, reflecting on the fact that she'd spent an awful lot of time climbing and letting herself into buildings in the last few days.

She glanced down into the alley below, where a particularly persistent policeman had been shining his flashlight every direction but up for five solid minutes. Hiding from the law with her fingers jammed into mortar wasn't what Emily had imagined life after school would be, but then, she'd been so completely focused on studying, training, and competing that she'd barely had time to imagine it at all. The calendar had been full and colorful up until graduation day, and after that, just an empty white space filled only with a vague promise that if she took care of school, the future would take care of itself.

At last, the policeman below muttered something to himself and left the alley. Emily waited until she heard the squelch of a radio and the roar of a starting engine before she let out the breath she'd been holding for the last five minutes. Another few deep breaths steadied her, and she began to inch her way along the wall.

She'd made it up to the third floor easily enough but getting over to the window of Treat's office had proved more difficult than she'd expected. The old bricks of the Guild Hall hadn't been repaired in ages and seemed to crumble away at the slightest wrong touch. A particularly large chunk had hit the ground before Emily could catch it and jam it back into place, summoning the diligent policeman as surely as in a story.

Finally, she reached the office window. Peering in, she found it draped in an inviting darkness. Nothing moved, and the cloaked shapes she could make out matched comfortingly to the objects she remembered from her time in the office that day. All that was left was to force the window and open the drawer that had been the focus of her thoughts for the past six hours. It seemed a little anticlimactic, but then, Emily was ready for something to go simply.

The window opened without so much as a squeak. Too easy? No, Emily decided, just easy enough. After all, it hadn't been very tough to get in the front door, just some old metal hinges that needed bending. The Lancers clearly weren't too concerned about security; after all, they were obsolete, bound to be forgotten in another generation or two, and probably didn't have much worth guarding.

She let herself in.

Emily gasped as she barked her shin against something in the darkness. A resounding crash sounded in front of her, followed by a sloshing noise as water seeped under her feet. Her shoes were soaked through immediately, and something smelled terrible. She looked around wildly, but it was nearly black, not the welcoming half-darkness she'd seen through the window. Looking back, she saw a tiny barred window high up in the wall. Had she really come in through that?

Gingerly, she spread out her arms, only to pull them back in surprise when they touched wood shelving less than a foot to either side of her. She half-knelt, keeping her knees out of the water, and felt a toppled bucket and mop at her feet.

Emily cursed quietly. She was in a maintenance closet, probably where her dad kept his cleaning supplies. And the fact that she'd gone through a window and ended up in a closet could only mean one thing: magic.

She thought back to the classes she'd paid the least attention to freshman and sophomore year. Harkness had a lot of required courses that covered—as fully as was possible with magic and monsters—the weird situations fighters might find themselves in. But it had been a while since she had finished the required stuff, and maybe spending the last two years taking every elective she could about obscure and forgotten fighting styles hadn't been the best idea. So far this first adventure had been sorely lacking in stand-up fights. She felt vaguely annoyed that nobody had warned her about this, then remembered that Montrose most certainly had, many times.

It was a reasonably common protection spell, she remembered that much. Once everybody left for the night, all the windows and doors in the building unhooked from each other and reshuffled. Circling around at random, you could get lost forever, or at least until the next morning when things realigned and somebody came to collect you.

There was something else about these spells, though, something Emily couldn't quite remember. She shrugged it off: there was nowhere to go but forward, anyway. She picked her way carefully around the mess she'd made on the floor, her shoes hopelessly soaked in the mop water, and opened the closet door.

Beyond was a room she didn't recognize. It was a sort of classroom— the door she'd come through was at the bottom of a small amphitheater of long tables and chairs in tiers. An old-fashioned green chalkboard and lectern stood lonely nearby. At the back of the room, up the tiers of seating, there were three doors to let out what had presumably once been a large mass of students.

Emily sighed. Keeping track of all these doors was going to be a huge pain, unless…she smiled. Whoever had last cleaned this room, years ago, had left plenty of chalk in the chalkboard.

She pocketed it all, then took the biggest piece and wrote "storage" on the door she'd come through. After a moment of doubt, she double-checked: the door did indeed return to the same room it had led from, the dark, sodden closet. That meant that most likely, if she could squeeze through the tiny window at the top of the closet she would find herself back outside Treat's office looking in. That cut the nonsense in half, at least.

Emily stepped back into the auditorium just as all three doors opened, which reminded her of the other thing about these door-shuffling spells: they were way more effective with guards around.

Three old suits of armor clanked into the room, one from each door. They were beautiful—Emily loved old armor and weapons—with ornate scrollwork depicting swirling, battling dragons raised on their breastplates and greaves. Two raised sword and shield, while the third held a long axe-ended halberd in both gauntlets. The shields were battered, but all three weapons gleamed as though brand new.

Emily was in trouble, she knew that much immediately. There was no telling how strong these things were without getting close to them—magic was tricky like that—and in an ideal world she would do as little damage to the Lancers' defenses as possible. She was here for a smash and grab, not a smash and smash.

Emily jumped, clearing half the risers of the auditorium and landing on a chair that promptly collapsed under her. She hit the ground hard, but on her feet. The constructs were closer than she'd expected—they moved fast. The halberd wielder was coming down the stairs between desks nearest her; the other two moved along the rows in her direction.

She jumped again; the halberd glittered razor sharp an inch beneath her feet as the nearest construct lunged. She landed one tier above it and bounced back off a desk to the steps. A kick to the armor's back toppled it forward.

She ran for the door it had come through, pausing just long enough to mark a slash on it with her chalk, then hustled through and slammed it shut behind her.

Emily was surprised to see the portrait hallway from her first visit with her father. A few doors at least opened out of it, leading to who knew where, and for a moment she saw trees reaching out across her vision, every branch splitting into even more, smaller branches, endlessly.

Emily shook her head. She'd studied this one, a classic in the world of breaking and entering (or, conversely, security, which had been the purported topic of her sophomore seminar). The spell didn't create or remove portals; it couldn't. It just rearranged them. There were no more doors and windows in the Guild Hall than there had been by the light of day. They were just laid out impossibly, that was all.

The door at her back half-opened, and without thinking Emily slammed against it to hold it shut. A gauntleted fist pounded briefly on the other side, shaking her, then Emily hopped back as three inches of sword and half the halberd's axe blade bit through the wood simultaneously. All three constructs had caught up.

She ran for the door to the drawing room, chalking it on the go, and found herself in a dusty, unused bedroom. She shut the door quietly, bolted for the single window, and found it locked. The door creaked open as she fumbled with the lock, and she saw half a sword poke through from the portrait hall as she threw herself through the window into…another closet?

It was dark here as well, but her searching hands found a doorknob. She eased the door open to reveal a view into the room she'd just left, with the two sword-wielding constructs in it. A view in from a window. Cursing her ridiculous luck, she eased the door shut, trapped in the darkness.

So the only way out of the closet led back into the same room. At least the living armor seemed not to have noticed her. One of them clanked in the room beyond, moving…towards her? Away from her? It was impossible to tell, and who knew what happened to sound caught in the bizarre defensive spell.

The closet door opened, and Emily exploded out into the light, falling back in through the bedroom window past a suit of armor that she would have sworn had a surprised expression on its helmeted face. A sword whistled over her head as she hit the ground and rolled. She sprinted for the door to the portrait hall, passing the second armor, which was looking through the closet door at the alley beyond.

Thirty breathless minutes later, Emily ran confidently through an illogical mess of doors and windows, all chalked up. She'd checked and marked every door and window she could find, and could almost find her way around by memory now, ducking through unexpected routes to avoid or ambush the persistently stalking suits of armor. There was only one problem: none of the portals led to Treat's office.

It made sense that it would be the hardest room to find. The spell worked by confusion, security through obscurity, so letting an intruder open randomly on what was surely the most sensitive, valuable room in the building would defeat the whole purpose of the thing.

Emily sighed as she caught her breath in a second supply closet that exited into the drawing room via the front door she'd taken apart. She wasn't panicking, not yet. She'd found a few more ways that would lead her outside, including one door off the portrait hallway that opened dizzyingly onto a third-floor window above the nighttime alleyway. So she wasn't trapped, just frustrated. Plus, she'd made a pretty big mess, between the door she'd torn from its hinges, the water she'd spilled in the closet, the chalk everywhere, and half a broken sword that had snapped off in a hastily shut door. There was no hiding the fact that someone had been here, and Emily was pretty confident that Treat would know exactly who it had been.

That was a whole other problem, one that she hadn't quite thought through before letting herself in by Treat's window. It had seemed simple: into the room, open the drawer, find a helpful clue, and out again with nobody the wiser. That wasn't happening. Well, she couldn't go back in time, so she just had to make the most of the mess.

Maybe it would all be worth it, this time.

Emily bit her lip. The number of doors and windows couldn't

change, that was the rule. If there was one door and one window opening onto Treat's office, that meant that there had to be two matching portals hiding somewhere in the building. Of course they would be hard to find, that was the point, but they had to be there.

But where?

She stepped back out into the drawing room, ready to start running again. At the same moment, the door that normally led out to the hall opened, and all three suits of armor rushed through. Emily cursed, caught off guard. The halberd wielder lunged for her, his wicked axe blade leading. She slapped the polearm away and stepped back. They had her cornered, her back to the wall—or at least to a tiny closet that led nowhere.

The living armor advanced on her, wasting no time. They probably wouldn't kill her if she surrendered, Emily thought. Better to keep an intruder alive for questioning. What a miserable failure this stupid adventure had been. Emily sighed, stepped forward, and—

There was a small decorative window above the hallway door. It should have passed through to show the hall beyond, glowing with warm light from the night-burning lamps. But it was dark, as though it opened on a room with all the lights shut off. It was maybe a foot high and two feet across…

The halberd came at her again, and she hopped onto it, forcing it down to bite into the carpet with a splintery *thunk*. Running up its length, she kicked one sword from its wielder's gauntlet and cleared the other as she hopped again, onto the helmeted head of the lead armor. From there she leapt towards the decorative window, throwing her feet forward and her head back, tucking her arms at her sides to make herself as small as possible.

Shattering glass barely scratched her skin as it rained down around her. She hit carpet in a welcoming darkness and sprang up to find herself alone in Treat's office.

Throwing stealth aside Emily ran for the desk and tore open the target drawer. Somewhere in the building, a siren—more magic, or just a good old-fashioned security system?—began to wail. Triumphantly she took in the contents of the drawer: pens, a box of staples, a half-worn pink eraser.

"What the shit!" Emily yelled to the empty room. She pulled the drawer completely free of the desk and turned it over. Its meager contents spilled onto the floor, revealing a blank wooden bottom. Emily slammed it down on the desk in anger.

A scratching noise drew her attention to the broken window, where she could see the helmet and sword-blade of one of the living armors starting to climb through. The perspective of looking into a full-sized window and out a tiny one was baffling and made her a bit queasy. She turned away, to the door leading who knew where.

Something about the question of perspective—relative size—turned over in her mind.

"Ha!" Emily punched two fingers straight down into the empty drawer, hooked them, and pulled out a false bottom. A huge, ancient book, bound in blood-red dragon leather, was waiting for her. With a quick glance at the window, where the living armor was almost halfway through, she picked up the tome and began riffling through it.

It was a book of heraldic symbols, none of which matched the designs on the shields on the wall to her left. Each was carefully and clearly labelled with a name, and each was different. Secret symbols for every man of the Lancers? Near the end of the book, she began to see names she recognized: Cecil Howe, Trevor Leslie-Yost…and there it was. The dragon sign from her parchment, painted carefully onto a thick vellum page that looked as though an older design had been removed from it before the new one was laid down. And above it, in straight, neat letters, a name: Marshall Alder.

Alder—she knew that name. He was the one big-name Lancer who still lived. The man who'd killed, perhaps, the last dragon in the world. The man who was stationed—what had Treat said? Finalhaven. And her dad had mentioned him, too, said he was somewhere in Maine.

63

With a wrenching crash, the first of the living armors tumbled into the office. Behind it, Emily stole one last glance at Alder's old shield, hanging unmarred on the wall with its motto visible even in the gloom: "RESURGAM."

She dropped the book, leapt for the office door, threw it open, and dove through to find herself in summer shadows on the roof of the Guild Hall. Laughing, she ran.

CHAPTER 6

Emily stood on a small sandy cove surrounded on three sides by high rocks, watching a small fishing boat come in across the flat gray sea. The late-afternoon sun touched her back, a thin cloak of warmth against the chill that would come in with evening.

She stretched, yawning, still working out the cramps of a day of travel. The train had taken her from Boston as far as Portland, and most of the Maine coast from there was covered by a series of buses, but eventually Route 1 had turned away from the coast, leaving her to hitchhike, then just hike, the last few miles to the sea.

The trip had given Emily plenty of time to reflect on her actions the night before. The farther she got from the scene of the crime, the worse things seemed. By now, Treat and her father had come in to work at the Lancers' Guild Hall to find the scene of destruction she'd left behind. Her father was probably paying for the damage she'd caused, almost certainly furious with her, and most definitely fired. The only question was whether Treat had made him clean up before kicking him out on the street.

The fishing boat was getting near to shore. It was a little boat, barely more than a dinghy with an outboard motor and a canvas canopy for shade and protection from the rain. Emily could make out a pilot standing with one hand on the tiller of the motor, and at the prow, a man who appeared to be an old wizard of the hat-and-robes sort.

Maybe it hadn't been that bad after all, Emily thought. She'd only broken a window and a desk drawer. And chalked up a bunch of doors and windows. The living armors were all intact—she was proud of that one—and she hadn't stolen anything, not really, just an idea. Somehow she didn't think Treat would see it that way. Well, you couldn't argue with success. She'd just have to figure out what was happening on Finalhaven, impress the Sabre & Torch Society, and let everything else work itself out.

Emily had no doubt that the answers she was looking for waited on the island. It all fit: dun Raven finds a message in a bottle in the ocean between Nova Scotia and Maine. It contains a symbol that leads, however indirectly, to the man in charge of the garrison of a castle off the Maine coast. So the bottle must come from the castle.

And yet—why such an abstract, roundabout message? The dragon's symbol wasn't exactly public knowledge, and the fact that it was linked somehow to Alder was obviously a highly guarded secret. If it was a call for help, it was sure an obscure one. Writing "Help! We are at the Castle Forlorn on Finalhaven in Maine" would have been a lot quicker for any would-be rescuers.

Well, that last missing piece of the puzzle would be on the island, and then Emily could find someone from the S&T to make her report with all the questions answered and loose ends tied up. Much more impressive that way, she thought.

The crunch of fiberglass on sand brought Emily out of her reverie. The old wizard stepped carefully from the fishing boat to the beach, his long robes hitched up to his knees, revealing pale, spindly legs and sandaled feet.

"Hello!" Emily called with a smile as she headed down the beach to meet the boat. "Just come back from Finalhaven?"

"Oh, ah, it certainly appears that way, doesn't it?" replied the wizard, his brows pulling together in obvious thought.

"Yes, were you on vacation?" asked Emily politely. This one had clearly cast one too many astral projections.

"Yes, vacation, that had been the plan. Hmm, hard to say. For now, perhaps home is the best option. Thank you, Edmund!" With a wave back to the boat pilot and a nod to Emily, the old wizard trudged up the beach. Emily watched with a smile as he whirled his hand in a lazy arc and lifted straight off the sand to be deposited gently at the top of the rocks.

"Wizards, huh?" said Emily to the pilot, who was waiting patiently at the waterline. He had heavy black brows beneath a mop of equally black hair, and a gut hid under his dirty T-shirt, though his tattooed arms were ropy with muscle.

"I suppose," he replied. "Actually, he's no stranger than the rest of them."

"What do you mean?" asked Emily.

The pilot shrugged. "Here, give me your bag and hop in. I'll tell you on the way. The name's Doughty, by the way," he continued as he heaved Emily's bag into his boat with a grunt. "You can call me Ed if you like."

"Nice to meet you, Ed. I'm Emily Sledge." They shook hands, then Ed held the boat steady while Emily clambered aboard. Normally she would have insisted on hauling her own bag, and getting into boats was nothing compared to running up a moving polearm, but she'd taken an immediate liking to Ed, who was plainly a regular man in the world of the Gifted.

Ed grabbed an oar from the bottom of the boat and was about to shove off when a shout from the top of the rocks turned both their heads. A woman in blue stood there holding a large canvas bag in one hand and waving with the other.

"Hey, the mail! That's lucky," said Ed. "Emily, do you mind?"

"Not at all," replied Emily with a smile. She hopped out of the boat, crossed the beach, and climbed quickly to the top of the rocks, where the mailwoman had her sign a receipt stating that she'd take the mail the rest of the way.

"Anything outgoing?" asked the mailwoman. Emily looked back at Ed, who showed them empty hands, apparently anticipating the question he couldn't hear.

"Guess not," said Emily.

"Well, pleasure unburdening myself on you!" The mailwoman tipped her hat and headed back across the short grass above the beach. Emily grabbed the mailbag—it would be heavy to a regular person, she figured—and slid the fifteen feet or so back down to the beach. At the waterline she tossed the mail into Ed's boat, which settled an inch or two deeper into the water. Before she could climb in again, Ed stopped her with a raised hand.

"Hey, are you sure you wanna go over there?" Genuine concern lined his weather-beaten face.

"Yeah, why wouldn't I?" Emily asked.

"Well, that old wizard—everybody who comes back from Finalhaven is like that. Confused, you know? Can't remember anything about their visit. It's pretty unnerving, if I'm being honest."

"You think there's something weird going on?"

"I know there is, kid," said Ed with a shrug.

"Well, I'm trying to figure out what it is. Let me on."

Ed moved aside for her to climb in. "Not like I could stop you. At least you can deliver the mail for me. I just started tossing it on the shore. Someone always comes to get it as I'm heading off, so I figure it's fine. They always look kinda sad about it, though."

"Huh," replied Emily, settling onto a bench. "They ever try to communicate with you? Ask for help or anything?"

Ed shoved off from the beach, then took up his place at the tiller.

"Not that I can remember," he said.

An hour over flat, empty waters brought them in view of the little island of Finalhaven. It was a low, sparse thing, with little greenery to define its rocky shores against the gray sea. At its northern tip, on a rock outcropping connected to the main body of the island by a stretch of sand perhaps a hundred yards long, sat the Castle Forlorn. It seemed to have grown straight up from the stone, with the same moss and barnacles that covered the seaweed-strewn rock climbing a few feet up the stones of the castle. A few feet above the moss-line, arched windows opened into the castle. A warm light burned in one row, but the rest of the castle was dark and empty.

"Tide's coming in. It's a sandbar, see?" said Ed. "When the tide's up there's just water between the castle and the island proper. Good for defense, I suppose."

"So is that the high water mark?" Emily asked, indicating the point where the moss reached on the castle.

"You got it," said Ed with a nod. "Here, I'll take you around to the town landing. Wanted to give you the proper tourist view first, though."

Ed guided the boat south, paralleling the shoreline and moving away from the castle. They soon rounded the southern point of the island and headed north again, keeping the eastern shore on their left hand. Ahead, Emily could see a break in the rocks and a surprisingly bright white sand beach stretching out like a long tongue into the water. On the far side of the beach, a long wooden walkway ran along the foot of a rocky cliff; multiple short piers, crowded with boats, stuck out perpendicular into the water.

Ed guided his boat around the white beach, heading for an empty spot at one of the piers. As they passed the break in the rocks, Emily saw that the beach sloped uphill to what looked like a paved town square. She could make out the top of a fountain or statue peeking out above the slope, and buildings that walled in the square on three sides, the beach making the fourth. A few seagulls hung in the air above the beach, spiraling slowly in search of food, but otherwise nothing moved.

Ed parked the boat handily and hopped out to tie off. Emily followed him, with her duffel in one hand and the mailbag in the other. Looking back over the sea, she could just make out the sun touching the line of the mainland.

"You staying the night?" she asked Ed. "It's gonna be dark before you can get back."

He shook his head as he untied the boat.

"Well, in that case, thanks for everything. What do I owe you for the ride?"

"Don't worry about it," Ed replied, hopping down by the tiller. Without another word, he started the engine and was off. As he headed back out to sea, he looked back at Emily with an expression of…it wasn't concern. Confusion, maybe?

Ed shook his head and turned his back on Finalhaven and Emily.

Emily shouldered her duffel and grabbed the mailbag in her other hand. The walkway brought her along the rocks to the white sand beach, which rose as she expected to the paving stones of a lovely, quiet town square.

A woman with pale skin and short-cropped, coarse black hair leaned against the low wall of the fountain at the heart of the square, her arms crossed, clearly waiting. She wore casual clothing, a fitted black zip-up sweater and jeans, but Emily knew instantly that she was a fighter. She had the combination of perfect balance and coiled-spring tension that any other Combat Gifted could identify in a second.

The woman levered herself away from the wall and intercepted Emily. She was about Emily's height, but broader and more obviously muscular. It was hard to place her age, but she was definitely older than Emily by at least a decade.

"And who might you be?" she asked.

"Emily Sledge," Emily replied, trying to stay polite. "I'm with—I'm here on a mission for the Sabre & Torch Society."

"Aren't you a bit young for the S&T?" The woman was openly sizing Emily up, clearly also recognizing a fellow fighter. "I thought they didn't take kids. Is anybody else coming behind you?"

"No," said Emily. "Is Marshall Alder here? I need to tell him I got his message."

"Ah, shit," the woman sighed. Some of the aggression left her body as her broad shoulders slumped. She stuck her hand out suddenly for a shake. "You mean my message. I'm Bronwyn Queen, captain of the Irregulars of the Castle Forlorn."

"Nice to meet you," Emily said, shaking. "So you sent that symbol thing? The S&T intercepted the bottle and asked me to figure out what it was all about. It led me here to Finalhaven." Aware of the obvious disappointment on Captain Queen's face, she added, "If you just fill me in on what's up, I can get back home and make my report. I'll get out of your hair."

"Yes, I'm sure you'll want to get out of here as soon as you know what's going on." Queen shrugged. "Well, I guess it won't make any difference if you meet everyone first. Come on. You can carry the mail."

It was about half a mile's walk to the castle, on a well-trodden dirt road that led north from the small cluster of buildings in the town square. They passed a few houses outside the town proper, but it was clear that Finalhaven was not a densely populated island.

"Do many people live here year-round?" Emily asked Captain Queen as they passed a low farmhouse with its roof partially collapsed in.

"Not really," said Queen. "It's more of a tourist destination, or it was. The wizards call it a thin place. The Veil is like tissue paper here. We get a lot of weird stuff coming through, hence the castle. Though nothing like…"

"Like what?" Emily asked after a moment.

"Well, you'll see."

They reached the sandbar that separated the castle from the island. Ed had been right; the tide was coming in. Luckily there was enough solid ground left for the two fighters to pick their way around pooling seawater to a short flight of stone steps that led up to the castle door, which was ten feet of solid oak studded with iron spikes.

Queen opened it easily and let them in. The entry hall was mostly in shadows, with only a few run-down torches sputtering on the walls. Queen led them to a plain wooden door in a back corner of the hall, and swung it open to reveal a long, straight hall with a few wooden doors opening off it to the left. Warm light showed beneath them.

Captain Queen stopped at the first door and turned a heavy black iron handle. The door swung inwards on a large, long dining hall that must have run the entire western wall of the castle. Dusty sunlight slanted in the row of arched windows that ran the length of the wall across from the door, and a low fire burned in a great hearth, but the ceiling was in gray shadow. Two rows of rough wooden tables ran parallel down the length of the hall, with low benches on either side, clearly enough to feast far more people than the handful currently in the room.

Anticipation was written on nearly every face in the hall, all of which were aimed at Emily. About ten people sat around the room, a couple near the hearth but most on benches around the remnants of lunch. There was a moment of awkward silence, then a tall young man near the fire said, "Well, well, new blood."

"Don't be morbid, Ernest," scolded Captain Queen as she ushered Emily inside and shut the door behind them. "This is Emily Sledge. Emily is from the S&T. They got my message and this is all they sent. So we're going to give Emily the royal treatment tonight and send her on her way tomorrow, first thing."

"Is that the mail?" asked a pale young man who sat on a bench with a guitar in his lap.

"Oh dear," said Ernest morosely.

"Yeah," said Emily. "Here, let me get the bag open and I can hand it out." There had to be somebody friendly in this damn castle, Emily decided, and she was going to find them. She untied the drawstring of the mailbag and began pulling out letters.

"Let's see…Ernest Graves, that must be you. Oh, it's postmarked from Harkness! You're not related to Professor Graves, are you?" Ernest stood up from his armchair near the fire and snatched a bound stack of letters from Emily's hand. Emily could see something of Professor Graves's mobile face in Ernest, though where the professor had been compact and short, Ernest had the too-small head and slightly droopy look of a big man who has recently lost weight.

"Professor Graves? I suppose it's possible, but I don't know everything." Ernest tossed his mail into the fire without even glancing at it. "There, that's done! Now then, what about the rest of you damned souls? Let me help you, Emily."

Ernest grabbed the bag from her and began rifling through it. "Aha! Michael Fletcher, multiple letters! Mysterious! Let me apply myself here. They can't be from your family, so you must have some friends squirreled away that you haven't told us about. For shame, Michael. Here you go." He tossed the letters to a young man with dark skin and long black dreadlocks bound back from his head in a white ribbon. Michael caught the pile in his lap, laughing, and began to eagerly open them.

"Who's next? Aha, the brothers Blodring." Ernest pulled out a battered cardboard shipping box bound up in packing tape, plus two tied bundles of letters in heavy, yellowed envelopes. "Looks as though Ma Blodring still misses you as much as ever, boys."

From the group near the far end of the room, two men, clearly brothers, stood up to accept their mail. Both had a swarthy European look, with heavy brows and thick black hair, and both wore clothing with an old-fashioned, almost medieval, cut. Emily immediately pegged them as fighters like Captain Queen. The taller one had a few gray hairs at the temples of his Roman-cut hair, and a long nose that gave him a slightly haughty, intellectual air; Emily was certain this was the older brother. The younger was shorter and heavier, with a neat buzz cut. As they stepped up to take their letters, Emily saw they were both covered in old scars; the older brother in particular had a long line on each cheek that she recognized as the mark of someone with experience in the duels that were traditional among Combat Gifted from Teutonia.

"Uther, that's for you," said Ernest to the younger brother, holding out a bundle. "Oh, no, you're Wulf! I can never tell you two apart. Wulf, of course, I simply must remember that. And Uther, those are yours. The care package you'll have to fight over." As the rest of the hall laughed, Uther, the tall older brother, took the battered package.

"That's the boys sorted," Ernest continued. "Let's see, what about our Jack?" Ernest sniffed the opening of the mailbag to more general laughter. Even the previously glowering Blodring brothers were smiling at this. "Yes, I do believe I'm getting a whiff of perfume—mmm, at least two different brands, I would say—perhaps a hint of rose petals?"

The guitar player who had asked about the mail originally played a spirited, ironic few notes, then set down his instrument, leaning it gently against his bench.

"Come on, Ernest," said Jack with a weary smile. As he unfolded from the bench, Emily saw that he was a few inches taller than she was, but nowhere near her weight. He was pale and thin, with rich brown hair spilling around his eyes. He wore a loose white shirt tucked into tight black jeans, like a Romantic poet. Emily could guess who all the perfumed letters were from.

Ernest placed the envelopes into Jack's waiting hands with exaggerated care, saying, "I now bequeath these into your care, the only one amongst us poor souls whom anyone actually misses. Unless you've been sending these to yourself to protect your image."

Jack bowed low over the letters, like a priest accepting a blessing at the altar, and as his long white fingers wrapped around them, Emily was amazed to see a sixth finger on each hand. They seemed perfectly functional as he sorted through the perfumed envelopes, and she wondered how useful they would be with his guitar.

"Well, that's it for us, children," said Ernest. "Squires, nothing for you, but there are some letters here for your knights, so why don't you take these upstairs after dinner?" Scattered around the room, four teenagers stood up. Teenagers? Maybe not; to Emily, they barely looked old enough to have been freshmen at Harkness. There were two boys and two girls, all dressed in matching tunics that looked even more medieval than the Blodrings' outfits. The royal crest of Arthur XXX, king of Albion, was stitched on each, showing five red dragons on gold.

So there were four Albian knights here somewhere, Emily thought, and these were their squires. Ernest, Michael, Jack, and Captain Queen seemed to be from the American Gifted Nations, at least going by their accents, and Uther and Wulf were clearly from Teutonia. Whatever was going on in this castle, it sure seemed to involve a lot of people from all over the place.

As the members of this strange group settled down to read their mail, Emily realized she had been completely forgotten about. Ernest and Captain Queen were talking quietly by the fire, and the four squires had congregated around a chessboard after splitting up the letters for their respective knights. The Blodring brothers sat apart on one of the long wooden benches, swapping letters back and forth as they finished them, and occasionally pointing out certain lines to each other; at one point, they huddled together over a crumpled page, and when they both looked up, Uther murmured something quietly to his younger brother, who sat with a faraway look in his eyes.

"Thanks for getting the mail. It's nice not having to haul it back from the beach."

Emily jumped at the sudden voice at her side; she wasn't used to people sneaking up on her. She looked over to find Jack smiling at her side as though they had been watching the room together; he rested one hand on his chin in a thoughtful pose that somehow drew attention to both the clean line of his jaw and the extra finger that rested lightly on his upturned lips.

"You get the mail?" asked Emily, happy to be making conversation with someone. The perfumed letters Jack had received were nowhere to be seen. "I'm pretty sure that bag is heavy. Shouldn't they send one of the fighters?"

"It's good to make yourself useful." Jack crossed his arms in comic indignation. "And what makes you so certain I'm not a fighter?"

Emily couldn't help but laugh. "Because I am, and I've broken all of my fingers at least twice." She nodded at Jack's guitar, which leaned against a table. "You'd never be able to explain it to her. Or any other special ladies in your life."

"I tell you what," Jack replied. "You can get the mail next week."

Before Emily could respond, a clattering of dishes turned every head in the hall. Two more young men—*is everyone in this castle under thirty?* Emily wondered—set down a huge tray of food, carried between them, on a side table that seemed to groan audibly under the weight of the meal.

"Where's the wine?" called Ernest from the fire. The group laughed, and one of the young men grinned and bowed in mock apology. He had the swarthy, central-European look of the Blodring brothers, but was light where they were heavy, with aquiline features and smooth skin.

"Wentworth, dear, the wine, please, and hurry," he said to his assistant, who among all these romantic youths was shockingly normal looking. He was waspy white, with buzzed blonde hair and a neat polo shirt, and reminded Emily of so many high-school boys she'd seen the few times she'd ventured outside the Gifted bubble of Harkness into the normal world around her.

"Sure, Julian," said Wentworth, and disappeared through an archway to some stairs that Emily figured led to the kitchen or wine cellar.

"Now," said Julian, "no sense in waiting for the wine. Please, come, help yourselves. It's especially good tonight, if I may say so."

They did, loading battered old silver plates with plentiful servings of Julian's rich meal. Smelling the delicious scent of seasoned chicken, Emily realized suddenly that she hadn't eaten since before breaking into the Guild Hall the night before. For her metabolism, it may as well have been a year. Gratefully she got in line for the food.

When she made it back to feasting tables, she found an empty spot on a bench between Captain Queen and Michael. The group all sat at the same table, close together despite the many benches left empty in the hall. Ernest sat at the head, like the father of some old-fashioned family at holiday time, and gestured with his fork.

"Now! We all know the tradition on mail day. Before we eat, we read. Your most heartbreaking, please. A sentence or two, no more than a paragraph; we're all hungry. Jack, you start."

Jack obliged, picking up a sheet of paper covered on both sides with tight, neat handwriting.

"There's a lot here—where was it? Here we go: 'I'm counting down the days until I see you again.'" There was a sort of collective sigh from the group, as though the sentence had special meaning to all of them.

Jack must have noticed Emily's curious stare, because he said, "Only seven days left," as though that explained everything.

Uther was up next; he stabbed his fork into a chicken breast, where it stood upright and quivering, and read from a letter on the table in front of him: "Mama writes, 'Little Karl—'"

"Little Karl!" The entire table shouted the toast, raising glasses and food-laden utensils to whoever Little Karl was. Uther smiled without looking up from the letter, then cleared his throat.

"'Little Karl has had his first duel. The boy was two years his senior, but your brother was not afraid at all. He is—what is the word—ecstatic, ecstatic to show you his scar when you return home.'" Uther grabbed up the fork and took a huge bite of chicken. Jack, next to him, put a hand on Uther's shoulder in a comforting gesture.

"He took mine," complained Wulf, rifling through the stack of letters that sat between the brothers. "Damn. Ah, here's one. 'Your father is ill again. We all fear that he shall die in his bed. Won't you come visit before…before…'" He faltered to a stop, staring down at his food. Uther didn't look at his brother, but he did stop chewing.

The moment was broken by Wentworth returning with four wine bottles, two in each hand. Julian helped him serve, pouring generous glasses for everyone at the table. When that was done, the two cooks helped themselves to food and joined the table, sitting across from each other.

"Where were we?" said Ernest. "Ah, Julian, no mail for you, I'm afraid. Of course, if your mother wants you she can just come up here and pinch your ear! Now then, I burned all my mail, as is tradition, but I can tell you what it said from memory." He looked straight at Emily. "Quit wasting your time with poetry, boy. Your mind is going to waste, filled with romantic dreams. Join my great purpose." He paused. "Sound like anyone you know, newcomer?"

Emily flushed, finding the attention of the whole room suddenly on her.

"Um, no," she said truthfully. If Ernest really was related to Professor Graves, his version of the professor was nothing like the spritely man she'd met.

"Thought not," said Ernest. "Who's next? Captain?" Captain Queen, sitting on Emily's left, shrugged and turned her hands up to show she had no letters. "Emily doesn't count, so, all right, Michael, let's have it."

Michael, on Emily's right, gave a nervous smile. "Actually," he said quietly, "I got one from my parents."

The table got quiet for a moment, and then Ernest said, "You don't have to—"

"No, it's fine. If you want to eat you have to play, right?" Michael flashed a grin. "Um, there was a good line at the end. 'Whenever you get home your father is gonna beat your ass.' All things considered, I think I'll stay here with you guys."

Nobody had anything to say to that. The silence stretched out painfully, until Emily found it unbearable.

"What's that?" she asked, pointing. At the far end of the hall, there was a door. She hadn't really noticed until just now, but it was standing independent of the wall, like a door leading to an imaginary second room in a cheap theatrical set. It was a pretty normal-looking door, at least for the dreary Castle Forlorn, made of plain wood in an unpainted frame.

The others at the table looked to Captain Queen. She put down her fork and turned to look Emily straight in the eye.

"That," she said, "is why you're here."

CHAPTER 7

As they ate, the young men and women of the Irregulars filled Emily in on the story of the door and the doom that hung over the Castle Forlorn. Captain Queen told most of it in short, factual sentences that almost concealed her obvious tension.

"The door has always been here," Queen began, "at least as long as anybody can remember. In all that time, it never opened, and couldn't be opened. Until ninety-two days ago."

"You opened it?" Emily asked, perplexed.

"No." Queen shook her head emphatically. "That night, one of my Irregulars was killed. His name was Alexander Cho, and we found a dagger in his back."

From the end of the table, Julian the cook piped up. "As far as we can tell, Alexander was, um, unlucky. I think he went to the great hall to grab a midnight snack and someone came through the door and stabbed him."

"Most likely," agreed Captain Queen. "We believe that someone, whoever they were, was an advance scout for an invading force." She cleared her throat. "Before he died, Alexander wrote a message on the floor: '100 days.'" Captain Queen glanced briefly at the door, then turned back to Emily. "We're assuming that's when the real assault is coming through."

"Eight days from now." Emily nodded, understanding. "I don't get something, though. Why haven't you sent for help, or even told anyone? Your message in a bottle wasn't exactly easy to understand. Honestly, I went through some shit to get here." It was hard to believe she'd broken into the Lancers' Guild Hall less than twenty-four hours ago. It had been a really long day.

Jack spoke up. "We've tried, Emily. There's some kind of spell around the island."

"A memory wall," said Michael.

"A memory wall, right," Jack continued. "Any communication that goes out gets, ah, forgotten."

"Forgotten?" Emily blinked.

"Apparently, people just can't retain the information," put in Ernest. "When you leave tomorrow, you'll forget everything about your little visit here."

"What about sending a letter? Or hell, an email?"

"Okay, we clearly don't have Wi-Fi here," said Jack with a gentle smile. "But we've sent plenty of letters, to friends, family, old teachers, you name it. They either get lost, or whoever reads them isn't really getting the drift. Not totally sure which, but when they write back they think everything is normal."

That explained the somewhat macabre tradition of reading letters from home, a little bit of gallows humor shared among the Irregulars. How horrible, Emily thought, to be trying to communicate with the rest of the world and have them just refuse to understand.

"What about phone calls? Texts? I mean, come on—"

"Believe me," Captain Queen said with finality. "We've tried it all."

"Phone calls are awful," said Michael without looking up. He was folding something out of white paper. "You're having one conversation and they're having another."

"So what about the symbol, your message in a bottle?" asked Emily.

"That was my last hope," said Captain Queen. "General Marshall

Alder is…General Alder is in charge of the castle's defenses. A few Lancers, the knights from Albion, the castle's garrison, and us, the Irregulars."

"The symbol you saw is his personal sigil, his secret name among the Lancers," interjected Ernest. "He…took it from the dragon he killed. It's an old name, quite a lot of residual magic tied up in it. It was also neither a direct request for help nor a straightforward explanation of our predicament."

"So it was able to make it through this wall thing?" asked Emily.

"Yes," said Queen, standing. "We'd hoped the Lancers would track it down and send help. If you'll excuse me, I need to inform the senior staff that my plan failed."

As the dinner broke up and Julian and Wentworth cleared dishes, Captain Queen gave Emily directions to the castle's residential floor. Having been built to hold far more soldiers, staff, and visitors, the Castle Forlorn had no lack of available rooms. As Emily made her way down a long, blank hallway, the Irregulars' situation boiled in her mind.

It was impossible to know what kind of force was going to come through the door in a week. But leaving your knife behind, buried in some kid's back, was a pretty clear message: *we don't care if you know we're coming.* It didn't inspire confidence in the castle's chances for beating back an invasion.

And it didn't really inspire confidence in Emily that she'd be much use. They had a bunch of Gifted fighters already: Captain Queen, the Blodring brothers, presumably the four Albian knights, probably some of the Lancers with General Alder. One more wouldn't make a difference.

And besides, it wasn't her mission to die in some random castle. She'd been asked to find out what was going on, and she had. The fact that she would forget it all when she left was frustrating, but Emily found it hard to imagine. Would she really lose all her memories of the day when she pushed off from the dock? She couldn't even take notes? It felt impossible.

But the confused faces of the old wizard, and Ed Doughty when he'd left her on Finalhaven, had seemed very real. And Captain Queen had been pretty clear that getting any message out at all had taken a dose of old dragon magic, and even then the message had been about as cryptic and vague as possible.

The extent of the magic wasn't clear, which was annoyingly common for magic. The more Emily thought about it, the more she was afraid that if she stepped off the island, she wouldn't just forget the evening she'd spent there, but also all the work she'd done in figuring out Queen's message in a bottle. Which now resided somewhere in Mr. Treat's office, never to be seen again.

Emily was startled out of her reverie by a plaintive meow. She looked down to see a group of cats lined up by the blank wall of the hallway. There were four. A fat brownish one lounged on its back while two orange and white cats, clearly littermates, scratched and cried at the corner where wall met floor. A scrawny black one, no bigger than a kitten, noticed Emily and came over to twine around her legs.

"Found the castle cats, huh?" said Jack from behind her.

"Huh? Oh, yeah. I'm not really a cat person." She tried to shoo the black one away. Jack picked it up, wrapping its tiny body in the long fingers of one hand while the other scratched behind its ears.

"You're missing out," he said with a smile. "Anyway, I just wanted to tell you not to let Bronwyn—Captain Queen—get to you."

"Oh, I didn't—"

"No, I mean it," Jack interrupted her. "She's a good person and a good leader. She's just tired of false hope. She's been carrying the Irregulars on her shoulders since this whole thing began a few weeks ago and she's exhausted."

"It's pretty awful, huh?" Emily said. The fat brown cat stretched lazily on the floor, revealing a wide stretch of white belly. Emily kneeled down and hesitantly pet it, and got a loud rumbling purr in return.

"It sure is," said Jack. "But I've got hope, even if Bronwyn doesn't. I've gotten out of worse scrapes in my day."

Emily didn't know what to say to that, so she didn't say anything. Jack released the little black cat, who went back to winding between her feet.

In the wan moonlight glowing from a single narrow window, Emily could just make out the blocky outlines of her bedroom. It was small, dominated by a four-poster bed, with a low desk by the window and a chair in the corner by the door. Emily slouched to the bed and dropped heavily on it, feeling clean sheets on a comfortable feather mattress.

She hadn't brought much, but as she peeled off her travel-spoiled clothes, Emily felt a familiar weight in the pocket of her jeans: her phone. She paused a moment, staring at nothing in the darkness of the room, then slipped the phone from her pocket and turned it on. The signal indicator showed a red X.

Sighing, Emily stood and moved to the window, where she held the phone over her head and turned a slow circle. She faced the bed, then the door, the wall, and finally the window again, with no response from the phone. Shaking her head, she lowered the phone, and was about to toss it onto her pile of clothes when the red X changed to a single stubby white bar.

Emily crouched cautiously, unwilling to shift the phone out of position. Hunched awkwardly by the window, she opened her contact list and tried to guess who might still be up this late. One name jumped out: Chris McLeod, who had always been a night owl at Harkness.

She tapped his name. There was a long pause, then a digital ring came tinnily from the earpiece. Emily tapped the speaker button, and the ring loudened, then cut off suddenly.

"Emily, hey!" It was Chris, crackly but audible. "Where are you? Kayo said you—"

"Hey!" Emily said, moving the phone close to her face. "Bad signal, I need to talk fast. I'm on an island called Finalhaven."

"Finalhaven?"

"Far north Commonwealth, almost Madawaska. Not too far from you, I think. But look, there's something really wrong here."

"Nice!" Chris's voice was cheery.

"Nice?" Emily blinked.

"Maine is great in the summer."

"Chris, I'm not on vacation. This is related to that symbol I showed you, the one the S&T asked me to look into."

"Oh yeah, did you find Graves?"

"Yeah, it's dragon magic."

"He couldn't help, huh?" Chris snorted. "That's Graves for you. Knows everything except what you just asked him. Sorry for the wild goose chase."

"What?" A pit was forming in Emily's stomach, as though she were on a roller coaster just cresting a tall rise, balanced in the moment before it began its wild hurtle back down to earth. "No, he told me it was dragon magic. I was able to—look, that doesn't matter. There's something wrong here. There are people here, about to be invaded. They said there was a spell around the island called a memory wall. They need help."

"Em, you there?"

"Yeah." The bottom was falling out of the pit, collapsing into open nothing. "I'm here, Chris."

"Oh, I was just saying I'm sorry Graves couldn't help you. Bad connection out there, huh?"

"Something like that," Emily said.

"So how long are you on vacation?"

"Chris, everyone here is going to die!" Emily moved the phone away from her face, as though she could somehow fix the thing if she just got a better look at it. The white bar in the corner flickered in and out of life for a moment, then became a red X again.

"Chris? Chris…?"

7 Days

Emily woke late the next morning despite her intentions to get up early and get moving. Daylight streamed in through an open window, carrying fresh ocean air with it. All in all, not bad, she thought, though clearly not designed for long stays if the narrow dimensions and spartan furniture were anything to go by.

The jarring phone call of the night before felt like just one part of Emily's jumbled dreams, and she still held some vague conviction that the memory spell shouldn't work on her. But that conviction wasn't actually based on any evidence, which meant her next step was to figure out how to get around the wall of forgetfulness surrounding the island.

She had no clue.

After she dressed, Emily peeked out into the hallway. She saw a long row of evenly spaced doors, suggesting a series of rooms more or less identical to hers. The hall dead-ended to her left, but on her right it came to a T-junction where Michael Fletcher stood talking with a young man Emily didn't recognize.

He was as tall as Jack, but bigger. He wore loose training clothes, but a very real longsword was belted at his hip, and he kept one hand on it as he spoke to Michael. When the man turned his head, Emily got a glimpse of a handsome face marred by a cruel smile. His rich chestnut hair was cut in what Emily guessed was a trendy style from the non-Gifted world, and he apparently kept one eyebrow permanently raised as he looked down his long nose at Michael, who was shorter by a few inches.

Whoever this guy was, Emily hated him immediately.

As she got closer, she could make out their conversation, which was really more of a monologue by the handsome young man.

"Come on, Fletcher," he was saying. He had a snooty Albian accent. "Let's see the letter."

"No," said Michael, quietly but firmly.

"I know you've got it. Luke told me you've been carrying it around with you since last night."

"Max, come on." Michael opened his hands as if to show that they were empty.

"That's Sir Maximilian to you, Fletcher. It's a hereditary title, not that you'd know anything about that. Tell me, did your parents kick you out for being a freak, or did they—what the hell do you want?"

Emily had reached them, and silently put herself between Michael and this Sir Maximilian. One of the Albian knights, apparently, and his squire must have been one of the kids in the great hall during dinner.

"You looking for a fight?" asked Emily. "I'm always in a bad mood before breakfast."

Sir Maximilian looked her up and down, clearly sizing her up. He sneered. "I don't fight women. Besides, you're unarmed. It would hardly be sporting."

"It's your best chance at not getting your ass kicked," Emily replied.

"Emily, leave it," said Michael behind her.

"Don't worry, Fletcher," said Sir Maximilian before Emily could speak. "I'll be the bigger man here. Come find me later if you need a shoulder to cry on." He turned on his heel and headed off down the hall, tapping the pommel of his sword and whistling.

"Wow, what an asshole," said Emily loudly while the knight was still within earshot.

"Don't worry about it, really," said Michael. "He's just sick of being cooped up here waiting for the end. Come on, let's get breakfast."

As they walked, Emily asked, "So why is Sir Maximilian sticking around, anyway? He doesn't really seem like the whole romantic lost cause type."

Michael laughed. "It's not his choice, actually. He's not the leader of our little Albian delegation, no matter how much he thinks he is."

"Oh, who is?" asked Emily. They were in the long, empty hallway where she'd seen the cats the night before, but they were nowhere to be found.

"Another knight, Sir Richard Peakey. He's, um, antique? He's got them staying on here to do the honorable thing and help out, but it's no secret Max wants to move on."

"Move on where?"

Michael was quiet for a long time, as they turned a corner, passed through a crumbling archway, and headed down a long, spiraling flight of stairs.

"Have you ever heard of Elizabeth Pendragon?" he asked finally.

"The lost princess, right? Or queen, I guess, depending on who you ask."

"That's the one," said Michael. "The rumor was always that Arthur XXIX had a daughter first, before the current king of Albion was born. Well, apparently the rumor is true."

"Really!" Emily laughed, thinking of how angry Miss Scrivener had gotten when Emily had asked about it. She'd just been trying to tweak the uptight woman; she had no idea there was any truth to the old story.

"So apparently, Sir Richard and the others are in America hunting her down. They stopped off here at the castle first and Sir Richard decided to stay, but Max is itching to keep moving. I keep hoping he'll win the argument."

"Hunting her down?" Emily couldn't keep the surprise from her voice.

"Yup. She's a threat to the line of succession. They went twenty-nine generations without a girl, and I guess Arthur the Thirtieth wants to keep the tradition going. So they're here to kill her."

Emily had thought they were headed to the great hall again, but Michael had led them directly to the kitchen, where the castle's two cooks were hard at work on breakfast; Wentworth put a knife in Julian's left hand as he flipped an egg with a spatula in his right, then swapped the tools between hands to chop an onion. Captain Queen was halfway through a heaping plate of bacon and eggs, and Ernest waved at them with one biscuit while chewing another.

Emily made herself a plate to match Queen's and sat down next to her. She was very, very hungry all of a sudden, and she lifted her fork with relish.

"Come on, Sledge," said Captain Queen suddenly. "Get up. You're meeting with the senior staff."

Emily sighed.

"Better go," said Julian from the stove. "Don't worry, I'll keep your eggs warm. In case you make it back alive."

Emily's stomach growled audibly as she stood before the senior staff of the Castle Forlorn. Six men and two women sat along either side of a long table in a small room hung with rich tapestries. Emily stood at one end of the table; across from her an ancient man sat dozing at the head.

She recognized Sir Maximilian immediately. He had changed out of his training clothes into a very impressive, if old-fashioned, tabard bearing the arms of King Arthur split with what Emily guessed was Sir Max's family crest. To the knight's left sat another old man with a drooping white mustache, dressed similarly, who Emily figured must be Sir Richard. To Sir Maximilian's right were two more knights who had both been introduced as Arthur, which seemed to be a popular name for Albian boys. One was tall and thin and the other short and stocky, but neither spoke, seeming to defer to Sir Max.

Across the table from the knights sat the other four members of the senior staff. The man nearest to Emily was Nadim Dhar, Poet-Captain of the Castle Forlorn, which apparently meant he led the castle's small garrison of men-at-arms. He looked up at Emily with one thick black eyebrow raised beneath somewhat messy black hair with just a few strands of white, and then an amused half-smile broke within his trim beard, as though he couldn't hold it back anymore. Emily smiled back reflexively as the Poet-Captain crossed his muscular arms and leaned back in his chair. Unlike the knights, Dhar was dressed informally in only a black T-shirt and jeans.

Next to Dhar was Lancer Colonel Liu, who looked every inch the executive officer she was. She was small but muscular in a tank top and camo pants, with sleek black hair pulled tight back from a sharp, intelligent face. A big chunk of her left ear was missing. Emily tried not to stare.

Captain Queen had taken the seat next to Colonel Liu. Last, sitting across from Sir Richard near the head of the table, was Lancer General Sir Marshall Alder. He took Emily in with a long, challenging stare. His hair was snowy white, and pale gray eyes burned in his lined face, but unlike Sir Richard or the sleeping old man, General Alder had lost nothing to age. Like the knights, he wore an old-fashioned tabard, this one in all black and bearing the dragon-and-lance crest of the Lancers stitched in silver. A high collar covered his neck to the chin, and soft gray gloves hid his hands.

Colonel Liu cleared her throat. "So, Miss Sledge. To put it bluntly: you're all they sent?"

"Uh, yes," said Emily.

"Why don't you explain how you ended up here?" said Captain Queen.

Emily gave them the short version, though she left out how exactly

90

she had finally identified the dragon symbol as—belonging to? related to? she still wasn't clear on that part—General Alder.

"It seems to me," said Sir Maximilian coldly when Emily had finished, "that if you had told somebody—the Sabre & Torch, some of your friends from Harkness, anybody really—where you were going, you might have brought enough people to actually make a difference."

"How was I supposed to know I was headed to a castle under siege with a bunch of spells around it?" Emily snapped. "And besides, Mr. Treat knew, and he obviously wanted to bury it! You're really going to blame me when your Lancers are leaving you out to dry?"

There was a long awkward silence. Sir Richard coughed quietly, Colonel Liu stared at the table, and General Alder stared at Emily. It was unnerving, how he did that.

Finally Poet-Captain Dhar spoke. "I'm sure you did what you thought was right, Emily."

"I'm not sure she thought at all," said Sir Maximilian with a sneer.

"Enough," said General Alder. The others fell silent immediately. "Miss Sledge, is it your intention to stay here with us?"

"Ah…" Emily started, then found she didn't know how to answer the question. They were all staring at her now, Captain Queen most intently of all.

Emily looked Queen in the eye. "Yes, I'm going to stay. Until I can figure out how to get a call for help out."

"In that case," said Colonel Liu quickly, "you can make yourself useful. We've begun preparations in the great hall. The Blodring brothers are overseeing the construction of some physical defenses. Please go help them. Dismissed."

As the senior staff stood, Captain Queen pulled Colonel Liu aside for a private word, leaving Emily to find her own way back to the great hall.

After only two wrong turns, Emily found herself at the great hall. As she entered, a small group of people she didn't recognize were just finishing stacking the long tables and benches against the left-hand wall, beneath the row of arched windows. The hall was echoing and empty; the hearth was cold and black, and a chill seemed to have settled over the room despite the blue summer sky visible through the windows.

Emily recognized Uther and Wulf Blodring directing the last of the stacking. She caught Uther's eye and gave him a small wave; he nodded in reply, then returned to giving orders. Wulf split off from the group and came over to Emily.

"They've sent me to help out," said Emily as Wulf got near.

"Ah," the younger Blodring replied. He ran a scarred hand over his buzzed hair. "Frankly we are okay here, thank you." He spoke in a heavy Teutonic accent that forced Emily to really pay attention if she wanted to follow along.

"What are you doing exactly?" Emily asked. "Maybe I can help."

Wulf looked over his shoulder, where Uther was issuing new instructions to the small group of workers.

"We will be building defenses here, surrounding the door. We put a chokepoint here, to bottle them up, then direct them along this line so our guns can pick at them."

"Seems a bit close for guns," Emily said, looking around the room. Wulf shrugged.

"Close up is where the real fighting shall happen, anyhow," he said.

"Huh," said Emily. "So, um, why not just block off the door? Board it up or something?"

Wulf thought for a second, then laughed. "It opens inward, not out."

Emily wasn't sure what that meant for a door to another dimension, but she didn't want to press the issue. She was about to make another suggestion when she heard a sort of grunting shuffle from the doorway behind her. She turned to see another group of workers struggling with a large section of wooden palisade that looked like it had been brought out of storage somewhere deep in the castle.

"Come on, let's help them," she said to Wulf.

"No," he replied. Emily stopped in her tracks.

"I'm sorry?"

"We are directing, they are working," said Wulf with a shrug.

"You could help them, you know," said Emily coldly.

"Not our job," replied Wulf. "We are Gifted. We fight. We will be working hard enough in seven days, don't you think?"

"That doesn't—are you serious?"

"We owe these people a duty, yes, and we will risk our lives to protect them. They repay us by their labor. It is the way of things." Wulf scratched his chin, where a few days of stubble had grown.

"Then things are going the wrong way," said Emily, as she turned on her heel.

A few hours later, a dozen palisades had been set in a complex spiraling pattern, centered on the door, that earned Uther Blodring's nod of approval. Emily was about ready to add a few more scars to his face, but she wasn't sure if she could take him, considering she'd been hauling multi-ton barricades around for hours while he gave occasional directions and at one point, left and came back with a glass of lemonade.

At least the servants—that's who they were, the servants of the castle—were grateful for Emily's help. To the last man, they thanked her, and one older man who lived in town told her she was always welcome to stop by for a taste of his wife's cooking, an invitation Emily accepted with a smile.

As she stood toweling sweat off her forehead, Emily heard Ernest Graves's voice ringing out across the hall.

"Brothers Blodring! Put aside your labors and join the Irregulars for a drink or three! Uther! Wulf?"

"Probably on another lemonade break," Emily said, joining Ernest by the door.

"Emily Sledge! How sweaty you are." Ernest raised an eyebrow.

"The strength of ten men isn't that great when you need twenty people to lift one of these things," Emily replied, gesturing behind her. Ernest pursed his lips, but said nothing, so Emily continued, "Anyway, I could definitely use a drink. If I'm invited, that is."

"But of course. Truth be told, I didn't expect you to still be here. Visitors to our poor castle have a tendency to disappear upon learning what we're up against."

The Blodrings never showed, so Emily and Ernest headed across the sandbar and into the town of Finalhaven. The sun was setting huge and red behind the distant mainland, and their bodies cast long shadows out towards the open sea. As they walked, Ernest told Emily how one Madame de Luna, mother to chef Julian, ran an inn and tavern in town called the Twisted Wrist that was a favorite of the Irregulars.

"Time was," said Ernest, "she did quite the trade with wizards come to experience the thin place that is Finalhaven. Now, of course, the permeability of the Veil here on the island has proven to be something of a liability. Business hasn't been so good these last few weeks, and it doesn't help that the few guests she does get can't remember their stay afterwards. Bad for word of mouth, you know."

Emily snorted. "I can see that, yeah."

"Ah, she laughs! That's more than I've gotten from the Blodrings in nearly a year."

"Yeah, what's their deal anyway? There was a lot of leading from behind going on in the great hall today."

"Don't mind Sturm und Drang. Teutonic warrior culture isn't exactly the great meritocracy of the Secret Commonwealth."

"How did you know?" asked Emily, surprised.

"Well, you sound like a northeasterner, for one. But more to the point, I caught you in the act of helping the Giftless masses. Not everyone would do that."

"Well, they should," said Emily stubbornly.

Ernest sighed, then looked up to the fading sky as if searching for inspiration. "There once were two brothers Teutonic, who though rather strong were moronic—"

"Ernest! Emily!" Emily looked up to see Jack waving to them from the long shadow of the fountain in the town square. When she waved back, Jack jogged across the cobblestones to meet them, then walked by Emily's side as Ernest led them toward the Twisted Wrist at the other side of the square. He had thrown an open vest on over his loose poet's shirt, and pulled his hair back into a lazy ponytail.

"Where have you two been? Everyone else is here already. Not much to do other than drink these days, and the great hall is occupado, so..." Jack shrugged.

The Twisted Wrist was a three-story Tudor inn straight out of a fairy tale. A painted plank showing a hand contorted into a spellcaster's awkward claw hung above a heavy oaken door, which Jack opened with a sweeping bow. Warm light and muffled sounds of speech and drinking spilled into the summer night.

Beyond the door, two steps led down into the common room of the inn, where the Irregulars had all gathered just as Jack had said. Emily relaxed a bit when she saw that neither Captain Queen nor Sir Maximilian was there. In fact, the various Irregulars were the inn's only patrons, lending truth to Ernest's assertion that the inn wasn't doing too well.

It was clearly built to hold far more people, with perhaps a dozen large round tables arranged in a rough L shape around a bar in the far-right corner. Most of them had their chairs still upside-down on them for cleaning the floor, and the Irregulars fit comfortably at only two: Michael and Wentworth shared a table with Jack's guitar, while the four Albian squires sat chatting one table over.

95

"We are arrived!" Ernest announced to the room. "And look who's decided to stay!"

"For now," Emily said, but it was drowned out by the ragged cheer and clinking of mugs from the Irregulars. Michael pushed a chair towards Emily with his foot, and even as she sat, a woman who could only be Julian's mother appeared with a tray of full mugs. She shared her son's long nose, rich complexion, and thick black hair, though hers was streaked with white and crow's feet wrinkled the corners of her eyes.

"You must be Emily," she said. Her accent was more pronounced than Julian's, too; Emily guessed that he'd grown up in the northeast while Madame de Luna was a transplant.

"Thank you," said Emily, taking a mug. "I am. I guess news travels fast on a little island, huh?"

"Good news does," replied Madame de Luna with a smile, then turned away to continue serving.

A few drinks later, Emily had told the story of her break-in at Lancer Hall twice, once to the older Irregulars and then again to the squires. Then Ernest made her tell the assembled group about the Blodring brothers refusing to help in the great hall; the four Albian squires seemed to especially revel in Emily's imitation of Wulf's accent.

"Why do you guys put up with them?" she asked after the laughter about Uther's lemonade break had died down.

"Ah, they're not all bad," said Jack. "They're just…particular."

"What Jack means is that they come from a sort of hero culture," put in Ernest. "They don't really like to use their strength unless it's in a fight. To them it's like using a sword to spread butter."

"That's why they're here," agreed Michael. "For the fight that's coming."

This comment triggered a round of contemplative drinking among the Irregulars, broken only when Emily asked, "What about the rest of you? Why are you all here?"

"Ah, the age-old question," said Ernest, leaning back in his chair. "Why do the young ones stay for the fight, even as the old prepare to flee? The folly of youth, perhaps, and the wisdom of age?"

"I think it's because of Queen Bronwyn, the first of her name," Jack said. "And not just because she's cute—I'm not exactly her type, if you know what I mean."

"Queen Bronwyn?" asked Emily with a smile.

"Her wish is our command," explained Ernest. "Has someone given you the talk about cutting her some slack?"

Emily nodded towards Jack, who smiled. She had to admit, it was a charming smile. He had an easy sort of self-confidence of the type that you usually found among fighters and very powerful wizards. And the way he carried that guitar with him everywhere…Emily would have bet her dad's job that Jack was a spellsinger, the formal name for magic-users who employed music to cast their spells.

Most mages, like Kayo Jackson, earned their power through a combination of innate talent and grindingly hard work. Others attributed their gifts to various great and petty gods and goddesses, whose avatars on Earth they claimed to be. But a very few had a Gift that short-circuited these paths to power and flowed directly from melody and rhythm.

Jack's twelve fingers didn't hurt his overall image of Arcane prowess, either.

Ernest slammed his mug down on the table and leaned forward in his chair. "If I'm perfectly honest, which as a poet I must always be, the lot of us aren't really what you'd call joiners. Queen B just has a knack for making the best of a bad lot. As a matter of fact, there are nearly as many tragic backstories as there are Irregulars." He raised an eyebrow at Emily. "Assuming you had parents who loved you, you're going to bring our average down."

They all laughed, and Emily retorted, "Well, what's your sob story, then?"

Ernest put his drink down with exaggerated seriousness. "I think you've met my father."

"Professor Graves, at Harkness? Honestly, he seemed…nice."

"As long as he's talking about his research," replied Ernest. "No interest in anything other than facts."

"Like poetry," said Emily, understanding.

"Like poetry," Ernest agreed. "A waste of a great mind, in his esteemed opinion. And he's right, of course. I just happen to believe that wasting my mind is as good a use as any for it."

"So how'd you end up here?" Emily waved, taking in the Twisted Wrist, the island, the castle.

"Ah. The professor, my father, suggested that it might be a romantic setting to inspire my verse. When I got here I discovered he'd signed me up for the Irregulars without my knowledge."

"So you're here by accident?" Emily said, horrified. Ernest shrugged.

"I've had worse accidents than landing here. I don't have to work hard, friendly natives bring me food and drink at my call, and I know the exact time and place I'm going to die. And besides, if you think that's bad, imagine being a squire." He nodded to the four teenagers at the other table. "Hey squires! Introduce yourselves, already."

The two girls were Merry and Flora; the boys were named Daniel and Luke. Merry, a tall, broad girl with a crooked nose and a half-healed split lip, was Sir Maximilian's squire. Luke, a squeaky, nervous boy who by all appearances hadn't gone through puberty yet, squired for Sir Richard. That left Flora and Daniel to the two Arthurs.

"These poor souls were dragged across the Atlantic on a royal hit job and washed up on our little cursed island, the poor things," said Ernest. Luke, Flora, and Daniel smiled shyly and sipped their drinks, but Merry glared openly at Ernest following his characterization of their fate.

"If you think that's bad," said Luke quietly, but with a small smile, "you should ask Michael where he's from."

Emily looked at Michael, who shrugged and said, "Detroit."

There was a round of sympathetic laughter, and Madame de Luna brought Michael another drink, which she said was on the house.

Jack stood up, holding his mug up for a toast. "We've heard a lot of terrible things tonight," he said gravely. "Ernest is estranged from his father. Poor Daniel and Flora have to squire for the Arthurs, and God only knows what Luke has to do for Sir Richard." Luke blushed a bright red and looked at his boots.

"Emily had the bad luck to find our message in a bottle, and Michael, well…" Jack raised his glass in a brief salute. "But I can top you all, I think. I've actually never told anybody this, or at least I try not to." He looked at Emily, catching her gaze and holding it as he spoke. "But I'm feeling open tonight." Jack looked away, but Emily was more interested in the fact that Ernest and Michael had straightened up in their seats and looked completely transfixed.

"Probably drunk." Jack took a healthy swig from his mug. "Okay, here goes: my dad is Baron Wasteland."

There was dead silence in the Twisted Wrist, as the Irregulars tried to rationalize their understanding of their friend against what they knew of the strange, powerful leader of the Gifted Nation of Deseret.

Then Emily blurted, "The guy with the dreds?"

There was cheering, which eventually dissolved into more drinking.

Splashing blearily across the half-submerged sandbar in the midnight darkness, Emily wondered through an oncoming headache what would have happened if the castle's mysterious intruders had decided to come a few nights early, while the entire force of Irregulars was dead drunk in comradeship. Luckily, she came home to find the castle silent and asleep.

She was learning her way around, at least between the rooms that mattered, the great hall and the kitchen and the staffroom and mercifully, her bedroom. As she dragged herself down the featureless gray brick hallway leading to what she had started thinking of as the dormitory, she nearly fell as the little black cat of the night before twined between her feet.

"Dammit, you little—" Emily slurred. But something had caught her attention, something out of place. Lined up against the wall that the cats seemed to haunt were four small, handsome white porcelain bowls of milk and four matching dishes of fish. The fat brown cat and the orange-and-white siblings were happily gorging themselves, having no time to spare for Emily.

"Who put food?" she mumbled, then picked up the black cat and placed it back by its bowl.

CHAPTER 8

6 DAYS

The morning sun glared cruelly through Emily's window. Neither the flimsy white curtain nor all the sheets on her bed could block it out or reduce it to anything less than an intense white glow. Muttering curses, Emily wrenched herself out of bed and pulled on yesterday's clothes. It was time for a sortie downstairs to the kitchen, in search of the breakfast she'd been denied the day before.

Come to think of it, she hadn't eaten anything at all yesterday, between sleeping late, hauling defenses around, and drinking the night away. No wonder she felt like crap. Combat Gifted were plenty resilient; she'd gone three days without food in the tunnels under Harkness. But they weren't invincible, least of all when they hadn't eaten the massive amounts of food they needed to feed their raging internal fires.

Emily burped, tasting stale wine, and pushed open her door. The hallway beyond was mercifully quiet, and a bit dimmer than the bedroom. Down the hall, at the T-junction where she'd seen Michael and Sir Maximilian arguing the previous morning, Captain Queen looked up at the sound of Emily's door.

They paused for a moment, staring at each other, and then Captain Queen silently raised a hand in greeting before continuing around the corner. Emily felt a rush of gratitude. As a fellow fighter, Queen surely knew the warriors' unspoken rule: no business before breakfast.

Of course, that left Emily to find her own way to the kitchen. The routes around the castle that had seemed so clear in her mind yesterday were blurred now, and she paused at more than one intersection, looking haplessly back and forth between identical stone-flagged halls before choosing whichever one felt right in the moment.

It didn't take long before Emily was lost. She stopped abruptly when she realized she'd been wandering for a solid ten minutes without finding a single staircase down. In fact, as far as she could tell she'd ended up back where she'd started, in the long dormitory hallway. The thought of finding her bedroom and just sitting down for a minute before making a second attempt at breakfast began to call to her.

"Okay, um…" Emily said to herself. On second glance, the hallway didn't look so familiar. There was a banner hanging on one wall, which she was pretty sure didn't exist anywhere near her room. It was awfully bright, too, the colors so loud, red and gold blaring out from the wall.

Emily realized where she must be: the dormitories of the Albian knights and their squires. In all likelihood, she wasn't too far from her own hallway, assuming all the bedrooms were near each other. So all she had to do was get back to the last T-junction before anybody unpleasant woke up and wanted to have a conversation, or worse, an argument, before she'd had a suitably huge breakfast. Worst of all would be running into—

Sir Maximilian threw open the door of one of the bedrooms, which crashed agonizingly into the hallway wall, and sprinted halfway down the hall in the other direction before skidding to a halt.

"You!" he shouted, whirling around.

"Me?" asked Emily. Even for a headachey morning, that seemed unusually aggressive.

Sir Maximilian stalked down the hall to her. He grabbed her by the arm and looked her in the eye, anger burning in his brown eyes.

"What are you doing here?" he hissed.

"Easy, killer, I was just leaving," Emily replied, throwing her hands up in a gesture of surrender.

"Killer? You think that's funny, do you? Reckon you'll have a laugh at my expense whilst you frame me?"

"Frame you? What the hell are you talking about? Come on, I'm too hungry for this—" Emily was cut off as Sir Maximilian hauled her bodily towards the open door. "Hey, hands off, guy! Oh—oh, shit."

The dead body of Sir Richard Peakey lay curled up on the floor. He looked very small and pale in an old-fashioned nightgown.

"What the hell happened?" Emily asked in surprise.

"Why don't you tell me, Sledge?" hissed Sir Maximilian. "You show up here out of nowhere, and barely a day later Sir Richard is dead. And I find you skulking about, no doubt having just done the deed."

"Skulking? *Skulking?* I was lost! You were the one who came out of his room just now. That doesn't seem a bit suspicious to you?"

"And why on God's green earth would I kill Sir Richard?" retorted Sir Maximilian.

"Michael told me about your—your mission. He said you were all for getting out there and killing some innocent girl, but Sir Richard was making you stay. Well, you're free to leave now, aren't you?"

Sir Maximilian let go of Emily's arm, which she reflexively began to rub where he'd grabbed her. A look passed over his face that she couldn't place: horror at having his plan discovered? He was silent, and Emily was about to press her advantage when the two Sir Arthurs appeared at the door.

"What's all this?" said the tall, skinny one.

"Sir Richard!" cried the stocky one.

"Arthur—no, not you, you—go fetch General Alder," ordered Sir

103

Maximilian. "Arthur—yes, you!—stay with me to keep watch over the body and this girl. She's our prime suspect."

Emily was too angry, and way too hungry, to rehash the argument. She sighed as she realized that she'd be missing breakfast yet again.

Five minutes later, General Alder, Colonel Liu, Captain Queen, Ernest Graves, and Julian de Luna came clattering down the hall, all led by Sir Arthur. From the half-eaten biscuit in Queen's hand, Emily guessed that Arthur had found them at breakfast. Her stomach gave a sympathetic rumble.

General Alder silently pushed between her and Sir Maximilian to survey the body of Sir Richard. He checked for a pulse at both wrist and neck, listened for breath at the old man's mouth, and did a quick sweep of the room for any obvious signs of struggle or murder. Then he stood crisply.

"Death by natural causes," he declared flatly. "Sir Richard, God keep him, was an old man. The strain of our current crisis was too much for him, and he collapsed in the night."

Captain Queen turned and murmured something to Ernest, who hustled back down the hallway the way they had come. Colonel Liu gave a few short orders to the Arthurs, who began gently straightening out Sir Richard's body.

The assembled crowd watched the young knights at work, showing a shocked reluctance to disperse from the scene of such a tragedy. After a few moments, Emily began feeling awkward, as though she had interrupted the funeral of a family she didn't know. She turned to leave, but Captain Queen caught her eye and gave her a firm, short shake of the head: no.

"So I suppose you'll be leaving, then?" said Julian to Sir Maximilian. He sounded angry, and Emily couldn't blame him. Everything she'd heard about the Albian knights and their mission made it sound as though Sir Richard was the only decent one among them. It was hard to imagine the already meager defenses of the Castle Forlorn being stripped of four good fighters, but it was clearly common knowledge that Sir Maximilian was eager to go after Elizabeth Pendragon, and he was just as clearly now in charge of the small group of knights.

Sir Maximilian frowned, and his eyes flickered over to Emily for just a moment. "No, I don't think so," he said slowly. Everyone in the small group turned to him at this pronouncement. Captain Queen was openly staring, her eyebrows raised. "It was Sir Richard's wish that we help defend the Castle Forlorn. We will finish what he started, in his memory and in his honor."

There was a moment of quiet, then Colonel Liu said, "Thank you."

Ernest came back up the hallway, leading Michael Fletcher behind him.

"Ah, Michael. Good," said Captain Queen, turning. "Sir Richard passed away in the night. Would you examine the body, please?"

"Examine the…?" Michael looked confused and more than a little alarmed. Captain Queen gave him a significant stare, and then understanding dawned on his face. She guided him past Sir Maximilian and General Alder and into the bedroom where Sir Richard's body lay, straight and cold, the Arthurs standing on either side of it.

Michael knelt at Sir Richard's head and placed a hand gently on each temple. He whispered a few words under his breath, and even as his hands began to glow with a soft white light, Emily felt the tell-tale prickle of magic creeping up her spine. Michael had to be giving off a lot of power for her to feel it from out in the hallway; the quiet boy from Detroit was clearly more of a mage than he let on.

After a few moments of focus, the white glow around Michael's hands began to take on a greenish tint, like vomit or the skin of a very sick person. He waited, his lips pursed, until the glow was entirely green, then brought his hands together with a decisive clap. He opened them again quickly, and a thick greenish liquid spilled out from between them, splattering all over the carpet.

"Ah, sorry about the mess," he said. "Couldn't hold onto it for too long."

"Poison?" said Colonel Liu, crossing her arms.

"Poison," nodded Michael. A sheen of sweat had broken out on his forehead.

"Are you certain, young man?" asked General Alder with a frown. "Drawing poison is no easy magic."

"Yes, sir," replied Michael. "That's probably the first spell I ever learned." He gave an unexpected smile, from some secret place within, and shrugged. "Michigan tap water."

"I caught Emily skulking around the hall just now," said Sir Maximilian suddenly.

"*Skulking* again? Really?" snapped Emily.

Everyone began to speak at once. Julian said, "Do you think it was her?" as Colonel Liu said, "Miss Sledge, perhaps we should—" and Sir Maximilian retorted, "Yes, skulking, that's what you were doing—"

"No," said Captain Queen in a voice of command. The babble stopped immediately. "No, I saw her leave her bedroom as I was heading down to breakfast not long before Arthur came to get us. Michael, correct me if I'm wrong, but a poison like this would have taken more than five or ten minutes to take effect, right?"

Michael nodded. Silence fell again as the group digested this alibi.

"Besides, you only saw me because you were coming out of Sir Richard's room," said Emily quietly, looking straight at Sir Maximilian.

"I don't have to take this from you," he replied hotly. "And if Captain Queen is right about the poison, why would I have been in Sir Richard's room just now? My God, I came to fetch him to breakfast, not murder him."

"What's clear," said Colonel Liu, "is that we have a killer in the castle. Max is right: as far as we know now, it could have been anybody. Come on, let's get Sir Richard taken care of."

Emily stood among flat, worn stones marking graves from a hundred years ago or more. She leaned on a shovel, chest heaving, sweat sliding down her cheeks. Madame de Luna had guided her to a small graveyard on the outskirts of town, where an open plot that would soon be Sir Richard's waited. As she left Emily to the digging, the innkeeper had paused at a fairly new-looking headstone nearby before heading back to the Twisted Wrist with her eyes on the ground.

Emily had volunteered to dig Sir Richard's grave. She had no interest in hanging around in the castle while news of the murder spread, and the summer sun helped clear out the last cobwebs that hadn't been shocked from her head at the sight of the dead knight. She pushed herself hard, sweating out the alcohol and anxiety, and was done in a little over an hour. That gave her plenty of time to wait as Sir Richard's body was prepared.

She momentarily considered checking out the beach, but there was no denying her curiosity. A few steps brought her to the recent headstone. Emily was heartbroken to read the name "Andoni de Luna" with a death date of about twelve years ago. Julian must have been just a kid.

Looking up from Julian's father's grave, Emily found Ernest standing quietly at her shoulder.

"He's a lifer," he said. "I'm not sure he's ever even left Finalhaven, other than a few trips for kitchen equipment."

"What killed his dad?"

Ernest shook his head. "Heart attack, I think."

"Oh," said Emily. "Hey, why is Sir Richard being buried here, rather than back in Albion?"

"The memory wall," said Ernest. "We're not sure if…we're not sure anyone would understand if we tried to explain what happened. And honestly, I'm not sure Ed Doughty would take a corpse on his boat, even if he remembered the instructions we gave him."

"I just thought maybe it was, I don't know, symbolic. It seems like nobody really expects to make it out of here alive, so…" Emily trailed off, embarrassed by her flash of emotional insight.

"A sort of funeral for all of us, huh?" Ernest stroked his chin, an act that would have seemed ridiculous on anyone else but seemed to fit him naturally. "You know, Sledge, I don't think you're wrong. Anyway. They're still getting things ready at the castle, and the grave's obviously done, so shall we have a drink while we wait?"

Sir Richard's funeral wasn't officiated by General Alder, as Emily had expected. Instead, the ancient man who had slept through the senior staff meeting Emily had attended reappeared in musty, oversized clothes of somber black. He had to be older even than Sir Richard was, Emily guessed, and reminded her of Headmaster Knowles back at Harkness.

"Who is he?" Emily whispered to Ernest, who had had more than one drink before the funeral and smelled like it.

"Ah, that's the Marcher Lord," Ernest replied a bit too loudly. Captain Queen hissed and elbowed him. He continued in a slightly more modest whisper, "He's the lord of the Castle Forlorn. They trot him out for things like this, but mostly I think he sits by the fire with a hot water bottle."

"Are there a lot of things like this?" Emily asked.

"Not really," Ernest admitted.

Sir Richard's body had been washed and dressed in his armor. Someone had made an attempt at polishing it, but nothing could make the patchwork of old scars and dings shine again. An equally battered longsword lay down the length of his body. He looked better in his armor, Emily thought, bigger than the frail old thing she'd seen curled up on his carpet. He looked like he might have died in battle rather than from poison.

Sir Richard lay in an open coffin that had obviously just been constructed of some light wood. It seemed inappropriately flimsy to bear the heavy weight of the dead knight, but Emily imagined they didn't just have nice coffins lying around the castle.

The Marcher Lord drew himself up at the head of the coffin and cleared his throat. The whispering of the crowd died away.

"We are gathered to commit to the earth a knight of Albion," began the Marcher Lord. His voice sounded as though he were squeezing it from his throat with an effort. It was loud, but had a deep, uneven quaver. "Sir Richard Peakey represented the best of Albian chivalry, and committed to the aid of the Castle Forlorn in our time of need. It is our great sorrow to lose him now, but his fight is over, and we wish that he may find his youth again in the eternal summer of Avalon."

Sir Maximilian nodded at these words, his handsome face blank.

"Does anyone else wish to speak at this time?" asked the Marcher Lord. A few moments of silence passed, and nobody moved. Emily was surprised that Sir Maximilian had nothing to say. Was it sorrow, she wondered, or guilt?

Michael Fletcher stepped forward, holding something cupped in his hand. Gently he placed it on Sir Richard's chest, to one side of the hilt of his longsword. It was a red rose, and it stood out like a spot of blood against the knight's polished armor.

Michael receded into the crowd. Another moment passed, then the Marcher Lord nodded to General Alder. He set a lid, little more than a sheet of plywood, over the knight's body, then moved to the head of the coffin. Sir Maximilian moved to its foot, and together they lifted the box and slowly lowered it into the grave Emily had dug.

Everyone else seemed to recognize this as the end of the funeral and began to depart. Emily followed, heading back towards the castle. She looked back once to see Sir Maximilian, alone, shoveling dirt slowly down into the open grave.

On the sandbar, Emily caught up to Michael, who was walking alone. He had the air of someone who didn't want to be disturbed, but she couldn't help herself.

"I liked the rose," she said, matching his pace. They walked for a moment in silence before Michael replied.

"There's one for everyone in the castle," he said. At Emily's blank look, he continued, "They're enchanted. I have one for each of us." He pulled a white rose, somewhat crumpled, from the pocket of his jeans, and held it up for her. "See? This one is mine."

"Where did they come from?" Emily asked, transfixed.

"I've been making them, ever since Alexander died. Mine is white; they all are. It'll turn red when…if I get hurt."

"That's useful," Emily replied, then added, "and sort of beautiful."

"It won't bring Alexander back, though. Or Sir Richard."

Emily had nothing to say to this, so they walked on in silence until they reached the portcullis of the castle, when Michael said, "I made one for you, too. The night you arrived."

"But I was supposed to leave the next day," Emily said. Michael shrugged. "No, really," she continued. "I still might leave, if I can figure out a way to get out with my memories."

Looking around, Emily realized they were heading towards the dormitory hall. She had been following Michael without really thinking, assuming they would go to the kitchen with the rest of the mourners for Sir Richard's memorial feast.

"Where are we going?" she asked.

"I want to introduce you to someone," said Michael. Soon they reached the long, blank hallway that seemed be home to the castle's cats. All four of them were there, curled up at the base of the wall in a sleeping line.

They didn't stir as Michael approached the wall and knocked sharply three times. A door-sized section of the wall promptly slid aside, revealing a young woman of about Emily's age. She was pale, with straight, white-blonde hair that reached her lower back. She stood barefoot in a simple white dress, looking like someone out of a fairy tale, and smiled when she saw Michael.

"Emily, this is Elizabeth Pendragon."

Chapter 9

"You've been here the whole time?" Emily gasped. "Does anybody know? Do the knights know? You know they're trying to kill you, right? This is—oh, what a beautiful room."

Unlike the simple, heavy stone bedrooms she'd become accustomed to in the Castle Forlorn, Emily found Elizabeth Pendragon's apartment more like the master suite in a beach house. A large bay window showed a sparkling view of the ocean breaking below the castle, and sported a wide, cushioned reading seat built into its alcove.

Two walls were lined entirely with bookshelves, all overflowing. A small upright piano sat in one corner, across from a comfortable-looking wooden rocking chair. Beside the piano, a closed white door led, Emily guessed, to the bedroom.

It was neat and clean, but the room had a very lived-in feel; a blanket stitched with birds that lay across one arm of the rocking chair looked especially well loved, like a baby blanket that had been carried into adulthood.

"Have you lived here long?" asked Emily, cringing inwardly at how stupid the question sounded as it came out of her mouth.

"Since I was a baby," said Elizabeth with a smile. "The King of Birds carried me across the ocean on the trade winds and set me down on the sand."

"I see," Emily lied.

"Aside from us, only the Marcher Lord knows she's here," said Michael. Elizabeth put her hand on his arm with a smile.

"Us?" Emily repeated. "Just us?"

Michael smiled. "Me, you, Jack and Ernest. You know: *us*."

More than anything, Emily wanted to ask why Michael had trusted her with a secret of this magnitude, but she didn't know how to ask.

"So the Marcher Lord is keeping you safe from the knights," she said instead.

"Yes." Elizabeth nodded. She indicated the rocking chair with a slender hand. "Please, won't you sit?"

Emily sat, still a bit too stunned to object. Elizabeth and Michael sat together on the window seat, the mysterious Albian woman leaning against the young wizard. It was a cozy, protective pose; they could have been siblings, best friends, or lovers.

"Isn't it lonely?" Emily blurted out suddenly. The thought of friends had brought back a flood of memories from the last four years with Kayo, Chris, and Andrea, whom she'd all somehow forgotten in her rush to solve the riddles of the Castle Forlorn.

"Lonely? No." Elizabeth smiled again; she seemed to do it a lot. Waving a hand at her overloaded bookshelves, she added, "How could I be lonely with so many friends?"

Emily had never really thought of books as friends before, but she nodded. "But do you get to explore the castle much?"

Elizabeth's smile didn't waver as she said softly, "I cannot leave my suite."

"Not at all?" said Emily, shocked.

"When the Marcher Lord took her in, he cast a pretty heavy-duty spell around these rooms," explained Michael. "Apparently he used to be quite a wizard, before his mind started to go. But the Albians have a lot of big magic, too, tracking Elizabeth. If she set foot outside her door, they'd be on her pretty much immediately. So to stay safe, she stays put."

"At least you've got the million-dollar view."

A silence fell, but it was somehow not awkward, Emily thought. It had a certain warmth to it. She could see why Michael liked Elizabeth. She was like the heroine of a fairy tale, Emily realized, a lost princess locked in a tower for her whole life. She seemed as though she belonged to an entirely different reality, as though the magic and monsters of the Gifted world would be as pedestrian to her as mundane people were to Emily.

Despite the obvious tragedies of her life, Elizabeth had a steadiness you wouldn't expect from someone who'd lived her entire life in two rooms. It said something about the Marcher Lord that he'd clearly not only taken in an infant queen, but put enough love and care into raising her that she'd turned out all right, considering. He must have been quite a man before old age broke him.

It was still hard to imagine, though. Emily wanted to see the world; she burned to. She'd go nuts, cooped up in here. Just the thought made her a bit claustrophobic. She stood and stepped behind the rocking chair to one of the smaller windows, thinking she'd let in a nice sea breeze.

The window was stuck, or jammed, or something. Gently Emily put her arms, then her back into it—she'd broken a few windows that weren't meant for the Gifted, back when she'd first been growing into her strength—but the thing just wouldn't go up. It looked like it should, it had two parts, but it stayed tighter than if it had been nailed shut.

Finally Elizabeth stopped her with a small cough. "You'll find it won't, I'm afraid."

Emily turned, blushing. "I'm sorry, I just thought I'd let in a breeze."

"I've had that thought too," replied Elizabeth, her ever-present smile showing that she wasn't annoyed. "It might be a nice thing to experience. But you know how magic is."

"I'm not sure I do," said Emily, dropping back into the rocking chair.

"Michael, you're much better at explaining these things than I am. Would you mind?" Elizabeth gave Michael's arm a squeeze.

"Sure, sure. So, um, imagine you're making a submarine. So you get a big metal tube, but you have to have some exits. So you put a door in it, so you can get in and out." Michael gestured as he spoke, sketching out the imaginary sub in the air. It was fun to watch him explain; he was more animated than she'd ever seen him. "But you have to work extra hard to make sure the door closes really, really tight. Otherwise water will get in. Two doors will be an even bigger pain. Three is worse, and so on. Those are always gonna be your problem spots; water is always gonna get in there first. So to make the tightest submarine you can…"

"You want as few doors as possible," finished Emily.

"Exactly," said Michael. "I mean, you need one, because how else will you get in and out? But any more than that is…" He shrugged.

"The walls that hold them out hold me in," said Elizabeth. Her eyes were lowered, fixed on something cradled in her cupped hands. Emily blinked, realizing it was the crumpled white rose Michael had referred to as his. "But it's necessary, I can see that. The true spells of protection are always this way, with only one passage."

"The true spells," repeated Emily. She had butterflies in her stomach. Michael and Elizabeth both nodded. "The best spells, the tightest spells. Like a memory wall?"

Michael's brow furrowed. "Well…yeah, if you do it right."

"I'm guessing our mysterious attackers did it right," Emily said, gesturing around her.

"You bet." Michael nodded. "I've checked."

"So then, what you're saying is there's only one way in or out of here. Like Elizabeth's spell. In other words: we have to go through the door."

They found Captain Queen in a small yard off Finalhaven town square. She was leading a group of sweating townies through a basic drill with spears that looked like they hadn't been used in a hundred years. Queen had barely broken a sweat, even in the hot summer sun, but the volunteers looked about ready to collapse. Emily noticed Madame de Luna among them, going through the motions of the drill with a look of hellbent determination on her face despite her shaking arms.

Emily and Michael waited anxiously at the side of the yard until Captain Queen called a break. The grateful townies sank to the ground in a gasping mass as Queen sauntered over.

"What's up, Mike?" she said, barely seeming to notice Emily.

"You'd better ask her," Michael said. Captain Queen turned to Emily with a raised eyebrow.

"We should—we need to go through the door. Out through the door. I don't know where it goes but I bet it'll let us through the memory wall. The way in has to be the way out, right?"

Captain Queen opened her mouth, closed it, opened it again, then settled on closed as she regarded Emily with a furrow between her eyebrows.

"You're suggesting not only surrendering our defensive line, but bringing a hundred soldiers, support, and civilians into enemy territory," she said finally.

"What? No, no, like I said, we don't know what's on the other side. We need to send an expeditionary force. A small group. Get the lay of the land, get out quick, report back. Then we can decide what to do, like if we think we can send someone through to get help."

"We? No, Miss Sledge, the senior staff will decide what to do. And, frankly, would be the ones to approve or deny this plan of yours."

"Well, let's ask them, then," retorted Emily. This wasn't going quite as she'd imagined. There was a lot less complimenting her brilliance than she'd expected.

Captain Queen shook her head. "Let's make a real plan first. I suppose you're volunteering for the expeditionary force?"

"Of course I am," said Emily. "And so is Michael."

"No chance," said Captain Queen. "He's our only wizard. Sorry, Mike, not expendable."

"What about Jack?" asked Emily.

"What about him?" retorted Captain Queen. "You and I can go, Sledge."

"Two fighters? That's it? We need somebody who can understand whatever we run into over there…" She trailed off, thinking. "What about Ernest? I know his thing is poetry, but he's a Mental. He's got more brains than the rest of us combined. Plus he can remember everything we see on the other side."

"Well…" Captain Queen looked doubtful. "We can ask him. This shitshow is volunteer only. If Alder even approves it, that is."

"Okay, let's ask him! Or, I'll ask him. Your recruits are starting to get their breath back, Captain. You're going easy on them."

Queen showed the briefest hint of a smile at this, then turned and headed back into the yard without another word.

"Wait!" shouted Emily. "Where's Ernest, do you know?"

"Where is he ever?" Queen called back.

Watching her yell at the townies, Emily realized that somewhere in there, the gruff Captain had come around to support her plan. Or at least Emily thought she had.

"She just agreed with me, right?" Emily asked Michael.

"Yeah, she's not big on praise. I think she thinks it's a waste of time."

"Huh. Well, I'm sorry you can't come along." Emily gave Michael a playful punch on the shoulder as they headed towards the Twisted Wrist. "But you wouldn't want to give Elizabeth anything to worry about."

Michael smiled and looked at his shoes.

"It's exciting, isn't it?" Emily went on. "We have no idea what's on the other side of the door."

"We're all gonna find out soon enough," Michael replied. "I've got no particular yearning for spoilers. I'm happy to stay here and work on the defenses."

"Your loss, wizard," Emily said brightly. It felt good to be moving forward again, into the unknown. Of course, first she had to recruit Ernest, and then convince Alder and the others her plan was a good idea. But at least she had a plan.

Inside the Twisted Wrist was dim and cool against the afternoon sun. It looked closed; most of the chairs were upside down on the tables. The place was empty except for Ernest and Jack sharing a drink at a back table, and Madame de Luna sweeping around them. All three looked up as Emily and Michael entered; Ernest grimaced at the sunlight but Jack gave a welcoming wave.

"Come join us! We were just toasting Sir Richard," Jack called. He pushed out the chair next to him for Emily, leaving Michael to take down one of his own. "Madame de Luna was good enough to let us in a little early."

"You pay," said the innkeeper with a shrug.

"So what's up, Sledge?" asked Jack. "You look like you've been looking for someone."

"Well, actually, yeah," said Emily.

"And you've found me," Jack smiled. "What can I do for you?"

"Uh, actually, we were looking for Ernest," Emily replied. At the sound of his name, Ernest looked up from his mug and raised an inquisitive eyebrow.

"So, we've got a plan. We want to take a few people through the door and see what's on the other side. I think we might be able to get out that way. With our memories intact, I mean."

"Mm," said Ernest noncommittally. "That could work."

"And since you're the brains of the Irregulars, Ernest, we thought— I thought—you should come with us."

"I see," said Ernest, frowning. "I must inform you, heading blindly into violence isn't really my style. I'm an Athenian, not a Spartan. Actually, I probably would have made a better Epicurean."

"Well, we don't know what's on the other side. It might be, I don't know…a library or something."

Ernest's eyebrow went back up. "You think we're being invaded by librarians?"

"Captain Queen and I are going," Emily said plaintively. Why did these things never go the way they were supposed to? "You'll be totally safe, I promise."

"Against the librarians."

"Against whatever! Come on, you're the only man for the job. I'm great at fighting but I don't have half the memory you do. I can't analyze information as fast. I can't think as quick. You're a Mental, right? So you're smart enough to know I'm right."

"So is General Alder," said Ernest. "I'm the bonus brain. Take him." Emily had never seen Ernest like this. Just how drunk was he?

"I think we both know this a job for the enlisted men, not the officers," Emily replied gently.

"Captain Queen is an officer," said Ernest petulantly. "Your argument is full of holes."

"Oh, for the love of God, Ernest," Jack snapped suddenly. "Will it make you feel better if I go with you?"

Emily sat back in her chair. Why hadn't Captain Queen wanted to bring Jack along? He was a magician, or at least Emily was pretty sure he was, what with the twelve fingers and all the musical talent. And his easy confidence and charm—people with hidden power tended to be like that.

"As long as you sing me a melancholy lullaby when I'm dying," Ernest said from behind his mug.

"I promise," said Jack, holding up two fingers. "Scout's honor."

"Is that a yes?" Emily asked, then decided just to treat it as one. Captain Queen could deal. "Thank you, Ernest. You'll see, it's gonna be fine."

"When are we going in?" asked Jack.

"Well, I need to convince the senior staff first," said Emily. "But I think we should do it tomorrow morning. No sense wasting any more time."

Jack nodded. "Makes sense. Want me to come back with you to help stare down the general?"

"No, that's okay," Emily said, thinking of Captain Queen. Better to spring it on her than rub it in her face that Jack was coming along. "Though I don't think management likes me very much."

"I'm sure you can trick them," said Jack with a smile.

Ernest looked up at Emily. "Tomorrow morning, you said?"

"That's my hope, yeah."

He pulled Jack's half-finished mug across the table. "In that case I've got to get a head start on my courage."

To Emily's surprise, Alder and his staff agreed to meet with her almost immediately. They all had other duties to complete, though, so for now she waited alone in the command room for them to arrive. With time on her hands, Emily paced the perimeter of the little meeting room, examining the tapestries on its walls. To her surprise, they seemed to tell the story of General Alder slaying his dragon.

As far as she could tell, the dragon had lived beneath the Castle Forlorn itself. The tapestries were a bit abstract, but she assumed that the thing must have been asleep for some long time, if they'd accidentally built a castle over it. Either way, it had woken up, presumably causing a lot of havoc and necessitating the Lancers' involvement. The woven pictures kind of skipped over the details, but it definitely ended with General Alder holding the dragon's severed head up in front of the cheering townspeople of Finalhaven.

It seemed a bit vain to have tapestries of yourself in your command room, but then again, Emily wasn't a general of anything, so she figured she could cut Alder some slack. He'd obviously helped a lot of people, and if he'd killed a dragon he'd earned whatever praise anybody wanted to throw his way.

The door opened behind her, and Emily turned to find that Poet-Captain Dhar was the first to arrive. He was wearing the same outfit she'd seen him in before, a black T-shirt and jeans. He looked just rumpled enough that she would have believed these were the very same clothes.

"Hello, Emily," he said warmly. He gestured at the tapestries. "Enjoying the Tale of Old What's-His-Name?"

"You probably shouldn't call General Alder that," Emily said without thinking, and then her heart stopped, but to her immense relief Dhar gave a huge, barking laugh.

"I meant the dragon, but I guess I should have been more specific." He dropped into the same seat she'd seen him in before and sighed.

"Tell me honestly, Emily. What do you think of our defensive preparations so far?"

"Well, it's hard to say. I mean, we don't know what we're up against."

"That's a very political answer," Dhar said leadingly.

"Okay, well, I think everybody is assuming this is gonna be a close-in, hand-to-hand kind of fight. The palisades in the great hall are good for breaking up a line or slowing down a column, but the second we have to fall back, the invaders get free cover against us. I mean, there's no kill zone for their approach."

"The great hall is a bit tight for guns, though, isn't it?" asked Dhar. Emily was reminded for a second of her tactics professors at Harkness grilling the class on chokepoints, fields of fire, and lines of sight.

"Yeah, that's true. But we're really focused on that one room when we've got the whole castle to play with. It's kind of like you're expecting us to be able to turn them back without any real damage."

"Actually, that's—" Dhar stopped suddenly as General Alder and Colonel Liu came through the door. He cleared his throat and continued, "Actually, that's why the post is called Poet-Captain. I'm a little of both, I'd say. Not the poet Ernest is, nor the captain Bronwyn is, but I guess I get the job done."

Colonel Liu smiled at him as she and Alder took their seats, but Emily was chewing her lip in confusion. Dhar had just picked up a conversation that they hadn't been having. To Emily, it sounded like he was hiding something from the senior Lancers, but she had no idea what or why.

She didn't have time to think about it, though, because the rest of the senior staff followed closely after Alder and Liu and took their customary seats around the table. Sir Maximilian took the seat that had belonged to Sir Richard last time, leaving a glaring gap between himself and the two Arthurs.

As before, Emily was left standing, trying to keep from twisting her hands nervously as she faced the silent faces of the staff.

"Well, thanks for listening to me," she said, then stalled out. From her seat next to Colonel Liu, Captain Queen nodded for Emily to continue.

"I want to suggest that we send a small group through the door in the great hall. I've talked to Michael, and he agrees that it's probably the only way to get through the memory wall without, you know, forgetting everything. We don't know what's on the other side, but if we send a recon team we can probably learn a lot about the invaders. And maybe even find a way out, to get help."

"And who should this team consist of?" asked Colonel Liu.

"Well, I'm volunteering, obviously. Captain Queen offered to go with me. And I talked to Ernest, who would be the brains of the thing, and Jack offered to come, too."

There were a few raised eyebrows at this, but nobody spoke up. Emily wasn't sure why anybody would be surprised that she'd want some magical backup, but she put the thought aside and plunged ahead.

"I want to do it first thing tomorrow morning. No reason to waste any time. We'll get in and out as quickly as possible, and then—"

"Are you sure you're coming back, Sledge?" Sir Maximilian interrupted harshly.

"Excuse me?" said Emily.

Sir Maximilian turned to the table at large. "Think about it. She shows up out of nowhere. A couple days later, Sir Richard is poisoned. Now she suddenly has this great plan to split our forces days before the assault, and of course she'll lead the way into enemy territory."

"Are you suggesting Emily is trying to escape?" asked Colonel Liu.

"I'm just saying, what if it's not enemy territory for her?" Sir Maximilian sat back, looking grimly pleased with himself.

"That's ridiculous—" Emily began, but Captain Queen cut her off.

"Max, you need to let go of this conspiracy theory," she said with a barely suppressed snarl. "It's got holes I could march a column through. Emily didn't appear out of nowhere, she got our message. If she's the only one who came, that's our bad luck. As I told you this morning, you didn't catch her in the act of poisoning Sir Richard, because I saw her right before you found the body. And as for her plan, it's the only damn thing we haven't tried yet and I think it's worth doing."

Sir Maximilian leaned forward. "If it was a slow-acting poison, the fact that you saw Sledge just before I found Richard doesn't mean she's innocent. She could have poisoned him overnight."

"So could anybody," said Poet-Captain Dhar. "Relax, Max."

Sir Maximilian snorted. "It's just suspicious, that's all." He crossed his arms and fell back into his chair.

"Can we return to the matter at hand, please?" said Colonel Liu. "Miss Sledge isn't on trial."

"Not yet," said Sir Maximilian quietly, but everyone ignored him.

"What do you think, General?" asked Liu. General Alder had been listening to the proceedings with his eyes half-closed. It might have made anybody else look sleepy, but Emily had never doubted that Alder was wide awake and taking everything in.

"I'm skeptical," said the general. "I don't like losing two fighters right before the fight, and I certainly don't like losing a Mind, even if he is just a poet. No offense, Dhar." Poet-Captain Dhar gave a relaxed shrug, and General Alder continued, "Miss Sledge has a point, but I see no reason to believe that she'll do anything other than get my people killed."

Emily opened her mouth to object, but to her surprise, Dhar beat her to it.

"With respect, sir, I think Emily knows what she's doing."

"Explain," said Colonel Liu.

"Think about it. She figured out our message in a bottle, which, let's be honest, was not exactly a map and some GPS coordinates with 'Help Us' written in big red letters. And it wasn't just a matter of solving a puzzle. From what I've heard, getting to us took as much guts as it did brains." He smiled. "And a little judicious midnight property damage."

"What's your point, Nadim?" asked Liu.

"My point is that if the rumors are to be believed, she's smart, she's tough, she thinks quickly on her feet, she knows when and whom to ask for help, and she sure as hell doesn't give up easy. In short, exactly the sort of person we want leading a sortie into unknown dangers. I vote yes."

"It's not a democracy, Captain," retorted Liu.

"That's Poet-Captain to you," replied Dhar with a smile.

"Very well," said General Alder with a frown, cutting off Colonel Liu's attempt at a comeback. "Sledge, you've got permission. Captain Queen, keep her out of trouble. Get in, get the lay of the land, and get the hell out. Miss Sledge, if I hear about any mission creep I'll throw you back in there myself, alone this time."

Chapter 10

Emily woke the next morning feeling rested, mercifully un-hungover, and only a little hungry. One thing she'd never had trouble with was sleeping; her late-night tower climb before graduation had been the exception, not the rule. Physical danger had never scared her, even after what had happened to her parents. It had just never really occurred to her to doubt herself in a fight, and that instinct had proven itself right far more often than not.

She swung her legs over the edge of the bed and dropped into a set of stretches, calisthenics and isometric exercises that got her blood flowing and her muscles warm. After a shower in the bathroom down the hall—only slightly out of date—she dressed in a clean set of fighting clothes and headed down to the kitchen for breakfast.

Emily wasn't surprised to find that Captain Queen had beaten her downstairs and was halfway through a massive plate of scrambled eggs, bacon, steak, and asparagus. The captain nodded to Emily, her mouth full, and went back to eating.

Emily turned to look for food and found Julian already headed her way, a plate loaded to match Queen's in his hand.

"Sit," he ordered. "I heard all about the morning you've got coming up. We don't know what's on the other side, so you'd better eat while you can."

Emily didn't need any more invitation, so she joined Captain Queen at the table and silently challenged herself to catch up with the other woman's position in her meal. They ate like that for a while, silent other than the sound of chewing and one request for Captain Queen to pass the salt.

Queen finished first, though Emily only had a few strips of bacon and maybe an egg's worth of scramble left.

"Ice cream?" the captain asked.

"I'm sorry?" said Emily around her eggs.

"Ice cream. Do you want it?"

"Oh." Emily swallowed. "No thanks, I don't love dairy before a fight day."

Queen shrugged. "Suit yourself. You might need the calories later."

"I'm fine, thanks," said Emily firmly.

Captain Queen disappeared into what looked like a walk-in freezer and emerged a minute later with a pint tub of chocolate ice cream and a spoon.

"Ready?" she asked.

"Sure," said Emily. "Are you?"

"I can eat and walk, thanks," Queen replied. "We need to go pick up Ernest, anyway. And I want to make a little stop before that. Come on, Sledge, move it!"

Emily stared in openmouthed joy at the walls and racks of weaponry that spread before her wide eyes. Captain Queen's little stop had turned out to be a trip to the basement of the castle, where a plainly underutilized armory waited behind an ancient oaken door.

"It's beautiful," said Emily. Captain Queen just shrugged. She was leaning against the doorframe, eating ice cream directly from the tub. Most older fighters had a weapon or two that they were particularly attached to, plus a back catalogue of old arms kept for sentimental reasons. Leaving the kitchen, Queen had strapped on a ballistic vest and hung a heavy sword from one hip and a long dagger from the other. All these were from her own collection, she'd explained, but Emily hadn't had the time, or the money, to amass any sort of arsenal of her own.

Slowly, Emily made her way along the shelves, picking up weapons here and there to test edges, balance, and all the hard-to-define characteristics that might make the difference between life and death on the other side of the door.

A rack of combat rifles grabbed her attention, and she grabbed one for a quick examination. She'd heard that out in the non-Gifted world, guns were the only weapons anyone used anymore. It seemed like a shame to abandon the martial arts, the hard-won skills of fighting with your body. Even shooting a bow was so much more physical than firing a gun, asking so much more of the muscles.

But Emily was well aware that her Gift of Combat was a more-than-adequate equalizer for the speed and power of a gun. She'd deflected a few bullets in her day, though it tended to shatter whatever you did the deflecting with. And anyway, a bullet could only travel so fast, so if you could dodge them, even the best gunfighter lost their advantage over you. Not to mention the fact that the combat suits, and most of the monsters, she'd faced down so far were pretty bulletproof.

Emily put the rifle back in its rack and moved on. Whatever was on the other side of that door, she wanted to make a good first impression, literally and figuratively. She needed something intimidating and powerful in her hands when she kicked the door in.

She paused. Hanging on the wall behind a rack of infantry spears was a long, two-handed hammer. Cobwebs hung between it and the spears, and when she pulled it off the wall, it left a hammer-shaped blank in the dust around it.

Emily had won her first Harkness Combat Tournament with a hammer like this; the obvious nickname "Sledgehammer" hadn't been far behind. That was why she'd won the second one with a pair of knives, to prove she wasn't a one-trick pony, but she had to admit that the weight of the hammer in her hands felt good. There had been faster fighters at Harkness, but nobody hit harder.

She came out from the racks with the hammer in one hand and a ballistic vest like Captain Queen's in the other. Queen, ice cream spoon in her mouth, gave her an appraising look and raised a doubtful eyebrow at the sight of the hammer, but kept her mouth shut.

"All right, Captain," said Emily. "Let's collect the boys and do this."

Collecting Ernest proved to be a bigger challenge than Emily had anticipated. They tried his room first and found it unoccupied. The clean bedsheets were neatly made; in fact the room showed no sign of having been slept in the night before. Emily somehow doubted that Ernest was a neat freak; he seemed more the type to have empty wine bottles and clothes everywhere.

From the dormitory hall, Emily and Captain Queen made their way back down to the kitchen. The rest of the castle all seemed to have woken up and gone for breakfast at the same time. The three Albian knights, plus Uther and Wulf Blodring, crowded the small table. The four squires stood at attention behind their knights.

Michael and Jack stood chatting quietly between bites of oatmeal from gray stone bowls. Julian and Wentworth rushed between the stove, the double oven, and the table, bringing new food as fast as the fighters could eat it and clearing the massive stacks of plates and bowls left behind.

As Emily scanned the crowded kitchen for Ernest, Poet-Captain Dhar snuck through the door, grabbed two hot biscuits in each hand and popped a fifth in his mouth, then headed out again. Everyone from the Irregulars, and at least part of the senior staff, seemed to be here—except the man they needed.

Jack caught Emily's eye and gave her a lazy wave and smile. His hair was pulled back in a neat ponytail, but instead of his usual loose poet's shirt he was wearing a black T-shirt that hugged his slender body. Michael looked up, his spoon bobbing in his mouth, and Emily felt a snap of electricity as their eyes met. In the excitement of her revelation about the door, Emily had lost track of the dangerous secret the young magician had shared with her. She shook her head, grabbed a couple biscuits, and went to join them.

"Nice hammer," said Jack as she came up. "Time to go?"

"Yeah, but I'm still looking for Ernest," she replied.

"Aren't you always? Well, I know where I left him yesterday. He probably opened the bar, closed it down, and poured himself into bed in the middle of the night. Sleeping it off, I bet. You try his room yet?"

"Actually, yeah," said Emily. "He wasn't there. Honestly, it looked like he hadn't been there at all."

Jack frowned.

"You don't think…" said Michael.

"Shit," agreed Jack. "Okay, Sledge, give us a sec to finish breakfast and then we'll go with you."

"Where are we going?"

"The Wrist, of course," said Michael with a slow shake of his head.

It was high tide, so Emily, Jack, Michael, and Captain Queen piled into a small rowboat and shoved off into the shallow sea. The clear blue skies of the last few days had been replaced by a cover of heavy gray clouds, and a chilly wind whipped their hair as they struggled through choppy water. Queen took one oar and Emily took the other, but despite their considerable combined strength, they seemed unable to find a good rhythm to drive the boat through the waves together.

"I've never seen the kitchen so crowded," said Captain Queen, speaking between two long breaths that made a counterpoint to the splashing of her oar. Every stroke brought cold, gray water up into the boat to soak their feet and chill their bones.

Jack shrugged in response. "Everybody got up early. What did you expect?"

"What do you mean?" asked Emily.

"Everyone wants to see you off," Michael explained. He was wearing a hooded sweatshirt, but he still sat somewhat huddled up, hugging his arms. "They want to know what's behind the door."

"Oh," said Emily, and nobody really had anything to add.

The little rowboat crunched into the beach on the other side of the sunken sandbar, and Emily hopped out into the shallows to haul it to dry land. Captain Queen nodded her thanks as she hopped out of the boat; Emily helped Michael and Jack over the gunwale, and was rewarded with an ironic half-bow from Jack.

As they trudged grouchily towards the center of town, Emily wished she'd thought to bring a sweatshirt like Michael had. She was in no real danger from the cold; part of being a Combat Gifted was a certain innate toughness against the weather, the same way she could take a hit that would crack most people's ribs. But the cold bummed her out just the same.

"This is what I get for spending my summer vacation in northern Maine," she muttered, but nobody heard her over the wind.

They made it to the Twisted Wrist just before the sky broke open and rain began pouring down. Piling through the door, they almost got caught in a knot half-in and half-out, but Captain Queen shoved them through with only a little cursing. The four stood for a moment to shake themselves off and adjust to the dim bar.

Blinking, Emily saw a tall, heavy shape hunched over the same back table, slumped in the same seat, as she'd seen him the day before.

Approaching, she said quietly, "Ernest?"

He snapped upright with surprising control and looked at her through eyes that seemed to be smeared with Vaseline.

"Why, hello, Emily, darling! Won't you pull up a chair and join me?"

Unnerved, Emily looked back at her three companions, who were picking their ways through the tables and chairs. Sighing, Jack sat across from Ernest and plucked a wineglass directly from his hand.

"I don't know how he does it, but he does it," said Jack. "Sometimes I think it's his real Gift, not his mind. Ernest, did you sleep at all last night?"

"Goodness, no," replied Ernest with a huge grin. "Sleep is the realm of dreams, which are far too close to truth. I prefer to close my inner eye with chemical assistance, thank you very much and may I please have my wine back?"

"No," said Jack.

"So, um…is he good to go?" Emily asked carefully.

Behind her, Michael shook his head. "Not at all, sorry. As far as we know he can keep going as long as he's drinking, but the second we drag him into bed he's going to black out for the rest of the day. He might be—might be—okay tomorrow, but…" He shrugged.

"That's not gonna work!" said Emily, who was starting to feel a bit panicky. She grabbed Ernest's shoulder and shook it, maybe a bit too roughly. "Come on, we've only got five days. Get it together!"

Ernest let out a loud, long, boozy belch that forced Emily and Jack back a step. "I'm afraid I shan't be attending tea with the enemy," he said. "Kindly convey my best regards and ask them on my behalf would they please kill me last."

"Dammit, Graves!" snapped Captain Queen. "What the hell got into you?" She pulled out a chair next to Ernest and sat in it backwards, her arms crossed over the back, her face close to his. "When I accepted you into the Irregulars, you promised me all this"—she waved a hand at him and all the empty glasses and mugs on the table—"all this shit was over. As I recall, your exact words were 'I have a cause other than myself now.'"

"Does not the Bible say 'a man can serve two masters?'" retorted Ernest blearily.

"*No* man," said Michael.

"Mm," said Ernest. "Maybe. How about, 'Render unto Bronwyn the things that are Bronwyn's, but please leave the booze for Ernest.'"

"I'm going to render you unconscious if you don't quit this bullshit," said Captain Queen. "But for now, you're obviously useless." She looked up at Emily. "Sledge, thoughts?"

"Well, I'm not sure," said Emily hesitantly. She hadn't expected Captain Queen to ask her opinion. Queen frowned at the noncommittal response. "But, if I had to choose, I'd say we still go through. For all we know Ernest wouldn't have been able to help anyway, maybe. And we're running out of time."

Queen nodded. "Good answer. Come on, kids, let's go have an adventure." She stood up decisively, and Jack did the same, leaving Ernest half-slumped over his collection of empty glasses.

The three Irregulars headed back towards the exit, but Emily lingered uneasily by Ernest's table. As she watched, he slowly deflated, collapsing onto the table. His cheek smushed against the sticky wood, and she could hear him breathing heavily through his open mouth, but his eyes were still slightly open.

Emily cleared her throat. "Ernest...please. Why?"

Without moving his head, Ernest slid his bleary eyes up to look Emily in the face.

"My goodness, Miss Sledge," he wheezed quietly. "But isn't it obvious?"

"Not to me it's not," Emily retorted, irritation edging her voice.

His eyes slid back down to stare blankly into empty space. "You're going to make me say it, aren't you?"

"I guess so. I really need to get going." Captain Queen was waiting in the doorway, silhouetted against the gray light outside, watching Emily and Ernest across the room.

"Very well," Ernest murmured. "But only because I like you. Between friends, then, let us put it this way: I am equally as drunk as I am scared. Which is to say, quite an awful lot."

His eyes closed, and his labored breathing became a noisy snore. Emily looked up at Captain Queen, who shook her head and went out into the rain. Emily spent a moment watching Ernest beginning to drool onto his hand, then followed the captain.

Jack and Michael ended up being right about the early morning activity in the kitchen. When they returned, soaked and grouchy, a huge group was gathered in the front hall waiting for them. The other Irregulars were there, as well as the Albian squires, the full senior staff other than the Marcher Lord himself, and a number of faces Emily hadn't seen before that she figured represented the support staff of the castle.

Emily headed straight for the stairs up, letting Captain Queen handle the explanations about the state they'd found Ernest in. That was what officers were for, after all. Her clothes were soaked, as were her good sneakers, and more than anything she wanted another shower to burn off the chill of the rain. She contented herself with toweling off and changing her clothes. Luckily, she'd left the ballistic vest and hammer behind, so she geared up and headed down to the great hall.

To her surprise, she found that the arrangement of palisades had been adjusted according to her conversation with Poet-Captain Dhar the day before. They now began about halfway down the length of the room, leaving the other half wide open as an approach from the door.

Thinking back, she didn't get the feeling Dhar had been all that surprised by her suggestions. It had felt more as though she was confirming what he'd already decided on, or validating an argument he had made before. Either way, it wasn't her business to design the castle's defenses. Her job lay ahead of her.

The door still stood, upright and alone, at the far end of the hall. A few people stood talking in a small knot just before it: General Alder, Captain Queen, Colonel Liu, and Jack. The rest of the crowd seemed to have taken their places just outside the first line of palisades, as though ready to retreat behind the huge wooden structures if anything should come leaping out of the door when Emily opened it.

She kept her eyes on the floor as she walked through the staggered defenses and out into the killing zone. She didn't feel self-conscious, exactly, but hearing any last-minute advice or good wishes from the crowd would throw her out of the fighter's mindset she was cultivating.

Emily approached the door. General Alder fixed her with a gray-eyed stare as she approached.

"Miss Sledge, are you absolutely certain that you all won't lose your memories when you step through this door?" Queen, Liu, and Jack turned to hear Emily's response to the general's question.

"No, sir," she said.

"Very well," said Alder with a nod. "You first, please."

Emily tore herself away from the general's gaze to look Captain Queen and Jack each in the eye, and received wary nods from both. Then, after a deep, centering breath, she readied herself for action and reached for the doorknob. She touched it gingerly at first, as though it might burn her, and finding it nothing more than metal, she turned it.

The door was locked.

"Um," said Emily.

"Did you try pulling?" asked Captain Queen.

"Wulf said it opened in," Emily said, turning the knob again and pulling. The door wouldn't open that way either.

"Maybe you need to jiggle the handle?" suggested Jack.

"Somehow I don't think that's it," said Emily. Behind her, whispers were starting within the crowd. Somebody laughed, then cut off short. Emily felt as though she could feel each individual pair of eyes burning into her back: Sir Maximilian's with mockery, Michael's with sympathy, Uther and Wulf judging her, Poet-Captain Dhar with kind concern.

"Dammit," she muttered. But she had pulled a door off its hinges not too long ago; raw strength had gotten her through that obstacle. Maybe, Emily thought, this embarrassment was just lacking some elbow grease.

She grabbed the doorknob again and twisted it with a savage jolt. It offered no resistance, and the door swung easily inward.

"Okay, that was…weird…" Emily trailed off. "Oh my God."

CHAPTER 11

Her first impression was of stars, a million, ten million, more. A huge red sun burned overhead, its surface leaping and bursting with flares. Slowly Emily pulled her eyes away from the sight, some part of her brain wondering how she hadn't been instantly blinded.

Looking down, she found that she stood on a flat, perfectly white surface that seemed to stretch out towards the stars before her. She was alone on a vast plain, stars above and emptiness beneath...

"Move it, Sledge, come on! We're scouts, not tourists!" Captain Queen pushed through the door behind her, shoving Emily forward and aside. Jack followed cautiously behind, but stopped at Emily's right hand.

"Oh, wow," he whispered. A smile slowly crept across his face, totally different from the ironic humor Emily had seen there so often.

"No time, kids, no time," urged Captain Queen. "We're out in the open here. Let's find somewhere to hide and then we can talk about our feelings."

Emily blinked, shaken out of her reverie by Queen's attitude. Taking a look all around her, she found that what had been a door on the other side was a huge semicircular gate here. It was about twice her height and maybe double that in width. The arch itself looked like a long, slender rod of metal bent into a curve, with purple and blue electricity playing along it in short, stuttering arcs.

Within the gate was a view totally unlike the one they'd left behind.

The built-up great hall of the Castle Forlorn and its anxious crowd were gone. In their place was a huge vista of waving red grass, spilling towards a glittering blue-black mountain that rose incongruously from the heart of a deep valley.

"Emily, dammit!" Captain Queen snapped, irritation now naked in her voice. "Feelings later, survival now! What the hell did they teach you at Harkness?"

The insult stung Emily into motion. A last, longing glance at the red-grass world showed it beginning to waver and change, but Emily tore herself away and followed Captain Queen at a trot.

They moved over the flat white surface, their footfalls echoing in the vast silence. It felt like plastic, Emily thought, or really smooth concrete. As her head cleared she started to make out small details. They weren't naked beneath an open void—long arched beams split what must have been a huge window on the black sky overhead.

They were in a dome, a dome of glass or something like it. The gate behind her stood at one point around the dome's circular base, and perhaps a dozen more matching gates in various stages of collapse marked equidistant points around them. A human-scale door, surprisingly mundane-looking, stood between each pair of gates. Captain Queen was leading them towards one of these, apparently chosen at random, her head swiveling like an owl's in a vigilant hunt for danger. Her weapons were still sheathed, but a ready hand rested on the hilt of her sword as she ran.

Jack was right behind Captain Queen, putting Emily last, so she was the only one who heard the sound of a door opening from across the dome. She skidded to a half-halt, turning to see a human-like shape start into the dome, then pause and turn back as if to talk with someone on the other side of the doorway.

"Run," Emily hissed as loudly as she dared. "Run!"

Captain Queen and Jack didn't hesitate, but sprinted for their chosen door; Emily caught up and passed them in a matter of seconds. She hit the door first, tearing it open with a silent thanks to whoever that it wasn't locked. As one, the three spilled into a long, straight metal hallway that ended at a T-junction about thirty yards down.

The hall seemed deserted, and Emily let out her breath in relief. Turning back, she peered around the edge of the door at what was clearly a small squadron of soldiers entering the dome from across the way.

There were six of them, and they talked as they approached the gate. They were all roughly human-shaped and human-sized, though they ranged from short and round to tall and extremely thin. Black-glassed vacuum helmets hid their faces. They wore partial ballistic armor, black plates over dull red fatigues; they had probably matched neatly at one point, but each set of armor had been customized with insignia, trophies, medals, and many battle scars.

A snatch of laughter, human laughter, reached her ears, along with a high-pitched, insectoid chittering. To get to the gate, the soldiers had to come closer to where Emily and the others hid, as they'd run instinctively to the nearest door. As they got near, she began to make out bits of their conversation, and by the time they stopped at the gate she could hear them perfectly.

"Bu, take the count," ordered a soldier with a blood-red handprint painted—at least Emily thought it was painted—over the black glass of his helmet.

"Aye, Captain Smiertkin," replied the short round soldier in a watery, warbling voice. He stood attentively by the gate, peering into it carefully. It showed a white city built into the side of a mountain in concentric circles, but the image began to waver again as Emily watched.

"Bilo, the weapons," ordered Captain Smiertkin. Another average-sized soldier began handing out sleek black rifles.

"That's Rul, Captain," said Bu. The gate now showed a craggy, storm-haunted mountain range through the mouth of a dark cave. "Number Thirteen. We're just about at the top of the cycle."

"Thank you, Bu," said Smiertkin. "Everybody armed? Good. You know the drill, boys. Once Bu calls Number Four, hustle. We all know where Number Five goes, so do not let the gate get away from you. Von-Drelle, you're on point." One of the soldiers nodded in acknowledgement.

"Number One," called Bu.

"Uppagu, Tooms, secure the perimeter once we're in," continued Captain Smiertkin. "Bilo, permission slips, please." The soldier called Bilo pulled a small black case, about the size of a deck of cards, from a pouch on his belt. From it he drew a series of flat, translucent sheets, which he handed to each of the soldiers.

"Number Two," said Bu at the gate.

As each soldier received his sheet from Bilo, he pulled off a glove and slapped the sheet onto the back of his naked hand. Captain Smiertkin pulled off his helmet and pressed his sheet onto the back of his neck, grimacing briefly as he did. He was human, probably in his mid-forties, with a flat, broken nose and clipped black-and-white hair.

"Stings every time, eh Captain?" said Bilo as he applied his own sheet to the back of his hand.

"It'll sting a lot more if the gateguard fries you," snapped Smiertkin. "You want to get where we're going, you quit your bitching and wear the patch. Uppagu, check your helmet, dammit. You've got a clip hanging loose." The tall, thin soldier pulled his helmet off, revealing a mantis-like gray head with compound eyes and three rows of clacking pincers.

"Number Three," called Bu.

Emily's breath caught in her throat. She'd seen plenty of monsters in her day, but they'd all been local to Earth, however weird and dangerous they were. This was her first glimpse of something truly alien. The creature called Uppagu chittered something that sounded apologetic as it snapped a clip into place on its helmet, then checked the other three clips.

"Here we go," said Captain Smiertkin. "Standard operating procedure. Shock and awe, boys, shock and awe. Dammit, Uppagu, hurry it up! On my mark. Three...two..."

Jack sneezed.

Six heads swiveled as one and locked on the doorway where Emily, Jack, and Captain Queen hid. Behind the soldiers, the gate flickered and changed to show the inside of what looked like an old lady's home, with cushy yellow armchairs arrayed around a low coffee table.

"Intruders!" yelled VonDrelle, shouldering his rifle.

"Lockdown!" shouted Captain Smiertkin. "Grab 'em!"

A resonant *thunk* sounded as the hallway behind Emily shook from some impact. She stole a hasty glance backwards to see that a heavy metal bulkhead had slammed into place only a few yards behind Captain Queen, blocking the hall completely and instantly putting their backs against the wall.

"Shit," said Emily.

"Make for the gate," said Captain Queen. "Come on, move it!"

They sprang into motion, dashing straight for the gate and the six soldiers who stood between them and it. Emily had to admit that Queen had made the right call—the other doors they'd seen around the dome were almost certainly blocked like theirs, and none of the other gates appeared operational. Still, the idea of fighting their way through the knot of soldiers and flinging herself into a strange land didn't hold a lot of appeal. She swung her hammer up to grip it with both hands.

VonDrelle was the first to fire, sending a blue beam of energy searing past Emily's cheek from only a few yards away. She sprang towards him shoulder first, crashing into his stomach and toppling them both over into a tangled heap. Her hammer spun away to the right.

"Get off me," VonDrelle growled, and shoved Emily up and to the side with surprising strength. Another Combat Gifted? Some kind of power suit? There wasn't time to think about it; she had to act.

Emily grabbed the barrel of VonDrelle's plasma rifle and yanked it from his hands. As he scrambled backwards and tried to stand, she flipped the rifle around and snapped off a shot, which glanced off the faceplate of his helmet and ricocheted up towards the starry dome.

VonDrelle tried to steal Emily's move, grabbing the hot rifle in his heavy gloves, and they struggled over it for a few seconds before it snapped clean in half. They both tumbled backwards; Emily threw her half at Von-Drelle and leapt to her feet as he batted it away.

"You bitch!" snarled the soldier. He jumped up into an aggressive fighting stance. Emily chanced a look over her shoulder to see Captain Queen squaring off against four of the soldiers, her sword and long knife in her hands. Jack had already been grabbed, and was struggling in the arms of short round Bu.

A hot flush of shame crept up Emily's face at seeing Queen doing the bulk of the work. She backstepped to the captain's side and dropped into a defensive stance, facing off two against five. Furiously she wished she hadn't dropped her hammer at the start of the fight.

From her left, VonDrelle came at her with a boot knife, as the tall blocky soldier called Tooms leapt at her on her right. She jerked her head to avoid VonDrelle's knife—he was fast, incredibly fast—and threw him past her with a tug on his leading arm. He stumbled and hit the ground behind her.

Tooms brought the stock of his rifle down at her head. She dodged, but not quite enough, and caught it on her shoulder with a disorienting thud. They were all that fast, she realized.

Trying to clear some space, Emily backed around to her right. Von-Drelle was shaking his head woozily on the floor at her left hand, but she knew he'd be up again before too long. Tooms came at her again, and as she sidestepped, her right foot hit something on the floor: her hammer.

She kicked it into her hand and caught it spinning, letting it continue its rotation to slam into the faceplate of Tooms's helmet. The black glass cracked and flaked away in a few places. An eerie red light glowed through the gaps. Tooms staggered back a few steps.

VonDrelle was on his feet again, and Emily spun to meet him, driving the hammer straight forward with both hands on the shaft. It took VonDrelle square in the chest, and Emily smiled at the familiar sound of ribs breaking. The soldier dropped, and didn't get up.

Turning on her heel, Emily saw Captain Queen on one knee, trying desperately to parry the flashing assaults of Uppagu, Bilo, and Captain Smiertkin all at once. Her sword and knife moved with glittering speed, but there was blood on the inside of her right wrist, and a sheen of sweat on her forehead. Her face was fierce with concentration.

Emily shoved her hammer at Bilo, letting it shoot through her fingers headfirst at him. He saw it coming at the last second and ducked to the side, throwing his knife as he did. Emily slapped it out of the air with her left hand, but felt a searing lash across her fingers and palm. Blood sprayed from her wounded hand in a red arc, spattering Bilo's faceplate and the slick white floor. Pulling the hammer back in, she snagged the end of the handle with the bloody hand just for a second, then released it with a curse. It burned with pain, and her fingers were quivering. She couldn't get a grip.

Stepping back, she swung the hammer one-handed in a wide arc, trying to keep the soldiers back while she recovered. The motion threw her a bit off balance, and Bilo ducked in under the whistling hammer with a nastily buzzing prod in his hand. Emily danced backward another step, but Bilo lunged and caught her with the tip of the prod.

Her body locked up, teeth chattering in her head, hammer clattering to the ground from her nerveless grasp. A brutal kick to the stomach from Bilo doubled her over and dropped her to the ground, where she shook helplessly. From her vantage point on the floor, Emily saw Smiertkin and Uppagu stabbing down with similar prods at Captain Queen. She knocked the tall insectoid's prod away with her long knife, but she'd lost her sword somewhere, and Smiertkin's prod struck home.

Queen dropped, her head bouncing viciously off the hard floor. She came to rest staring in Emily's general direction, her eyes swimming vacantly.

"I surrender! I surrender," Jack said from somewhere behind and above them.

Captain Smiertkin laughed. "I think that would be wise, yes."

It was a few minutes before Emily and Captain Queen could move again, and the soldiers had them tightly bound well before that. Their hands and feet were bound with polymer ties, and a short line ran vertically between the two ties. It took three soldiers to haul Captain Queen, spitting and thrashing, to her feet. Their brutality in getting the job done convinced Emily to stand with only Uppagu's help.

VonDrelle, prodding his ribs gently with two fingers, said, "Can we kill them yet or what, Captain?"

"Rein it in, VonDrelle," snapped Smiertkin. "The big guy is gonna want to have a little chat with them. Not to mention we've still got a job to do on Anganar. Cleaning up the mess would be a real pain in my ass right now." VonDrelle nodded but didn't say anything. "Bilo, what's the count?"

Bilo, watching the gate, said, "Number Eleven, Captain. We've got a minute or two."

Smiertkin crossed his arms and took in the three intruders. "In that case, maybe you three could answer a few questions for me. First off: you're all human, yes?"

"Suck it, mercenary," said Captain Queen.

"I'll take that as a yes," said Smiertkin. "And the ladies are both Combat Gifted. What about you, young man?"

"Pretty sure the captain said to suck it," Jack muttered. Emily noticed that he wasn't bound; the soldiers obviously didn't think of him as a threat. She hoped they were about to be proven wrong.

"Last chance, other girl," said Smiertkin to Emily. She shrugged as best she could, hunched over from having her hands tied to her feet.

"Okay, then." Smiertkin straightened. "Looks like we're gonna do this the fun way. VonDrelle, would you—"

"Number Two, captain!" called Bilo from the gate.

"Dammit, where's our backup? We're already thirteen minutes behind schedule," said Smiertkin. As he spoke, another squad entered the dome from the same door Smiertkin's group had used. "Aha, perfect. These guys'll take you three to detention until the big guy has time for you. Well, it's been fun, but we have a beachhead to establish."

Panic welled up in Emily's chest. She was sure Jack had something up his sleeve; he had a tense, loaded gun look that she associated with people about to take action. But their enemy count had just doubled. If it wasn't too late already, it was sure about to be.

Jack bolted. He made it between Smiertkin and VonDrelle before they could react. Bu brought his rifle up, but hesitated. Uppagu's grip on Emily's arm tightened painfully.

Jack had almost reached the gate when Bilo grabbed him in a full-body hug. They struggled for a few seconds before Bilo slapped him hard across the face and he dropped to his knees, still clinging faintly to the legs of Bilo's jumpsuit. A bright red welt was already starting out from his cheek.

"Bilo, break something of his, would you?" said Captain Smiertkin.

"Number Four!" shouted VonDrelle.

"Dammit! Move out, boys—drop him! I said leave him! Go, go, go!"

The mercenaries charged through the gate, storming the dainty sitting room Emily had seen earlier. VonDrelle's plasma rifle—he'd gotten a replacement somewhere—blazed blue fire as one of the cushioned chairs reared up with fanged teeth in a dripping mouth, but the scene shimmered and wavered, hiding the fate of the mercenary squad.

Somebody grabbed Emily roughly from behind, and she turned to see another six-person squad rounding up Captain Queen and picking up Jack's limp body. Two black-and-red-clad soldiers took Emily by the arms and dragged her away, as the image in the gate changed to Number 5.

The Irregulars were frog-marched mercilessly out of the dome through a third door. It led to another featureless metal hall that ended after about thirty yards in a sudden drop straight down. The mercenaries hauled them towards the edge without breaking stride, and the two holding Emily gripped her arms tight as she struggled against the fate apparently awaiting her.

Then the entire group marched straight over the edge, and Emily fought a sudden wave of nausea as her sense of what "down" meant reoriented itself violently. The near lip of the pit suddenly became the floor, and looking back, the hall they'd come from now looked like it was headed straight down instead.

"First time in artificial gravity?" Captain Queen whispered to Emily and Jack. Jack looked how Emily felt, green and unsteady.

"Where exactly are we?" asked Emily in the same quiet undertone.

"Haven't figured it out yet, Sledge? You haven't been out of our universe, have you?"

"Can you please cut the banter and just tell us what's happening, Bronwyn?" snapped Jack.

Captain Queen sighed. "I'll never stop being grateful for my Killoke education…Look around you. We're on a gatestation."

"A what?" said Emily and Jack together.

"A gatestation. It's a semi-mobile assault platform. They'll be sucking energy from that big sun we saw in the dome, using it to power the gate we came through. Good way to invade other universes."

"Why do you know this?" groaned Jack, but Captain Queen just raised her eyebrows suggestively.

Emily was well and thoroughly lost at this point. The mercenaries had led them around enough corners, both the usual and the vertical kinds, that her mental map of the station was totally scrambled. It occurred to her that that had probably been their goal.

They marched on for a while in sullen silence. They had reached a sort of straightaway, with doors on either side rather than more branching passageways, when Emily couldn't hold her question in anymore.

"Jack, were you trying to run away?"

Jack just shrugged, his eyes fixed firmly on the metal plating of the floor.

Emily tried again. "I mean, you didn't even know where that gate would have taken you. You probably would have been lost forever. And…you were going to desert us."

"I know what I did," said Jack quietly.

Emily had nothing to say to that. As they walked, she wondered what was becoming of the Irregulars she had befriended over the last few days. Ernest was a drunken coward; at least Jack seemed to be a sober one. Plus he was a definite disappointment in the magic powers department. Captain Queen wasn't so bad, though; she was brave, if bossy. She fought like a tiger and didn't seem to know what giving up was. Emily thought she could respect her, even if she didn't much like her.

Finally they stopped in front of a large double door. One of the mercenaries punched a code into a nearby keypad, and the doors rattled apart; the others shoved their captives through into an empty circular chamber. A series of small domes punctuated its otherwise smooth wall. The halls they'd walked had all been built from basic metal planking, and this room was the same, but the domes were of the blank white plastic that had been used as the floor of the large chamber that held the gate. They bulged from the wall all around, smooth and featureless.

"In here," grunted one of the soldiers, prodding Emily towards one of the domes. It slid aside in a sort of rotating motion, revealing a blinding whiteness beyond.

"What is this?" asked Emily.

"In," said the guard as he shoved her brutally forward. He was just as strong as the squad she'd fought, and she stumbled forward into the emptiness.

She was surprised to find her feet sticking to something just beyond the opening; she'd expected to fall forever. Taking a wary step forward, she found that she seemed to be walking on a solid, flat surface—she just couldn't tell how far, or in what direction, against the blank white all around her.

The mercenaries shoved Captain Queen and Jack into the space behind Emily, and both started cautiously stepping much as Emily had. As she watched, Emily was alarmed to see them head off in totally different directions. Jack was walking towards her, but veering off to the left and above her. Captain Queen seemed to be getting farther away, but she was walking perpendicularly to Emily, so that after a few steps, Emily was looking down at the top of Queen's head.

A whooshing sound made her head turn, and she barely caught the closing of the door they'd been put through. With it shut, everything was white in all directions. Disoriented, Emily sat down. Jack seemed to be headed right for her, but he was moving in a sort of arc above her head. Captain Queen was coming towards her from below, as though walking up a gentle slope.

"Got an explanation for this one, Captain?" asked Jack, taking a seat next to Emily.

"I think so," said Queen slowly. "An artificial gravity globe, and we're inside it. Every direction is down. Watch." She turned her back to Emily and Jack, and jogged straight away from them. They watched her run up the inner curve of a sphere, just as she'd predicted; first she rotated so they saw the top of her head, then she came around so she was moving towards them but upside-down, and finally she came towards them from behind.

"Good God, that's confusing," muttered Jack.

"That's the idea," said Queen, sitting with them. "No sense of space. No sense of time. No sense of direction. You could go a little nuts in here."

CHAPTER 12

4 DAYS?

"I really think it hasn't been a day yet," said Jack from above her. "They haven't fed us yet."

"We know," said Emily. "Better than you can imagine. Fighters feel hunger like you wouldn't believe. It's kind of a sixth sense. And that's how I know it's been a full day. I got lost in some tunnels under school once and this is how hungry I was after a day. That's about when we started eating moss."

"I didn't eat for four days, once," said Captain Queen.

"It was luminescent moss," Emily continued. "My pee glowed for weeks afterwards."

"I didn't eat for a week one time," said Jack.

"Seriously?" asked Emily. "The mighty Baron Wasteland let you starve?"

"He wasn't the baron of anything then. I was locked in a closet."

"How'd you get out?" asked Captain Queen, looking up, which for Emily was sort of to the right.

"I learned how to pick locks," said Jack. "That's why he locked me in there in the first place."

They lapsed back into silence. It wasn't their first argument about how much time had passed, but it had certainly been the most painful.

However long it had been, it had been forever, and Emily was feeling faint with hunger and thirst. She closed her eyes and let her head droop down onto her knee. She wanted to lie down and sleep for a long, long time.

Worse than the hunger, though, was the knowledge that this whole damn mess was her fault. She'd led them blindly into an overwhelming force and gotten them captured only days before the Castle Forlorn would need them. She'd been so sure that going through the door was the right move that she hadn't bothered to make a plan for the other side.

For some reason, Captain Queen kept making them talk to each other. She started up again. "Emily, what do you think of the strategic situation here?"

"We're trapped," said Emily.

"No, not us. I mean big picture. What are these guys doing here?" She said it like a Harkness professor, like she already knew the answer. Still, answering her was better than listening to her.

"Invading everybody through that gate, obviously," said Emily sulkily.

"Right. And how many troops do they have?"

"Um," Emily thought. "Twelve?"

"That's all we've seen, yeah. What else have we seen?"

"A lot of stupid hallways," said Emily.

"Exactly! A lot of stupid hallways, and only two six-man squads. Empty space. They're understaffed. And we know they're not up to the tech level of this place."

"How's that?" asked Emily.

"Because they only have one gate, and they can barely control it. Think about how the mercs talked about it. They were at the mercy of the gate, cycling through thirteen different locations. Couldn't stop it, couldn't slow it down, couldn't change where it was pointed."

"The other gates were all broken down," Emily agreed.

"And the captain mentioned some kind of guard on the gate, too," said Jack. "Made it sound nasty unless you had one of those patches." Something passed over his face, but Emily couldn't read it. Maybe he was just realizing he hadn't been wearing a patch when he'd almost run through the gate.

"Yes, that's a pretty standard safety precaution on gatestations," said Queen. "Stops guests like us from checking out early." She sighed. "So what does that tell us about our enemy? Did they build this gatestation?"

"No," said Emily. "They inherited it. Or stole it, or something."

"Exactly," said Queen. "They're squatters. Which means that somebody else probably wants it back."

"It explains the door on our side, too," said Jack suddenly. "We probably couldn't open it until the gate was pointed our way."

"Dammit, I wish we had Ernest right now," said Emily. "I bet a Mental could figure out how to point that thing wherever he wanted it to go. They must not have one either."

"No," agreed Queen. "Some of those mercs were human, but I don't think most of them were. Actually, I don't think any of them were Gifted. It's a human thing, but more to the point, it's an our-universe thing."

"Wait," said Emily. "Are you saying those guys were like, parallel-universe humans?"

"Um, not exactly," replied Queen. "As far as anyone knows, species don't repeat between universes. So humans, cats, dragons, whatever, only from our universe. Or they used to be. But then we got to exploring, and now there are communities of humans living more or less permanently in other worlds beyond the Veil."

"That's wild," said Jack. "That's really nuts."

"Sure," agreed Queen. "But they never seem to come up Gifted. I don't know if it's a magic thing or just some law of physics, but if you want a Gift, you need to be born in our home universe."

"Huh," said Emily.

Captain Queen's lecture seemed to have run itself out, and they fell back into a weary silence. Emily was about to fall asleep, for real this time, when Jack suddenly spoke.

"I figured it out!" he said, clapping his hands.

"What? What?" Emily said, blinking.

"I figured out what's been bugging me about Cho's death."

"You mean aside from the fact that he was murdered by a cross-universal mercenary who came through a wooden door?" said Queen, but Jack ignored her.

"He was left-handed. The note he left, the '100 Days' in blood."

"Yeah?" Emily encouraged him.

"It was by his right hand. But he was left-handed."

"So?" said Captain Queen.

"Well...it's weird," Jack finished lamely.

"Jack, all due respect, but I really don't think that's our biggest mystery right now." Captain Queen slumped down into a ball and shut her eyes.

3 DAYS?

Emily awoke with a heavy black boot in her ribs, giving her something that was not quite a kick but far more vigorous than a shove. Her stomach was painfully empty; she felt hollow and lighter than air.

"Up," growled a voice that she blearily recognized as VonDrelle's. For a moment Emily was stung with disappointment that he hadn't been eaten by that chair monster in universe number four.

"Five more minutes, Mom," she mumbled. The next thing she got from the boot was definitely a kick, and she rolled over and away from it, then slowly got to her knees.

VonDrelle and Bu stood over her, rifles in hand.

"Up, human," warbled Bu menacingly. A gesture with his rifle reinforced the command. Emily stood warily, keeping an eye on VonDrelle's gun.

Partway around the sphere, an upside-down Bilo and Tooms were rousing Captain Queen, and Uppagu was hauling Jack up by his elbow. Captain Smiertkin watched from the open doorway, which was directly above Emily's head.

VonDrelle and Bu marched Emily around the sphere to the door and pushed her through. The others followed. Even Captain Queen seemed resigned to getting pushed around; her eyes had lost some of their flash, though Emily was certain hers were just as dull from hunger.

In the circular chamber outside their prison pod, the mercenaries attached Emily's bonds to Captain Queen's with a polymer cable about two yards long.

"Just so you don't get any big ideas, ladies," said VonDrelle as he hooked one end of the cable to Emily's wrists and locked it in place.

They hustled the three prisoners out into the metal hallways and led them in another confusing march through twists and turns of all directions. At one or two points, Emily thought the stretches of hallway they were walking seemed familiar, but she couldn't have gotten back to either the gate or the jail cell even if she had been free and unchained.

"Where are you taking us?" asked Captain Queen. "One captain to another. C'mon, you can tell me."

Captain Smiertkin smiled. The faceplate was off his helmet, and hung from a belt clip, bouncing off his thigh as he walked.

"You'll see," he said. "We're almost there. Pick it up, boys!"

The mercenaries shoved Emily to move faster, and she bit her lip to keep from cursing at them. As they walked she entertained herself with fantasies of wrapping her chains around VonDrelle's neck, but she couldn't work out a way to do it without bringing Captain Queen along for the ride.

Eventually they passed through a large double door that was flanked by guards. Beyond was a massive chamber that was clearly the command center of the gatestation. They stood on a landing at the base of a huge staircase that swept up five or six tiers of computer workstations. Every one of the workstations was occupied by technicians of more species than Emily could have imagined.

The chamber buzzed with the noise of work, the chatter of quiet conversations, and the background hum of all the equipment. Keeping even that one gate running was clearly a labor-intensive task. Emily could imagine the effort involved in keeping the power flow from the nearby sun going, but her imagination ran out soon after that as to what the many techs could be doing.

At the bottom where they stood, the stairs were the pure white of the prison pod. Following them up, Emily saw that they slowly became pink, and as they reached the top and whatever waited there, the stairs were a deep blood red. A long, long light fixture hung above the stairs, top to bottom, apparently supported by nothing. Its light made the steps glow as if from within.

Pulling her eyes away from the arresting stairs, Emily looked up, and saw that the walls and ceiling were made of the same near-invisible glass as the gate room. The fat red sun was farther away and somewhat below them, but it was not at all alone in the galactic view afforded by the huge window.

Beyond the glass hung starships, hundreds of them, in all shapes and sizes. Small squadrons of fighters buzzed around huge carriers. Lean, wicked-looking warships bristled with what were clearly plasma cannons and missile tubes. Support ships, couriers, and personnel transports meandered between the capital ships, refueling, carrying messages, rearranging troops.

"I'll be honest," said Captain Queen, taking in the same view, "we may be a lot more screwed than I thought."

"Up," said VonDrelle, poking Emily with his rifle.

"How?" asked Emily bitterly, nodding at the ties around her ankles. VonDrelle sneered at her, then bent, shouldered his rifle, and pulled a gleaming knife from his boot. He cut through the bonds easily, but before Emily could act on her first impulse to kick him in the mouth, he pressed the knife into the small of her back. The message was clear.

They ascended the stairs, Emily and Captain Queen in front with their escort, Jack just behind, and Captain Smiertkin trailing them all with a watchful gleam in his eye. Queen's ankles had been cut free as well, Emily noted, and Jack didn't even have his hands tied.

As they neared the top, Emily felt as though she was walking in a river of blood, with pure crimson beneath her feet. At last they reached the highest landing, and as her head broke the line of the riser, Emily saw a huge glass sphere, twice her height, filled with a huge, curled shape. Brackish gray water sloshed and swirled as the serpentine form shifted within the orb. A few technicians stood to one side of it, checking readouts on a panel embedded in the glass.

"What the hell is that…?" breathed Jack at Emily's elbow.

The shape shifted again, turning, and a series of sharp clicks sounded as foot-long claws tapped the inside of the glass. From the coils, a head rose up. A huge gray head, covered in tattoos, red and green, black and blue. A head she had seen severed and stuffed on the wall of the Lancers' Guild Hall in Boston, on Earth, in a universe infinitely far away from this one.

The dragon smiled, revealing the same jagged, uneven teeth that were burned into Emily's memory.

"Hello, little invaders," it said.

"General Alder is a liar," breathed Captain Queen.

"Get us out of this," said Jack.

The dragon laughed, a low, resonant thrum that made the water in which it lay vibrate and ripple. "Little Marshall Alder…did he send you to finish his work, perhaps? He always preferred for others to do his dying for him. I'm sure the rank of general suits him."

Emily's head was spinning. If General Alder hadn't killed the dragon after all, what was the head she had seen? Why had he lied, if he'd driven the dragon out into a different universe all together?

"Now then," said the dragon. "Where are my manners? I would introduce myself, but my name is, of course, unpronounceable by your sort. And frankly, it offends me to hear it so butchered. But I suppose I'd like to know your names before I throw you away."

"Emily Sledge," said Emily, hoping she sounded brash instead of terrified. "Harkness Academy, and, um, Irregulars of the Castle Forlorn."

"Captain Bronwyn Queen of the Irregulars." She didn't sound scared at all; in fact, she seemed a little annoyed.

"Jack Twelve-Fingers," said Jack.

"And what brings you here, irregular humans?" asked the dragon, examining one of its gleaming claws as if in boredom.

Emily wasn't sure how to answer this, but Captain Queen said, "Scouting mission on behalf of the Castle Forlorn, which I gather is your next target. Wanted to see what we were up against."

"Oh?" The dragon sounded faintly amused. "And what did you learn in the comfort of my dungeon?"

"You've got limited resources," said Emily, forcing herself to stand up straight. "Despite all the ships out there, you have hardly any troops on this station. You sent six guys into Number Four, and they're the same guys who got us from the prison just now, so you don't have much in the way of manpower. They're probably all up here doing computer things."

"Computer things," said the dragon. "I see."

"You want to control the gate, but you can't," Emily continued. "You can't point it anywhere else, and you can't slow it down. Apparently it's taking everything you've got just to keep it running."

In a rush of gray water the dragon lunged towards her, nearly slamming its head against the inside of the glass sphere to get close to her. Its eyes narrowed and it gave her another flash of its twisted teeth.

"You think you know so much, little girl? Then tell me this: if I send only six men at a time to conquer my worlds for me, how is it that each time, they all come back?"

"Just lucky, I guess," said Jack.

The dragon turned its gray head and slit-like eyes to him. "It is because when they go through the gate, they know that they shall come back in victory or not at all. They conquer or they die. They fear me more than death itself, and in fear, they serve."

"What can you do that's worse than death?" asked Jack, stepping forward. Captain Smiertkin made a motion toward him, then subsided. "Splash them?"

"And who are you to speak to me with such impertinence, child?" The dragon pressed its body against the glass, front claws up, peering down at Jack from within the swirling water.

"The Honorable Jack Twelve-Fingers of Deseret, Son of the Healer, Keeper of the Secret Keys, Pathfinder and Waymaker, Singer of the Song of His Mother," replied Jack, raising his chin and squaring his shoulders to the dragon. He seemed like a wholly different person from the quiet, frightened young romantic of the last few days, and a few inches taller to boot.

The dragon laughed. "You think that impressive, boy? Don't you know who I am? I am the terror that sleeps beneath the rock. I am the ocean's devil. I am the wrecker of ships, the maker of widows, the madness below the surface of every man's mind…"

As the dragon went on, reeling off an impressively elaborate list of titles, Emily's thoughts started to wander. It was toying with them, that much was obvious. And when it got bored of them, Emily figured, it would have them killed. They clearly had no value to it. There wasn't much to say about the defenses of the Castle Forlorn; the dragon had made sure of that with the memory wall.

This was their last chance to escape. If only Earth-born humans were gifted, then the mercenaries must be wearing some sort of subtle power armor to be as fast and strong as they were. Assuming the technicians, who seemed to be ignoring the drama playing out above their heads, weren't dressed the same way, Emily, Jack, and Captain Queen only had to escape from six men. All of whom were up on the high dais with them...

"You were all of those things," Jack said. "Now you're just a lizard in a fishbowl." The dragon snorted in anger, and scuttled farther up the wall of the sphere, pulling itself up to its full height, glaring down at Jack.

Emily looked around, trying to keep her motions discreet. Behind the dragon was a drop into empty space, and beyond that, the glass wall of the huge command center like the face of a towering cliff. No escape that way. One end of the long, floating light fixture hovered about six feet over her head, then ran down the length of the staircase to the landing five tiers below. She could probably jump it, but not chained to Captain Queen.

"As a child, I convinced a chest of treasure to open its own lock," Jack was saying.

"My treasure is such that I would not miss a mere chest of it," retorted the dragon.

The mercenaries seemed distracted, watching the battle of boasts and insults play out between the young man and the dragon. Only Captain Smiertkin looked attentive, and a bit irritated. VonDrelle and Bu were behind Emily, slightly to her left. They were both in relaxed stances, their rifles down. Bilo and Tooms stood the same way just past Captain Queen. Uppagu had fallen back when Jack advanced on the dragon's sphere.

"As a boy, I convinced a woman to give up her faith," Jack said.

"The faith of a woman?" chortled the dragon. "Ha! I've drawn men away from their homes and families with false promises of gold and glory. I've set them to torch their own cities. I've commanded them to march into my waiting maw and swallowed them whole!"

Emily had fought with a chain before, a handful of times. Had Captain Queen? Did they teach chain-fighting at Killoke? Suddenly Emily wished she had gotten out of the gym more, traveled farther, met more people than just her tight circle of friends at Harkness. She didn't know anything about how Pacific Northwesterners fought. She'd heard about group fighting techniques developed by slaves on chain gangs, but had no way of knowing if Captain Queen knew the same stories.

"As a man, I sang to the sun to keep it asleep for a day, so I could longer enjoy the night," Jack said to the dragon.

"I was the sun!" the monster snapped. "I was the moon! When I came to a town at night, they would tell stories for years afterwards about the lights that danced in the sky. These were merely the fires of my eyes, the edges of my claws, the tips of my teeth!"

"And now you are a stuffed head on the wall of a house with nobody home," said Jack quietly.

"Kill him!" the dragon roared. Captain Smiertkin snapped to attention, raised his rifle, aimed it square at Jack's chest—

An earsplitting klaxon wailed, and the command center was bathed in the lurid tones of a red alert. The dragon whirled in its sphere, throwing up a wall of water that hid the beast from sight until it slid dripping down the glass again.

Beyond it, outside in the starry void of space, the thousand ships were coming to life. The searing lights of plasma fire scored lines between them that disappeared as soon as they appeared. Tiny, nimble fighter craft were scrambling from the huge carriers, taking off in hasty squadrons to engage with seemingly identical groups. Emily couldn't make out markings or colors at this distance, but there seemed to be a group of raiders in among the fleet, like wolves in a panicked herd of sheep.

"The Kleiborn Alliance, my lord!" yelled one of the techs at a station one tier down from the dragon's dais.

"Those damn pirates!" roared the dragon.

"Central Command is ordering us to scramble fighters," called another tech.

"Respond," ordered the dragon. Its attention was completely gone from the three prisoners as it began to rattle off a string of commands that made Emily's head spin. She tensed, sensing their moment had come.

With a snarl, Captain Smiertkin kicked Jack in the chest. Emily was close enough to hear the crack, then Jack flew past her head and down the long staircase. He hit the steps three tiers down and rolled the rest of the way, skidding across the landings, and finally coming to rest ten feet from the base of the staircase in an unmoving pile. Bright red blood glared against the pure white floor.

VonDrelle and Bu dove for Emily simultaneously; she leapt Von-Drelle's low tackle, kicked off his head, and made it halfway over Bu before she caught up short on the cable tethering her to Captain Queen. She fell suddenly onto Bu, and they collapsed together into a heap. The rifle skidded from Bu's hands, fell over the edge of the stairway, and came to rest a few steps down.

"Dammit, Sledge!" cursed Queen. "Close up!"

Emily scrambled off of Bu, but powerful hands gripped her ankles before she could stand. She looked back to see VonDrelle holding her left leg and Bu her right. Both were still on the ground. VonDrelle, his faceplate off, was openly snarling. His grip tightened, there was a faint whine of servos, and Emily's ankle crunched painfully under his hand.

Suddenly she found herself sliding along the floor. Captain Queen, a small ring of downed mercenaries around her, was pulling Emily in by her cable.

"No you don't," growled VonDrelle even as Bu let go and scrambled away for his rifle. Emily lashed out with the released leg and was rewarded with a satisfying crunch and a bright spray of blood. VonDrelle's hands flew to his broken nose and Emily leapt free.

Her broken ankle collapsed, dropping her back to her knees as Captain Queen closed up with her. Aside from the cursing, spitting VonDrelle, the mercenaries were on their feet, armed, and tightening the circle. Beyond the dragon's great glass sphere, lights burned in the starry sky as fighters chased one another in stomach-turning spirals around the lumbering capital ships. Emily tried to stand again, shivered, and fell.

VonDrelle stood, flicking blood from his hands that fell in a wide arc and was lost on the crimson floor.

"Shit," said Emily.

"Heads up!" Emily looked up to see Captain Queen leap towards her, throwing one knee high up—Emily caught on at the last second and rose onto her knees, her cupped hands in front of her. She caught Queen's boot and shoved as the captain leapt.

Queen catapulted up towards the hanging light. Ignoring her complaining ankle, Emily shoved herself up into a crouch. Just before the cable between them hit its full extension, she leapt straight up, following the captain. Her ankle gave a loud pop and went numb. Blue plasma fire blazed in a web under her feet as the mercenaries fired a half-second too late.

Queen grabbed the light with both hands and hauled herself over; falling down the other side, she yanked Emily up until they balanced for half a breath in a panicked equilibrium. Then they began to slide, dangling on either side of the light as they rode it down.

Thinking to gain some height, Emily began to scramble up her side of the tether, then lurched downward again as the action pulled Captain Queen up on the other side.

"Eyes front!" yelled the captain. Emily looked ahead to see the white floor rushing up toward them at an alarming rate. A plasma beam burned past her face. She heard yelling from the panicked techs below, and glanced down to see them stumbling around in all directions as the mercenaries shoved them about, trying to get line of sight on the moving target she presented.

The light lurched suddenly, its anti-gravity clearly not calibrated to support the additional weight of two heavy fighters. Up at the highest tier of the command center, the far end of the light tilted sharply up and crashed into the ceiling, spraying sparks down on the top row of ducking techs.

Emily and Captain Queen were dumped almost straight down and shot off the end of the light fixture, which righted itself aggressively and hung wobbling like a spear being shaken up and down. Then its artificial gravity gave up entirely, and a hundred yards of light came crashing down a few feet behind Emily and Queen where they lay dumped on the floor. Glass and sparks sprayed everywhere, and a few panicked techs rushed in to extinguish fires that were breaking out along the length of the staircase.

In a room now lit only by the glow of monitors and instruments, Emily and Queen scrambled to where Jack lay unmoving. Behind them, the mercenaries pounded down the stairs, trying to find safe shots at the escapees as techs ran all around them.

Gingerly, Emily rolled Jack onto his back and began checking for a pulse. One of his eyes was partially open, rolling up to show red where there should be white.

"Time to move, Emily," said Queen grimly. She had stood and was facing the stairs, waiting for the mercenaries. "Is Jack walking or are we carrying him?"

"Um—" Emily hedged.

"Just pick him up, then, dammit!" snapped the captain.

"No…" whispered Jack. "Was a good nap…time to wake up."

"Jack!" Emily cried, thrilled. She hugged him in joy, then loosened up a bit as he wheezed in her ear. "Can you walk?"

"Maybe," he croaked. "Help?"

Emily stood with Jack's arm over her shoulders. Her ankle was, mercifully, still numb. It wobbled a bit as she put her weight on it, but she didn't dare look at it until this was all over.

"Okay, Captain, we're ready," said Emily.

"About time!" snapped Queen as she sprinted past Emily and Jack. "They're on our asses, so keep up!"

Emily didn't need to look back to trust Captain Queen. She ran after her, hauling more than helping Jack as they went. Queen led them out of the command center through the double doors. One of the guards leapt to stop them, raising his rifle, but Queen grabbed him by the front of his jumpsuit and threw him over her shoulder, where he crashed into the mass of mercenaries at their heels.

They pounded down a metal hall to the nearest junction they could reach, and Captain Queen made to turn left, but Jack gasped, "Other way!"

"Other way!" Emily repeated, not sure if Queen had heard Jack. Queen spun on her heel and headed to the right, dragging Emily and Jack along behind her.

"How do you know?" Emily asked Jack as they ran.

"Trust me," he said between deep, ragged breaths. So she did. As they ran, Jack murmured something under his breath, a sort of rolling chant that occasionally rose up to become directions in Emily's ear, which she would call out for the captain to hear. Queen obeyed without question or argument, and soon they fell into a rhythm of twists and turns. Only once did Emily's ankle collapse completely beneath her, pulling Jack and Queen down into a panting mess and wasting precious seconds as they sorted themselves out.

But they appeared to have lost the mercenaries, even if it meant that Emily, at least, was totally lost as well. She hoped that Jack really knew what he was doing, and wasn't just calling out directions at random. His murmuring sounded magical, but Emily wondered bitterly if maybe he just had a Gift for running away.

Just as this thought crossed her mind, Jack called for them to make a right down a long hall that dead-ended in a closed door. They reached it in a flat-out sprint and Captain Queen kicked it open to reveal the gate room they'd originally come through, its great dome now showing the fringes of the assault on the fleet. The pirates, or whoever they were, seemed to have been turned back and were now fleeing, with a few pursuing fighters picking off the stragglers.

They made it to the gate in a few seconds, and Captain Queen spun to watch the many entrances to the dome.

"Where's it pointed?" she called over her shoulder. Emily was dismayed to see that it showed a world she didn't recognize.

"I don't know!" she shouted back. "I'm not sure what number this is."

"Just gonna have to wait, I guess," said Queen with bitter irony in her voice.

A door near the gate slammed open and VonDrelle came through it at a run. His faceplate was still off and he wore a manic snarl on his face. He skidded to a stop, unslung his rifle, and snapped off a shot at the three Irregulars.

Emily was jerked suddenly backward and up as Captain Queen yanked on the cable connecting them. Blue fire burned by an inch from her, singing the flesh of her wrists as it parted the tether. She stumbled backwards and nearly fell, suddenly disconnected from Queen, who was moving towards VonDrelle with a feral smile on her face.

"My turn," said the captain.

VonDrelle rose to her challenge, firing another plasma shot that Queen anticipated and dodged as she closed quickly on the mercenary. Too close for the rifle, VonDrelle pulled out his boot knife and lunged at Queen, who caught his hand between her bound wrists and twisted.

There was a sharp crack, and VonDrelle cried out in anger and pain as he pulled his hand free and backed up.

Glancing away from the fight, Emily realized that she recognized the world beyond the gate: Number Four, the sitting room that the mercenaries had invaded, now burnt black and scored with plasma marks.

"I think we're close!" she yelled. Queen glanced back over her shoulder, nodded, then turned quickly back as VonDrelle took advantage of her momentary distraction to charge.

The captain of the Irregulars stepped back, planted her feet, and whipped her bound wrists around so the five feet of tether dangling from them lashed out and looped around VonDrelle's neck. She tugged hard, pulling him stumbling in, then as they collided, turned the pull into a body throw that sent the mercenary over her shoulder and into the gate.

"Nahh!" was all he managed before he hit the gate, which had changed to Number Five. He hit the opening of the arch and seemed to stick there as a nimbus of blue lightning caught his body. He screamed briefly as his body fried; a moment later, a charred corpse fell smoking to the white floor.

"Permission slips," said Emily, her stomach sinking. "That's what the captain meant by a gateguard. We can't get through without—"

Yet another door into the dome crashed open, and the rest of the mercenary company spilled through, Captain Smiertkin in the lead. He shouted a few commands and his men took up firing positions, unlimbering their rifles and preparing to fire.

"Ladies!" yelled Jack. Emily turned to see him holding the small black case from which Bilo had first handed out the flat translucent sheets to his fellow soldiers.

"How did you—" Emily began, but Captain Queen was pulling her towards Jack and the gate. The first bolt of plasma fire seared over their heads.

"Halt!" called Captain Smiertkin from across the room. "You can't

166

get out through the gate, and we've got you covered. I suggest you come along quietly."

Shielded from the soldiers' view by Emily and Queen, Jack slid off the cover of the black case. Stacked within were four clear sheets. Quickly they passed the case around, slipping out the permission slips. Emily slapped hers onto the back of her hand, hissing in pain as it burned into her flesh, then stuck the case into her pocket.

"Last chance!" yelled Smiertkin.

"Everybody set?" asked Captain Queen quietly.

"Let's go home," said Jack.

"Blood Squadron, prepare to open fire!" Smiertkin ordered. "Captives, I am warning you, you have three seconds to surrender or you will all be killed!"

"I don't recognize this one," said Emily, peering into the gate, which showed a vague purple mist.

"Three...!"

"Come on, come on," Jack chanted under his breath.

"Two...!"

The hazy purple view began to waver and change.

"One...!"

Through the gate Emily could just make out the great hall of the Castle Forlorn, yards of open flagstone floor leading to the high wooden walls of the palisades.

"Blood Squadron, open fire!" came the voice of the mercenary captain as they dove through the gate.

Chapter 13

They stumbled out through the door into the great hall. A single beam of plasma fire followed them, hissing over Emily's head as she fell to her knees; it burst on the ceiling of the hall and left a smoking black mark.

"Oh, thank God," Jack began, but he was cut short by the thick voice of Wulf Blodring.

"Halt! Who is that?" His voice echoed down from over the top of one of the barricades. "State your purpose or you will be killed!"

"Wulf, you idiot, it's us!" yelled Captain Queen. The younger Blodring brother's face appeared over the top of the palisade, frowning in doubt, then splitting in a huge grin as he recognized his fellow Irregulars.

"It is you! Look, Uther, everybody, it's them!" Wulf leapt over the top of the palisade and landed heavily on the flagstones, then rushed over to engulf Captain Queen in a hug.

Slowly, the castle's defenders began to emerge from the maze of defenses in the great hall, which looked as though they had been rearranged yet again. Uther came around from behind another palisade and gave Captain Queen an attempt at a fierce warrior's handshake, which was hindered by the fact that her wrists were still tied together. Emily earned a somber nod, as did Jack, then Wulf mercifully pulled out a pocketknife and set to work sawing at Queen's bonds.

A few of Poet-Captain Dhar's guardsmen also appeared, looking suitably impressed by the Irregulars' sudden return. A pair of them were already at work on Jack, one snapping a brace around his neck as the other shone a flashlight in his bloodshot eyes, but a dark-skinned young woman politely indicated Emily's ankle, which she'd forgotten about during the crisis.

"Would you need a medic for that, miss?" she asked diffidently. Emily looked down.

"Oh, shit." Her ankle had swollen to the size of a softball, and her foot rolled at the end of it in a disconcerting, unattached sort of way. A moment after she saw it, it began to ache, as though her body had been reminded that it was injured. Soon the ache had turned into a roaring fire of pain, and Emily very suddenly sat down on the cold stone floor of the hall.

"Wulf," said Queen calmly, rubbing her chafed wrists. The yards of tether sat in a pile at her feet. "Would you please go fetch Michael? Leave your knife. And Uther, if you would find Colonel Liu for me, please." Wulf nodded happily and darted off among the palisades to make his way out of the great hall. Uther followed more slowly.

Captain Queen knelt by Emily and cut her wrists free. She could barely manage a sigh of relief at having her hands back, as the pain from her ankle seemed to be crawling up her leg and into her body.

Luke and Merry, the Albian squires, had come down from perches on palisades farther back in the hall. Merry stood frowning with her arms crossed, but Luke began to pepper Captain Queen with questions about what was beyond the door as she moved to examine Emily's ankle. She brushed off the squire's inquiries as best she could, but then paused in gently rolling Emily's foot and looked over at Jack, who lay staring up at the ceiling from a stretcher.

"Jack," she said slowly, "how did you happen to come into possession of those permission slips? We would have been dead if you hadn't had those."

"Oh," said Jack, a slow smile creeping up his face. He couldn't turn his head, but his eyes flickered over to catch Emily's. "Remember when I tried to escape, right when we were first captured?"

Captain Queen's eyes narrowed as she gave him a penetrating look. "Yes...?"

"Well, it just so happened that I was tackled by that merc called Bilo, the one who was handing out the cards in the first place."

Queen's dubious stare dissolved into a grin. "And you picked his pocket!"

"Yes, ma'am." Jack tried to nod, but only succeeded at squashing his chin.

"You—" Emily spluttered. "You weren't running away at all! Were you? You let him grab you on purpose! Ow, lay off!" Captain Queen had moved her foot in some way that created a horrible grinding sensation in her burning ankle. The captain raised an eyebrow by way of apology and went back to prodding the swollen joint.

Jack shrugged, an interesting motion in his position. "I figured I should make myself useful."

"But—" Emily shook her head in frustration. "But I was so mad at you!"

"I accept your apology," said Jack with another abbreviated nod. Luke and Merry were watching the whole exchange with the wide-eyed stares of an audience to a thrilling but absolutely baffling sporting event.

"Captain, I found Michael!" Wulf came jogging up among the palisades, Michael following close behind. He carried a small first-aid kit in one hand and a half-eaten roll in the other.

"Oh, jeez," he said when he saw Emily's ankle, and then repeated himself with feeling when he saw Jack.

"Yeah," said Emily.

The woman who had noticed Emily's ankle came jogging up to Michael's side.

"Sir, Poet-Captain Dhar told us to bring Jack to the infirmary. He's definitely concussed, and a rib or two is broken, but overall we think it looks worse than it is. The bleeding is mostly from where a lot of skin got torn off."

"Thanks, Tasha," said Michael with a smile. "Actually, would you wait for me? This should just be a minute." He knelt down by Emily's feet, gently pushing Captain Queen aside.

"It's completely shattered," said the captain, shaking her head. "I think there are a few shards broken off in there. Mostly dust, otherwise."

"What did you do, Emily?" asked Michael incredulously. Emily didn't have the energy for a biting retort, so she just lay her head back as he got to work. Soon she saw the same white aura he'd called up to draw the poison from Sir Richard begin to glow around his hands.

"Shouldn't you be helping Jack first?" she asked suddenly. "He got hit a lot harder than I did, and he's not a fighter."

Michael didn't look up from his work. "From what Tasha said, he'll keep for a while. This is actually a much thornier problem. Jack broke some ribs, but this...I need to deal with this before your ankle forgets what shape it's supposed to be."

Emily sighed, resigned to being treated first, and lay back to stare at the ceiling. The morning she'd come upon Sir Maximilian leaving the dead knight's room felt like a thousand years ago. The days they'd spent in the white prison were just a haze, and she was hungrier than ever. Between the pain, the dull roar in her stomach, and her ebbing adrenaline, she was starting to feel giddy.

"Michael, how many days are left?" she asked. His hands on her burning flesh felt mercifully cool. "Three, right?"

He looked up with his eyebrows raised. "Two, actually."

"Shit," said Captain Queen. "How did we lose track of time so badly? And where the hell is Maisie?"

"Okay," said Michael. "This might feel…weird." Emily sat up slightly to see what he was up to. The young wizard made a similar drawing-out motion to the one he had used on Sir Richard, but this time, he kept his hands loosely cupped instead of clapping them together as he'd done to release the poison. As he held that position, Emily's ankle felt as though it were ballooning up from the inside, trying to burst out of itself. Then all at once the pressure disappeared and the joint felt strangely loose and empty.

Michael opened his hands, and jagged fragments of bone fell clattering to the floor along with a handful of white powder. Sweat shone on his forehead.

"Okay, that's the easy part," he murmured.

"Um, is my ankle missing?" asked Emily.

"Temporarily, yes," Michael replied. His hands were shaking, and when he noticed Emily staring, he set them on his thighs. "The hard part is getting it to grow back. I don't mean to be rude, but if you could not talk to me for a few minutes, it would actually really help."

Emily lay back again to see Jack gazing down at her from his stretcher, which was being held aloft by two of Dhar's guardsmen as they waited for Michael to finish up. She was briefly reminded of their time in the anti-gravity prison; she'd almost gotten used to seeing Jack from below as he sat on the ceiling of the sphere, or she sat on the wall, or something.

"Jack, wait," Emily said suddenly. The guards glanced over, and Jack gave her a curious look from above his neck brace. Emily quickly picked up her line of thought from before Michael had arrived. "Why didn't you just tell us you had those cards? When that merc hit the gate and I realized what was happening to him, I just about peed my pants. You could have spared me a lot of terror." She frowned and looked away from his eyes. "And anyway, I spent the whole time in prison thinking you were…"

"A coward? I know," Jack said softly. His voice grew stronger as he continued, "But think about it. You don't think they'd put us in that crazy jail without any cameras or anything, right?" He raised his eyebrows conspiratorially. "I couldn't very well let them know we had a way out. They never would have let us rabbit in the first place, plus they would have blasted us into smoke the second we got anywhere near the gate."

"Huh," said Emily, a bit embarrassed. It actually seemed pretty obvious in retrospect.

"Okay, I think we're done here," said Michael. He sat back on his haunches, hugging himself. He was drenched in sweat and shivering visibly. Through chattering teeth, he continued, "Emily, try not to put any pressure on that ankle for a while. Ask the infirmary for a crutch if you need one."

A guard who had been milling around the barricades reached down a hand, which Michael accepted. With the guard's help, the young wizard climbed to his feet then blew out a long, weary sigh as he steadied himself. "Come on, Jack, you're the only thing between me and sleeping for twelve hours."

"Jack, one more question," said Captain Queen. "How did you know how to get back to the gate?" She had also clearly been waiting for Michael to finish up, Emily noted. She stood with her arms crossed, looking not so much impatient as impressed. "I tried like hell to keep the route straight but all those damn vertical corners screwed me up."

"Ah, honestly? I memorized it." Jack smiled shyly up at her. Somehow Emily felt as though she was seeing the real boy behind the act. "I used to do a lot of work in—how to put this—buildings that didn't belong to me. I'm good with floorplans. And air ducts."

"What were you saying while we were running away?" asked Emily.

"Just a little song," Jack replied, and he began to sing a simple tune.

"Left, down, right right down…Now for the love of God, you two, I have a concussion."

"Captain Queen?" said Uther, coming up behind them. "Colonel Liu and the others are in a staff meeting. She told me to just bring you all up for a debriefing. So follow me, please?"

"I think I know the way," Captain Queen said tightly.

The senior staff room was more crowded than Emily had ever seen it. The table was full with its usual occupants, and even the Marcher Lord looked relatively alert and attentive. A guardsman Emily didn't recognize stood behind Poet-Captain Dhar, taking notes. Daniel and Flora, the Albian squires not currently on guard in the great hall, flitted in and out, carrying messages to and from the senior staff; as the Irregulars took their place at the head of the table, Julian and Wentworth pushed past them, carrying away empty plates and glasses from a meeting that had clearly been going on for some time.

Emily's stomach growled at the signs of the just-finished meal. In all the chaos of their return through the door, apparently nobody had thought that she and the others might be hungry. In fact, she was starving, probably quite literally at this point. Her limbs felt somehow empty and incredibly heavy at the same time.

They waited for another few minutes, catching the end of an argument apparently about the number and placement of riflemen, until Captain Queen loudly cleared her throat. Colonel Liu, Poet-Captain Dhar, and General Alder turned their attention to her as Sir Maximilian and the Arthurs carried on a hushed conversation.

"Excuse me, boys, I think you'll want to hear this," said Captain Queen. "Emily, why don't you start?"

It was hard to say which caught Emily more off guard, being put on the spot to give a report or being called by her first name by Captain Queen. Still, she decided, she wasn't about to quail at telling her story when she'd only just barely lived through it. She shifted her weight to take some pressure off her ankle and began.

"We entered the door about three days ago. Actually, I'm not really sure what time it is right now."

"About eight," supplied Dhar, "at night."

"Thanks. Anyway, we entered the door and found that it was one side of a gate being operated on a gatestation orbiting a star some-where…somewhere. Long story short, we were captured and held without food or water for the better part of the time we were in there. Eventually we were taken to see the leader of the operation." Emily hesitated, and stole a glance at General Alder. He was leaning back in his chair, one hand resting lightly on his chin, his eyes fixed unwaveringly on her. She decided to gloss over the dragon for now.

"It was clear that they aren't operating with a full complement. In terms of muscle, we saw only two six-man mercenary squads plus two guards while there, though there could certainly have been more. The mercs have some sort of enhanced armor that makes them about as strong and fast as me or Captain Queen.

"They also had a few dozen technicians who were operating the gate. They seem to be running it, but unable to really control it. It runs through a predictable cycle of thirteen locations that it lets out on. The great hall is one of those thirteen, I think the eighth by their count.

"We figure they're squatters on the station; they took it over at some point and it just happens to have one gate that still works. They do seem to be part of a much larger space fleet, but not in charge of it. While we were being interviewed by their leader, the fleet was attacked by a group called the Kleiborn Alliance. It wasn't clear why, but the attack distracted their attention long enough for us to escape.

"Their goal is clearly conquest. We saw them assault one of the other universes through the gate with a six-man squad and come back victori-ous. As far as I can guess, they're taking out the other universes one by one, or at least establishing beachheads. I don't know if they only ever send one squad or if the assault is proportional to the defenses they expect to meet..."

She trailed off, unsure what else to add. Colonel Liu started to say something, but General Alder silenced her with a hand and leaned forward in his chair. His eyes were locked on Emily's, boring deeply as though he could mine the secrets out of her mind.

"Tell me, Miss Sledge," he said slowly, "who was this leader you mentioned? Who is running this program of conquest?"

Emily shuffled her weight around nervously. She couldn't quite say why, but General Alder made her really nervous.

Captain Queen came to her rescue. "The leader of operations at the gatestation was the dragon known as the Gray of Finalhaven, sir." She indicated the tapestries hung around the small chamber. "The same dragon depicted on these walls, if I'm not mistaken."

"I see," said General Alder, as though this news was no more than an inconvenience. He leaned back in his chair thoughtfully. "I had thought him banished for good, but I suppose when you're a thousand years old you develop quite the capacity for holding a grudge."

"Banished, sir?" Colonel Liu pursed her lips. "Not dead?" Loyalty and shock warred in Liu's expression, but her professionalism quickly won out. "Sir, is there...anything you can tell us about the Gray that might be of use in the upcoming fight?"

"I wish very much that there were, Colonel," replied the general. "He will not fight himself, I can tell you that much. I'm not surprised that he's been reduced to relying on mercenaries. Now then, Captain Queen, Miss Sledge. Based on what you saw, what recommendations do you have as we prepare for the assault?"

"Actually," said Emily, "there's one more thing. To get out through the gate you need these sort of key cards—they called them 'permission slips'—and Jack happened to, um, get his hands on a few. That's how we were able to get out. He really saved our lives. Anyway, we have one more.

"So I think we should send somebody back in. I volunteer. I could go in the door, then wait and see where I might be able to get to through the gate. Maybe one of the other settings also points to Earth. I could get out. I could get help."

There was a tense, expectant silence. Colonel Liu looked thoughtful; Poet-Captain Dhar looked hopeful. Sir Maximilian was watching Jack through slitted eyes.

"No," said General Alder.

"I—excuse me?" said Emily.

"It's a waste of time. Now, if you have nothing else—"

"I'm sorry, what do you mean it's a waste of time?" snapped Emily. General Alder sat forward again, his eyes blazing.

"Let us say that we send someone—we send you—in through the door again. And let us say that you are not immediately captured as you were three days ago. And let us even allow that this gate gives you access to somewhere else on Earth. Whom would you send to for help?"

"Well—the Lancers, of course," said Emily in confusion. "Won't they come to your aid?"

"The Lancers in the New World are a hollow shell of an organization. Their glory days ended with the reign of the Gray of Finalhaven and they are reduced to nothing more than a social club. And because I dared to expect more of our ancient brotherhood I was banished to this rock at the end of the world. No, we'll have no help from the Lancers."

"The Sabre and Torch, then. They live for this stuff!"

"Untrained, undisciplined, unreliable. We might get a hundred good fighters or we might get one young girl barely graduated from school. And for that you would have us risk one of the few Gifted defenders we have left? No. It's a fool's errand and I won't allow it. Miss Sledge, you are a good fighter, I'll give you that. But a fighter is a weapon, a tool, and must be used to maximum efficiency. You've told us that we're up against a conventional assault from a small strike team, nothing more—"

"I didn't say that," Emily interrupted. "They could have a dozen more squads for all we saw."

"—and therefore, your most useful place is on the front lines, not throwing your life away on a rash gamble."

"But—" Emily started. Captain Queen put a quelling hand on her shoulder.

"You are dismissed, Irregulars," said General Alder.

"Look, it's obviously personal between you and this dragon!" Emily babbled. "He hates you; he hates all of us. I think he's going to hit us with everything he's got. We need help!"

"Dismissed," said Alder again, with doom in his voice.

CHAPTER 14

Ten minutes later, Emily, Jack, and Captain Queen splashed across the sandbar in the last light of the long summer day. Leaving the senior staff to their deliberations, the two fighters hadn't said a word, but picked up Jack at the infirmary and set out for the destination they all had in mind.

The town square was full of shadows when they arrived. The fountain at its center loomed black against the low sun as they passed by, and the long stretch of sand leading down to the bay was blood red in the failing light.

Overall, the red-and-black world fit Emily's gloomy mood. Far from preparing her for the coming battle, their sortie through the door had made Emily more anxious than ever about what would be coming for them in less than two days. The hate she'd seen in the dragon's eyes made her sure that whatever it sent through the gate, it wouldn't be just six mercenaries.

General Alder's reaction had scared her as well. She'd assumed that he was a good leader—he was a Mental, she knew that much, and clearly had a long history with the Lancers. But something seemed off about him, and she was starting to think that some of the senior staff saw it, too. What if he was steering them all wrong?

She was pulled from her reverie by a movement among the shadows at the base of the fountain. Something had darted into hiding there, a dark spot hidden in the gloom.

"Did you see that?" she asked the others.

"See what?" asked Jack.

"Where?" said Captain Queen, turning.

"By the fountain," said Emily. "I don't know. I'm probably seeing things. I'm starving."

Queen frowned, thinking, then nodded. "We all are. It's been far too long. And frankly, I'm looking forward to some me time. Not that I didn't enjoy two days in a white bubble with you two."

"Three days," Emily said, but the captain ignored her.

"Here's a suggestion," said Jack as they started walking again. "When we get to the Wrist, we each get our own table. We eat as much as we want, no judgment. And we don't talk to anybody."

"See, that's a plan I can trust," said Captain Queen, putting a hand on the door to the Twisted Wrist. "I call back corner." Still looking over her shoulder at Jack, she opened the door.

A roar erupted from within the inn, rushing out on a blast of bright light that made Emily cover her eyes. She blinked, and the colorful mass on the other side of the door resolved into a common room full to bursting with cheering people.

The Irregulars were there to a man: the Blodring brothers stood shouting with raised mugs. Michael was by the door, pulling Captain Queen into the hug he'd been denied while rushing to fix Emily's ankle, a huge grin on his face. Ernest was standing on a table, red in the cheeks and looking like he'd been cut off mid-declamation. Somehow Julian and Wentworth had beaten them there; Emily saw them carrying plates piled with food among the tables as Madame de Luna served drinks. Even the squires had been released from their duties; Daniel, Flora, and Luke cheered openly from their seats, and Merry nodded a sort of grudging congratulations.

The rest of the crowd was made up of townspeople, many of whom Emily recognized from Captain Queen's training session. They seemed no less exuberant in welcoming home the errant Irregulars.

They spilled into the common room among hugs, pats on the back, and sloshing mugs thrust at them from all directions. Michael had released Captain Queen and was now hugging Jack, who looked no less relieved than his friend as they shared a long, heartfelt embrace.

The squires had caught Queen's eye and were calling her over, indicating an empty seat at their table and demanding the story of their time beyond the door. She held up a finger, telling them to wait, then turned back to Emily.

"Emily, come here a second," she ordered. Emily edged past a smiling Michael with a friendly squeeze on the shoulder and pushed her way to the captain's side.

"Emily, listen. I'm not big on speeches, so…you really impressed me in there. Sorry I didn't trust you before."

"Oh, it's okay, Captain Queen," said Emily. She could feel herself blushing. It surprised her how much the captain's praise meant to her, how much she cared in the first place.

"Please, call me Bronwyn," said the captain. "I mean, in a fight I still expect it to be 'Yes, Captain,' but when we're not in the shit I'd like to think we can be friends."

"Yeah, that sounds good." Emily laughed.

"Last thing, then I'll let you go. Even if it's only for the next day or so, I wanted to officially offer you a spot in the Irregulars of the Castle Forlorn."

"Oh…" Emily hesitated.

"What?" asked Captain Queen, frowning, but Emily smiled.

"I guess I'd already considered myself a member."

Captain Queen—Bronwyn—grinned and slapped her on the arm, then let herself get called away by the demanding squires. Emily watched as she joined them, visibly preparing herself for the barrage of questions she was about to endure.

At the next table, Ernest had gotten back into the rhythm of whatever poem he'd been spinning when Emily's entrance had interrupted him. His back was to her, but he gesticulated wildly with a slopping mug as he delivered some punchline that got a big laugh from the watching crowd.

Like an angel of mercy, Wentworth appeared at Emily's elbow with a huge plate of food. Two sizzling steaks sat atop a mountain of mashed potatoes and carrots, and a pile of asparagus spears threatened to roll off and fall to the floor.

"Keep it coming," Emily said, shoveling potatoes into her mouth with a spoon that seemed frustratingly small. Wentworth smiled and headed back toward the kitchen, passing Julian on his way. The handsome chef carried a similar plate of food in one hand, but turned back when Wentworth waved a hand to indicate the happily eating Emily. She considered calling out to Julian to bring it anyway, but her mouth was too full.

After a steak and a half, Emily felt up to some conversation, so she found Michael to thank him for the work he'd done on her ankle. He looked much better than when she'd left the great hall; Emily figured he'd also had a chance to eat since his magical exertion.

"Weren't you supposed to go sleep for twelve hours?" she asked him with a smile.

He shrugged and grinned at her. "And miss your homecoming party? I don't think so."

As they chatted, she kept one eye on Ernest, still regaling the crowd with a drink in his hand, which was looking more and more like his natural state of existence. She wanted to talk to him, to apologize. She had misjudged Jack's apparent moment of cowardice, and now she wondered if there were more going on with Ernest as well. It probably wasn't a secret plan to save them all, but after two hopeless days in a featureless prison, at the very least she could appreciate being afraid.

Finally Ernest finished his recital to a smattering of applause and a few drunken cheers. As he stepped down from the table that had been his stage, Emily put a hand gently on his shoulder. He turned with a wide grin on his face.

"The woman of the hour! And what can I do for you, my dear?" He gave her a bit of a bow, slopping ale from his mug onto the floor.

"Ernest, I just wanted to talk to you about the other day," Emily began.

"Ah, no need to apologize, darling!" Ernest patted her on the head. "Water under the bridge and all that."

"Well, I just—" Emily began.

"Now, now, if I'm not cross about it then neither should you be. Did you interrupt my lovely reverie? Yes. Yes, but as it happens I was able to get right back to my drinking after you departed, so I declare no harm to be done."

One of the townsfolk interrupted them to push a second mug of ale into Ernest's hand, which he gratefully accepted, clinking it messily against the one he already held.

"I see that my public forgives you as well," said Ernest. "Honestly, Emily, trying to get this island's leading poet killed! What on Earth were you thinking?"

"Excuse me?" snapped Emily.

"This benighted little rock needs my talents, dear. Ah, what's that? I hear them clamoring for another recital even now! I bid you adieu!"

With that, Ernest climbed awkwardly back onto the table and began loudly calling for attention. Emily had heard none of the clamoring he'd mentioned, but now she was too mad even to call him out on it. She couldn't imagine what he meant by accusing her of trying to get him killed. Maybe he really was a coward after all, she thought bitterly. He hadn't even thanked her for daring the door on behalf of all the people that he claimed depended on his talents.

Fuming, she stomped towards the door, having had enough of people and parties and wanting nothing more than to fall into her own bed and be left alone for a thousand years or so. She made it to the first step leading up to the door before someone in the crowd called, "Leaving so soon, Sledge?"

Emily looked back to see the crowd beginning to turn towards her.

"Don't go!" called one of the townies in the same voice that had first stopped her. She recognized him as the older man who'd invited her to try his wife's cooking after she'd helped set up the palisades in the great hall. He gave her a big, genuine smile.

"C'mon, have a drink with us first," called the squire Daniel.

"Speech! Speeeeech!" slurred a very drunk man whom Emily recognized from Bronwyn's training session.

"Speech!" echoed Madame de Luna, who had an overflowing tray in her hands and a devilish grin on her face. Soon the whole crowd took up the chant. Emily realized she couldn't pretend not to have heard it at this point, so she turned and patted the air to get them settle down.

"Okay, okay!" she said, but nobody seemed to hear her. "Okay! Take it easy!" That seemed to do it, and the crowd settled quickly into a quiet attention that was somehow more unnerving than when they'd all been shouting at her.

"So, um…" Emily stammered. She'd never really given a speech before, even when she'd won the Harkness tournaments. Fighters weren't big on speeches, usually, or at least not the fighters she'd trained with. "Well, first of all, I want to thank Captain Queen and Jack. We'd all be dead if not for them. Captain Queen really kept our sh—our act together, and Jack got us out with some really quick thinking."

Halfway back into the crowd, sitting at a table with Michael and the Blodring brothers, Jack raised a glass of wine and gave her a half-smile.

Somehow it made Emily feel much better and braver, so she swallowed and continued.

"Speaking of Jack, he was the one who made it so we could get back out the door when we escaped. We would have been plasma smudges otherwise." The crowd, catching the applause line, cheered heartily. Maybe giving speeches wasn't so bad, Emily thought. It was certainly easy on the ego. "He was the one who figured out how to go through the gate. And, actually, because of that, I think we could send somebody through the door again to get help—"

A roar from the crowd cut her off. Clearly hope was in short supply on the island of Finalhaven. Belatedly she wondered if she had said too much. Trying to stem the rush of enthusiasm, she added, "But we can't, we can't—Alder told me no."

Rather than dampening the mood of the crowd, this seemed to rile them up even more. A loud chorus of boos filled the common room. Emily had no idea how to react to this, afraid to get in any deeper if she opened her mouth again, and as the booing died away an awkward silence fell over the room.

"We should do it anyway!" called Jack into the hush. The crowd erupted in defiant cheers. Beneath the drunken bravado, Emily realized with a rush, they were desperate. Hopeless. These were average men and women, with no Gifts, who had been living for a month being told that an unknown enemy would be coming to kill them all. To them the mere thought that somebody, somehow, could even try to go for help was like water to a man in a desert.

"We *should* do it anyway! I think. But like I said, General Alder and the senior staff—" Emily stopped short. The crowd, wild a moment ago, had gone very, very quiet. All eyes seemed to be fixed on something, or someone, behind her in the doorway…

She turned to see Colonel Liu and Poet-Captain Dhar together on the top step, taking in the scene with naked apprehension on their faces.

"We come in peace," said Dhar. "Okay, no sudden movements, see?"

Slowly, he raised his right hand, which held a brown paper bag. With exaggerated care, he reached into the bag with his left hand. A tense hush had fallen over the common room.

"Maisie and I are just here to hear some poetry," he said. "I know we're not usually welcome among the Irregulars, but…well, I brought a peace offering." His eyes still on the crowd, Dhar drew out his hand from the bag.

He held a bottle of wine, expensive from the look of it.

The crowd's good cheer came rushing back like a river dammed too long. A roar went up that equaled or beat the cheer given to Emily's announcement about her plan to get help. Liu and Dhar stepped past Emily and into the eager crowd, who greeted them with comradely slaps on the back and words of welcome.

Emily found herself relieved to have the attention of the room off her for the time being. She considered slinking away under cover of Liu and Dhar's arrival, but once again she was interrupted in her plans by someone saying her name, quietly this time, but with a heart-fluttering calm confidence.

She turned to see Jack holding two empty wine glasses and a small, unopened bottle he'd procured somewhere.

"You looked like you could use a drink," he said with a smile.

"No thanks to you," Emily replied. "I was trying to calm them down, not rile them up!"

"I know," said Jack. He indicated a mercifully empty corner table. "Sit? Anyway, the thing is that you're right. I saw everything you saw on the other side of the door, and I don't think we stand a chance unless we can get some help. I just thought you needed a bit of a kick in the ass to actually do it."

"You think I'm going to do it? The senior staff…"

"Of course you are. You know as well as I do that there comes a time to stop doing what you're told." With a pop, Jack uncorked the wine.

"But—" said Emily.

"We'll talk plans later," Jack interrupted her. "But for now, ah, there's something else." Jack poured her a taste of the wine, then a much more generous helping for himself, which he downed half of before continuing. "Now, I'm not a poet like Ernest, but I have read quite a lot of his work, and I am a little drunk and feeling bold. So here goes. You are very brave, and quite clever, and you keep your shit together admirably in a crisis. You're one of the best fighters I've ever seen. Also, you are beautiful and only a little bit frightening." His mouth quirked in a sardonic smile. "As for myself, well, at the very least I am the son of a Baron. So I propose…ah, have you ever seen the desert?"

Emily was speechless. Her mouth moved up and down, but no sound came out. Jack was charming, mysterious, certainly good looking. After everything they'd been through—he'd seen her break a man's nose, for God's sake! What exactly was he proposing?

Things were moving too fast. The sortie through the door had been a complete disaster, saved only by everybody who *wasn't* Emily. Jack was already assuming she was going back through the door, but she'd rushed through every step of her little adventure up to this point and wound up in a bigger mess than ever. Now he wanted her to rush into some sort of—something—with him, too?

"Emily?" said a voice behind her. She half-turned, half-jumped to see the townie who had first asked her to make a speech standing abashedly by their table.

"Yes! Yes? What can I do for you?" She tried to make a normal smile happen on her face.

"Well, um, there's folks outside that weren't here just now when you made your speech, and they're all afraid, the same as we are, and I was just thinking…I was hoping, maybe you could say a few words to them as well?"

Emily swallowed her exhausted sigh and stood up. She opened her mouth to say something to Jack, realized she had no idea what to say, and shut it again. He looked up at her from the table like a lost dog, then abruptly took a swig from the wine bottle, his eyes still locked defiantly on her flushed face. Abashed, she looked away, and followed the townie outside.

True night had fallen, warm and heavy. A small crowd had gathered in the town square. They were buzzing quietly with nervous chatter as she approached.

A sudden motion caught her eye. It was the dark shape again, the shadow within a shadow, scurrying across the cobblestones to disappear around the side of the Twisted Wrist. The townie didn't seem to notice it, or at least didn't react, so Emily stolidly ignored it as well and allowed herself to be led to the waiting crowd.

They hushed quickly when she arrived, and once again she found herself uncertain of what to say. Looking out into the faces of the people who had gathered, she saw a different sort than she'd spoken to in the inn. There were children in this group, half-hidden behind fearful young parents with protective hands on little shoulders. Elderly people who had probably retired to this island community after a lifetime of service to the Gifted world. Frightened teenagers who would be at Harkness now if they'd been born Gifted, but instead worked the mundane jobs that supported the powerful figures who defined their world. She recognized more than a few of the workers who'd helped her set up the palisades in the great hall.

So she decided to tell them the truth.

"Okay, first, I should explain why we can't evacuate you…"

An hour or so later, Emily returned to the Twisted Wrist, exhausted. She'd told them everything she knew, down to the last detail, and then stood there answering questions and offering reassurances until every one of them had been, if not soothed, at least satisfied. Only when the last of the townspeople had started homeward in the night did she turn her back and head for the beckoning light of the inn's windows.

The common room she entered had changed drastically while she'd been outside. Most of the townies, and some of the Irregulars, had disappeared, leaving a remnant of quiet, pensive conversations where there had been a raucous party.

The Blodring brothers were among the missing, as were all four Albian squires. Emily's heart sank when she realized that Jack, too, was gone.

Bronwyn and Michael were sharing a small bottle of purple liqueur, which they sipped slowly from tiny glasses. Colonel Liu and Poet-Captain Dhar sat by the fire, which was now just embers and ash, listening to Ernest read quietly from a small notebook. Colonel Liu had a look of fierce concentration on her face, but Dhar noticed Emily's entrance and waved her over.

She carefully pulled up a chair in time to catch what seemed to be the end of one of Ernest's poems:

And if a lonely sparrow's call
Should echo once within the vast and various rafters of this hall
And turn a single lordly head
Why then, the bird shall live until the hearing lord himself is dead—Or goes
out in the storm and snow
And wraps his cloak against the troubles of the town and farms below.

A small sigh, or maybe the back half of a yawn, escaped Ernest's lips. The colonel sat pensively silent, staring into the fire. Dhar gave Emily a half-smile and squeezed her shoulder. They all sat motionless for a moment, until Ernest closed his notebook, pocketed it, and stood. He headed for the bar and struck up a low conversation with Madame de Luna, looking back over his shoulder at Emily only once.

"I never got a chance to tell you why my post is called Poet-Captain," said Dhar.

"I was wondering about that, actually," Emily replied.

"Well, a hundred and fifty years ago or so, the Marcher Lord—not the same one, at least I'm pretty sure not—the Marcher Lord who owned the Castle Forlorn got into an argument with his guard captain. History doesn't really tell us what it was about, but it seems the Marcher Lord thought the captain was making a tactical error of some sort. Specifically, he thought the captain wasn't being bold enough, or brave enough. Or something like that.

"Anyway, he tossed the guard captain out on his ear and sent around word that he was looking for a replacement. There was a catch, though. The new post was called Poet-Captain, and anyone who applied had to include a sample of poetry with his letter. It was still a job for someone with the Gift of Combat, of course, but it seems that the Marcher Lord felt that the defense of the Castle Forlorn required a certain, um, sensitive personality that was generally lacking among fighters."

Emily snorted in recognition. Fighters tended to be stereotyped as meatheads—she thought unfairly, but she did have to admit that many of them earned the description.

Poet-Captain Dhar turned in his chair to look her directly in the eye. "Specifically, he felt that the conservative sort of folks who become guard captains wouldn't quite recognize what makes the Castle Forlorn, and all of Finalhaven, such a special place. He wanted someone with a bit of a romantic bent. Someone who would see the castle as home, not just as a job. And as such, would do whatever it took to protect it."

Emily wasn't sure exactly what Dhar was trying to say, or how she was expected to respond.

"Do you fit the job description?" she finally asked. Dhar looked at the ground, then suddenly stood.

"I should get going," he said in a forced tone. "Long day ahead. Maisie, don't stay up all night mooning. Emily, I'll see you tomorrow."

He hustled to the door and out into the night, leaving Emily wondering exactly what had just happened. Looking over at Colonel Liu in hopes of getting some explanation, or at least a bit of sympathy, she found that the colonel's attention was somewhere else entirely. She was staring off into the middle distance—Dhar hadn't been kidding about her mooning, Emily realized.

Following Liu's gaze, Emily found that it landed squarely on the table where Bronwyn, Michael, and now Ernest sat sharing the purple liqueur. Emily shared the glance with her for a little while, then shook her head.

"You seemed to really enjoy Ernest's poem," Emily said politely.

"Hm? The poem?" said Colonel Liu, blinking. "No, that was one of Nadim's."

The door slammed open, and Sir Maximilian stormed in, flanked by the Arthurs.

"Where the hell have those bloody squires got to?" he raged at nobody in particular. "I've been in a damn meeting for twelve hours and all I want is a change of clothes and some bloody dinner, and those lazy kids are nowhere to be found. Well? Somebody answer me!"

Emily stood up, practically snarling. "They're in bed, you idiot! They're your squires, not your slaves!"

"And what would you know about the job of a squire?" Sir Maximilian stomped over to Emily. Behind him followed the Arthurs, who had the same irritable look that Emily recognized from many an underfed fighter. Maximilian stopped only when his face was inches from Emily's. "Word around the castle is that you're from a rather poor family."

Silence had fallen around them, and the faces of the few who remained in the common room had all turned to catch the show. Emily felt her face flushing. Angrily she wondered how she always ended up in fights with the snooty Albian knight when she was at her worst. Still, she wasn't about to back down.

"Better poor than a bully," she replied.

To her surprise, Sir Maximilian laughed, a short mocking bark. "A bully? A bully? Are we in the schoolyard? I'm sorry, did I hurt your feelings?" He gave her a cruel smile, looking down his long aristocratic nose at her. "You're just out of school, so I'll forgive you your ignorance. This is the real world. It's cruel, ugly, and violent. Especially here in the New

World, uncivilized as it is. As his majesty King Arthur the Thirtieth's representative on this godforsaken continent you'll forgive me if being considered a bully is the least of my concerns."

"And I guess killing girls is at the top of the list," Emily snapped.

Sir Maximilian stood stock still, his face frozen in a snarl. Slowly his eyes narrowed. Words escaped from between his teeth like air from a leaky balloon. "You understand nothing of my mission here."

"I understand that Elizabeth Pendragon is a wonderful, intelligent young woman!" Emily almost said it, almost gave her strange new friend away completely. But she bit off the words a second before they left her mouth, and instead they came out as a strangled snarl. Yet she had to say something, so she said the worst thing she could think of. "You brought eight people to kill one girl, you cowards."

The sound of steel sang in the air as Sir Maximilian's longsword flashed from its scabbard. Firelight glinted red along its blade as the tall knight swept it back and up, above his head. His left hand grabbed the front of Emily's shirt, holding her in position as a butcher might hold an animal for slaughter. She grabbed at his wrist, her fingers biting into his sinews, but she couldn't break his hold. Fury blazed in eyes that bored deep into hers.

"Stop it!" Colonel Liu's voice cracked through the air like a whip. "Both of you! Max, let her go, dammit!"

The hand on her shirt unclenched, but the knight's body was still tense, straining against his urge to let the killing blow fall.

"Don't ever call Sir Richard a coward," he hissed.

Emily backed up a step, and Colonel Liu rushed to fill the space between the two fighters. She shoved Emily back, then placed her hands gently on Sir Maximilian's arms, pulling the raised sword arm down as she squared him to look at her.

"Max, let it go. You're tired and hungry. Go to the kitchen and ask Julian about dessert."

"Dessert?" said the knight, as though he'd never heard of such a thing.

"Go," said the colonel, gently but firmly.

He took one more long breath through flaring nostrils, then pushed past Liu and headed for the kitchen door. As he passed Emily, he kept his eyes straight ahead, but hissed, "This isn't over, Sledge."

Colonel Liu turned to Emily. "Come on, let's sit down. Are you okay?"

"I'm fine," snapped Emily, brushing off the colonel's comforting hand on her shoulder. "What the hell is his problem?"

"Sit," Liu repeated, a little more harshly than she'd ordered the knight. Emily sat, furious and embarrassed. She didn't dare look back at the table where Bronwyn, Michael, and Ernest sat, as still and silent as they'd been during the humiliating incident. She stared at the fire, wishing it might leap from the grate and burn the whole inn to the ground, as long as it took her and Sir Maximilian with it. Her hand found a half-drunk bottle of wine nearby, and she took a long swig.

"You should go easy on him," said Colonel Liu softly.

"What?" Emily almost choked on her wine.

"I said, you should go easy on him."

"I got that part," Emily said. "I'm just trying to work out if you've lost your mind."

"I most certainly have not, Miss Sledge." The colonel's efficient personality seemed to be reasserting itself now that the crisis had passed. "Now shut up and listen to me. Sir Max is practically alone out here. His commanding officer is dead and now he's in charge, and he's thousands of miles away from his home, his family, and the whole world he was raised in. So it's no wonder he's playing the part of the hard-assed Albian warrior."

"How do you know?" asked Emily. "He just seems like an asshole to me."

Colonel Liu turned to stare into the fire. She was quiet for a minute, but just when Emily was about to apologize, the colonel said, "Do you know why General Alder is stationed all the way out here at the end of the world?"

"No," said Emily truthfully.

"The other Lancers hate him." Liu shook her head. "He was a genius, a Mental among fighters. So they sent him to solve the problem of this last intractable dragon, hiding under a rock in the freezing ocean. And he comes back less than a week later, not a scratch on him, and says the dragon is gone. Makes them all look bad.

"And what's worse, he'd taken the dragon's name for himself. For his personal symbol among the Lancers. They thought it was the height of hubris. Consorting with the enemy, they called it. Got all offended, but of course he was the golden boy as far as the public was concerned so they couldn't touch him." Liu sighed. "Well, that was almost thirty years ago. What the Lancers didn't realize was that with all the dragons gone, they had no purpose anymore."

"I've wondered about that, actually," Emily said. "The Lancers just called it a day after the dragons were dead? It's not like there's a shortage of other monsters."

"*Lesser* monsters, you mean." The fire danced reflected in Colonel Liu's eyes. "Beneath their glorious notice...or that's how they saw it. So they sat around reliving the past and rotting away, all except for Marshall Alder. He stood there yelling his head off that there was still work to be done, preparing for the next time something came through the Veil. But all they heard was that he was spoiling for a fight. So he kept yelling as he watched the Lancers turn into a...social club."

Liu snorted. "Finally, they got sick of him. And Treat said fine, you want to guard the Veil? You want to take the name of the dragon of the rock? Then you can die there for all we care. And they sent him here to live out the rest of his days where he could yell all he wanted and nobody could hear him."

Emily let out a breath she hadn't realized she'd been holding. "So...what about you?"

Colonel Liu smiled a secret half-smile. "I asked to go with him. My family has been in the Lancers for centuries. When I was finally old enough, and I found out it was all about reminiscing over cigars and brandy, well...you can imagine the appeal that an old lion like the general had."

"But you two are alone out here," Emily said.

"Exactly. That's why there's no point to you going back through the gate. Even if you could get a message to the Lancers, they wouldn't care."

Emily took a long breath and leaned back in her chair. She finally felt calm enough to look over to the table where the others sat, thinking she might even join them in another minute or two and try to make some joke about her fight with Sir Maximilian.

As she surreptitiously turned her head towards them, she caught Ernest watching her and Colonel Liu intently. He blinked and looked away, but she would have sworn that he wasn't drunk at all. His eyes were clear and sharp, his face pale in the fading firelight.

She was about to call out to him when the kitchen door opened and Madame de Luna entered bearing one last tray. Sir Maximilian followed a few steps behind her, looking sheepish and tired.

A large black cake sat on the tray, which glinted as she set it on a nearby empty table.

"Hmm, I'd hoped more of you would stick around for dessert," the raven-haired innkeeper said with a smile. "I'll try not to be offended. House specialty, after all."

"Where's Julian?" asked Bronwyn, standing.

Madame de Luna shook her head, still smiling. "Asleep, poor dear. He's been up and baking since before sunrise. The senior staff wore him out—no offense, Colonel."

Colonel Liu waved a hand to say that none was taken.

"Well, I for one wish to tuck in, that I might sooner tuck myself in," said Ernest, joining Bronwyn on his feet.

"That was a stretch even for you, Ernest," said Michael from the table. They all laughed, even Sir Maximilian, and Emily hoped that the gloomy mood left over from the fight had lifted.

"Now," said Madame de Luna, "I think the first bite should go to the woman of the hour. Not you this time, Bronwyn! Emily, would you like a slice?"

"You have no idea how much," said Emily. She got up from her chair and made her way to the cake. Sir Maximilian was watching her, his face tight and guarded, but he didn't move. Madame de Luna cut a generous slice from the cake—it had clearly been intended to feed far more people than the small crew that remained—and plated it for Emily.

She reached for it, and from the shadows beneath the table sprang a hissing, spitting black shape that latched onto her hand with tiny needle claws.

Shouting in surprise, Emily stumbled back from the table, shaking her arm, but the little black cat dug in even deeper. Blood started out from its clawpricks and trickled down her arm. The cat was still hissing, but eventually the black blur resolved into a head, hunched body, and tail, and Emily realized that it was facing away from her.

The cat's yellow-jade eyes were locked on the table—not the table, Emily realized, but the cake she had been about to eat. Just as she realized this the cat leapt from her hand, leaving four sets of bloody points behind, and knocked the little plate with Emily's slice to the floor. The plate shattered with a loud crack, but the cat, undeterred, began shoving the whole mess bodily towards the fire.

It made it about halfway before Michael grabbed it by the scruff and lifted it off the floor. No longer hissing, the cat looked about it at the shocked humans with something that Emily would almost have called embarrassment. It shook cake crumbs from its whiskers, then began calmly cleaning its face with one licked paw.

"What the hell was that all about?" asked Sir Maximilian.

"Emily, are you okay?" Bronwyn grabbed Emily by the wrist and began examining her wounds.

"I think so," said Emily. "Just rattled. Where did she even come from?" But even as she said it, Emily knew. The little black cat had followed her from the castle, flitting from shadow to shadow until she made it into the inn.

"Here, hold this," said Michael, and deposited the cat into Sir Maximilian's stunned hands. It promptly jumped free and ran out the front door.

"Michael, do you think—" Emily began.

"I know, I'm on it," he replied with mock weariness. "I'm getting quite a lot of practice, aren't I?"

Michael wove symbols in the air and murmured under his breath, until the now-familiar white glow reappeared around his hands. This work didn't seem to take as much out of him as the other times Emily had seen him do magic, because he quickly nodded and stepped back from the table, hardly seeming winded.

"Did anybody eat any of this?" he asked, looking especially at Sir Maximilian and Madame de Luna. They both shook their heads, and the rest of the room joined in in obvious relief.

"Good." Michael nodded. "It's rotten with poison. There's enough in here to kill all of us."

"Madame de Luna, who made this cake?" asked Colonel Liu sharply.

"Julian and Wentworth, but—"

"When?"

"This—this morning, I think. I'm not sure." Madame de Luna shook her head. "They were working all day, poor boys. You don't really think—"

"And could anybody else have gotten into the kitchen since they made it?" asked the colonel.

"Well, yes! It's a kitchen, not an armory." She sighed heavily. "I don't exactly keep it locked up tight. And they were in the castle most of today serving, and I was running errands off and on all day."

"Well, did you see anyone come in or out?" asked Bronwyn.

"I had a few folks from the town helping me." She looked up pleadingly at the Irregulars. "But they've been my assistants for years! Jeanette helps me chop vegetables for the stew, Thomas Breed brings me fresh meat, that sort of thing. Good townsfolk and friends, all of them."

"And nobody else?" asked Bronwyn, a curious leading tone in her voice.

"No, I don't think so, not that I saw. Oh, except…" Madame de Luna trailed off, her face worried and drawn.

"Except?" prodded Colonel Liu.

"Except when Sir Maximilian here came back to get some food." The innkeeper kept her eyes fixed firmly on the floor. "I told him to…to help himself."

"What the hell are you implying?!" Maximilian roared.

"Stand down, Max!" snapped Liu. "Nobody is accusing you of anything. There's no more evidence that you had anything to do with this than anybody else."

Emily couldn't help herself. "He seems a bit jumpy, don't you think?" she said to the room at large. Sir Maximilian rounded on her, fuming, his hand going for his sword. "But like the colonel said, there's no real evidence," she added.

"So we're left with either no suspects or too many of them, depending on how you look at it," said Ernest.

"That's one way to put it," agreed Bronwyn.

"Well, Max," Ernest said heavily, "it was such a lovely party until you showed up."

They reached the sandbar only to find it had been completely covered by a rising tide. The single small rowboat waited on the beach, looking rather inadequate. Nobody had spoken a word on the dismal trudge from the center of town, but Sir Maximilian quickly declared that he would be among the first trip over to the castle. Nobody had the energy to argue with him.

Emily felt horrible. She'd drunk much more than she intended, and she was starting to get hungry again. Her head was fuzzy with conspiracies, accusations, and worry. On top of all that, she felt like there was something she really needed to do before going to bed, but she couldn't remember what it was.

Maximilian, Bronwyn, and Colonel Liu took the boat over the black, choppy water with a promise that the colonel would return for the others. She'd offered Emily a spot on the first trip, but Emily didn't totally trust herself not to tip the boat over with Max in it.

Michael, Ernest, and Emily stood in silence watching them disappear into the night. Emily rubbed her arms and felt goose bumps rising up in the late-night chill. Ernest sat down heavily in the sand. She sighed.

Something furry pressed against her ankles, and a meow sounded quietly in the darkness. Blinking, she looked down to see the little black cat twining piteously around her ankles. It glanced down to the cold, black water lapping at the beach, then looked straight up at her, its eyes flashing with meaning in the wan moonlight.

Emily picked up the cat, which clearly felt free to make itself at home in her arms. It rumbled quietly and shut its eyes. Emily stroked its soft fur and closed her eyes as well.

Seemingly a second later, the crunch of the rowboat on sand snapped her back to attention. She opened her eyes to see Ernest stretched out on the beach snoring, Michael sitting huddled by his side. She had the unshakeable feeling that she'd been asleep on her feet for longer than she would have liked to admit.

Colonel Liu waved from the prow of the little boat. "Are you three ready?"

Michael shook Ernest awake, then stood and brushed sand from his pants. Emily looked down at the cat, which rolled over in her arms, stretching languidly and presenting a long black stomach to her.

"Four, actually," she said.

CHAPTER 15

1 DAY

The little black cat leapt from its nest among the sheets on Emily's feet as the insistent banging on her door continued. Wan gray sunlight filtered in through Emily's eyelids to help get her fresh headache rolling. The pounding was accompanied by a muffled voice calling her name, but it all seemed profoundly ignorable until the cat starting whining at the door to be let out.

Emily rolled out of bed, stumbling blearily to her feet, and made it to the door with one eye still glued shut with sleep gunk. She cracked it open, allowing the cat to slip eagerly out into the hall and revealing the irritatingly clean and bright-eyed face of Captain Queen.

"What?" said Emily, more an accusation than a question.

"Move it," replied Bronwyn with no apology in her voice. "Senior staff wants us. They're pissed."

"What?" Emily said again, shuffling over to the pile of last night's clothes and pulling on her jeans. The pounding at the door may have stopped, but it was replaced by a pounding in her head that promised to be much worse.

"Don't know. Come on, the longer we keep them waiting, the worse it's gonna be."

As they walked the sleepy halls of the Castle Forlorn, Emily realized what she had forgotten the night before. Out of all that she'd eaten and drunk at the Twisted Wrist, there hadn't been even a drop of water, or anything else that wasn't mostly alcohol. She squeezed her eyes shut as she walked, hoping that if she just gave in to the hangover it would somehow respect her acceptance and go easy on her.

It didn't, and by all appearances the senior staff didn't plan to go easy on her either. They entered the crowded staff room to find the people within irritable and impatient. General Alder was scowling, Sir Maximilian was shaking his head, Colonel Liu had a face like stone, and even Poet-Captain Dhar wouldn't meet Emily's eye.

Through bleary eyes, Emily saw that Luke, Sir Richard's squire, had taken the old knight's vacant seat at the table. His face was flushed and he stared intently at the table before him, as though trying to memorize the patterns in the wood grain.

"Is there something you'd like to tell us, Miss Sledge?" asked General Alder tightly. Emily was reminded uncomfortably of being grilled about some misadventure by all her least favorite professors at Harkness.

"I don't know what you mean," said Emily.

Colonel Liu sighed. "Luke?"

Luke shook his head, refusing to look up.

"Emily, Luke tells us that you're planning to disregard the general's orders and go back through the door." Liu's face was completely closed. Gone was the friendly smile of the night before. Emily wondered how much the colonel and Dhar had heard of her speech; had the two of them really learned of her plan from Luke, or had they already known? Emily could imagine that Liu felt bound to support the General's orders no matter what, but Dhar seemed to have a more flexible definition of the right thing to do.

Emily took a breath, opened her mouth to speak, and shut it again. She hadn't even been planning on really doing it—or had she? It was hard to be sure. But she certainly didn't like being tried for a crime she hadn't really committed.

Perhaps mistaking her inner turmoil for defiance, General Alder slammed his hands on the table and stood, nearly knocking his chair over. "You *dare?*" he roared. Emily instinctively took a step back in the face of his fury. "You *dare* disobey an order, a direct order from your command-ing officer! You *dare* disobey me!"

The rest of the senior staff were as still as statues; nobody could commit to looking at either the general or Emily. He gulped in a huge breath, no doubt to power the next roar, and Emily started to come to her own defense.

"It was my plan," said Captain Queen.

"What?" screamed Alder.

"What?" said Emily.

"I formed the plan after making it back through the gate," continued Bronwyn. "As a member of the Irregulars, Emily was acting on my orders."

"That's not—" Emily tried.

"*Thirty years!*" shouted the general. "Thirty years I have been a general, and never, *never* have I been surrounded by such incompetents!" He took in the whole senior staff with a wide-eyed glance. "Idiots, all of you! *All of you!* Fighters, ha! You're a lot of swords, weapons, tools, replaceable. The power is in the hand that wields the sword. *The sword does not disobey the hand!*"

At last the senior staff seemed to find their voices. Sir Maximilian protested that he had always followed orders; Colonel Liu started to say "Marshall, Marshall" in a pleading voice.

But Bronwyn's voice carried over them all. "General, please," she said calmly. "I very much regret going against your word. I assure you it will not happen again."

"No, it will not," replied General Alder over the babble. "Because I declare you banished from the Castle Forlorn and the island of Finalhaven."

A heartbeat of silence passed.

"*What?*" cried Bronwyn, open shock on her face.

"Banished," repeated the general. "Effective immediately. Guardsman?"

One of Dhar's guards, stationed by the door, approached Bronwyn, but at a furious look from her held his step.

Looking around at the fallen faces of the senior staff, all pinned to the table, Emily felt anger rise in her throat.

"Are none of you going to say *anything?*" she snapped. "This is insane! The fight is coming *tomorrow,* and Captain Queen is the leader of the Irregulars, not to mention the best fighter in the castle."

"You are only a child," said the general in a low voice that was possibly even more frightening than his rage of a moment ago. "You do not understand what it means to be betrayed. Guard?"

The guard hesitantly put a hand on Bronwyn's arm and, finding that she wasn't fighting back, guided her towards the door. Her previous fury had been replaced by a defeated misery. They reached the door, which the guard pushed open with one hand, keeping the other tightly on the captain.

"Wait," said Emily. General Alder raised an eyebrow. "Wait!" she continued. "I can guarantee that nobody will try anything. And give you a useful tool, too."

"How?" asked Alder.

"But in return, Bronwyn gets to stay," Emily continued.

"How?" Alder repeated.

Emily slipped a hand into the pocket of her jeans and drew out a flat plastic card, the last permission slip. "This is the key to getting through the gate. If Bronwyn stays, it's yours. Keep it, destroy it, I don't care."

General Alder's nostrils flared with heavy breaths as he stared at

Emily, calculating. His eyes were like ice, cold and still. His lower jaw jutted out momentarily as he pursed his lips.

"Agreed," he said, reaching out for the card. Emily leaned over the table and placed it into his waiting hand.

"Thank you, girl," said the general. "Now, guard, take Captain Queen to the shore."

They watched from the walls of the Castle Forlorn, all of them, as Captain Queen was led, without protest, to the water. The tide was low, the beach wide and the sandbar naked under the gray sky, and Ed Doughty's small boat was still a speck on the horizon.

The Irregulars stood together, clumped up for warmth against an unseasonably cold wind. Jack and Michael were side by side at the battlements, the tall romantic in a long black coat and the young wizard in a battered leather jacket. Ernest stood behind Emily—she didn't have the energy for anger now, not against him in addition to everyone else—and wrapped his arms around her in a brotherly gesture, full of family grief. Wulf Blodring was at the battlements too, watching open-mouthed; his brother hung behind, his arms crossed, his face closed.

Many of the castle's servants had come, including Julian and Wentworth, who stood apart from the Irregulars. The cook's glossy black hair whipped in the wind, and he tucked it away with a gloved hand. Wentworth's hands were shoved deep into his jacket pockets, and he shivered.

From the senior staff, all but General Alder himself had come. Sir Maximilian whispered something to the taller of the Arthurs, who snorted quietly. Poet-Captain Dhar, wearing nothing heavier than his usual T-shirt, looked openly disturbed. But his face was nothing compared to that of Colonel Liu, who seemed to be on the verge of tears. She leaned desperately over the battlements, clinging to the stone, apart.

Four of the castle guards led Captain Queen the short way from the open gate to the high watermark. They let her go, then stood back, uncertain. The boat grew nearer, rolling slightly on the water as Doughty killed the motor and coasted in.

Bronwyn looked back once, over her shoulder, only for a moment. Emily followed her glance up the castle wall and saw that it rested on Colonel Liu. The colonel stepped back from the battlement with a small gasp, as though hit by an arrow. The captain looked away.

The crunch of the boat on sand was clear in the quiet of the moment. Her head bowed, Bronwyn walked to it, and placed a hand on the bow. She took a breath, then climbed aboard. As he fitted oars into their locks, Doughty said something to her that was lost on the wind, and she shook her head.

A guardsman came down the beach and shoved them off. With a few long strokes, Doughty backed and turned the boat until it pointed due west. He started the motor with a sudden roar.

A few yards out from the shore, Bronwyn raised her head, looking around her. She gazed back at the castle for a moment, and her face was confused. Doughty asked her something, to which she shook her head and maybe said a few short words. Another two or three questions were met with the same response, and finally, Bronwyn Queen shrugged her shoulders helplessly and lapsed into silence.

"You!" said Emily.

"Me?" asked Sir Maximilian with a smirk and an arched eyebrow. Emily wasn't deterred; she stalked towards the tall knight with her fists at her sides. She'd found him alone in a long hallway on the dormitory level. He hadn't worn his sword or armor to see Captain Queen's banishment, and despite her raging headache, Emily was feeling rather clear-minded.

"Did you send your squires to spy on us?" Emily asked, stopping only inches away from Maximilian.

"I beg your pardon?" said the knight.

"Merry didn't seem too happy to be at the tavern last night. She's yours, right? And Luke betrayed us to the senior staff. And now Bronwyn is gone, because of that."

"I certainly didn't," said Sir Maximilian, his lips pursing in something that almost seemed like amusement. Emily decided he wasn't taking this at all seriously enough, and hit him in the stomach.

The knight staggered back into the wall, bent almost in half by the blow. He wheezed raspingly for a moment, his face red, then choked out, "How dare you...?" His hand searched briefly for his sword, but finding only air, it balled into a fist.

Catching his tension, Emily stepped into the blow as he swung, pressing him bodily into the wall. She couldn't quite get a grip on him, and he shoved her away with both hands. They squared off, falling into fighting stances.

Growling, Emily charged him again, low, trying to take him down at the knees. He sidestepped; she caught one leg, but he pivoted and kicked her soundly in the head as she dragged at him. She rolled away, shaking her head to clear out the sound of bells ringing.

"I'm not kidding around, Max," gasped Emily, standing. "Did you or did you not send your little minions to spy on us?"

"I should kill you where you stand," sneered Maximilian, watching her warily from behind raised hands.

"As far as I know, you've already tried," Emily said coldly. "Poison, Max, really? That's such a coward's weapon."

To her surprise, he didn't take the bait. "I know you're upset, Sledge, so I'll let the insult slide. But you're talking nonsense."

"Actually," said Emily, "it makes perfect sense. Your mission here in the New World is to kill Elizabeth Pendragon. Sir Richard made you stay here to defend the castle, but now he's dead. So why would you stick around? You have nothing to gain from a suicide mission. Unless you're really working for the dragon, and you're trying to kill us all."

Emily's fists tightened until her fingernails bit into her palms. Sir Maximilian dropped his guard a little and opened his mouth to respond. Emily charged, feinting low at his legs. He dropped his guard, and she closed on him in an instant. Her fist hit his jaw with a satisfyingly solid crack; his head snapped back and smacked into the wall behind him, bouncing forward again to put his chin on his chest before he could catch himself.

Sir Maximilian blinked, shaking his head, clearly rattled. Emily loomed over the slumping knight, who tried to back further into the wall and couldn't.

"Emily, please, that makes no sense." He actually seemed a bit frightened now. "If I wanted to leave, I would have left. If I had wanted to weaken the castle's defenses, I would have left! And taken six good fighters with me! Why would I keep trying to poison people all the time?"

Emily had no answer to that, so instead, she kept up the attack, pressing her advantage, venting her rage and her shame at Bronwyn taking the fall for her mistake. "You don't need to stick around on our behalf. Dying to protect some forgotten castle isn't part of your little mission."

"I don't plan on dying," retorted Maximilian, wiping blood from the corner of his mouth, but Emily ignored him.

"The moment you set foot off this island, you'll forget all about us. You all will. Your consciences will be clean, and we'll be rid of you. Sounds like a win-win to me."

"Is it really so hard for you to believe that we're staying because it's the right thing to do?" asked the knight, squaring his shoulders and straightening up.

"Yes," replied Emily honestly. She raised a fist threateningly.

Something passed over Sir Maximilian's face, a shadow of sorrow or maybe the look of a man making a painful decision. "Fine," he said heavily. "You want to know the truth?"

"Yes," said Emily.

"The other morning, when you happened to be in the hall right after I found Sir Richard—"

"Or poisoned him," Emily interrupted.

"Funny, I was about to say the same thing about you," the knight replied. "Anyway, I had just discovered him there, not dead, but dying. I was about to go for help, but he grabbed me. He pulled me down and whispered something in my ear. His dying words."

"Okay," said Emily doubtfully.

"You know what he said? 'She's here somewhere.' Elizabeth Pendragon is here somewhere—in the castle, on the island, I'm not sure. But Sir Richard was sure. He used his last breath to tell me, to charge me to complete his mission."

"And that's why you're still here." Emily hadn't thought she could hate the Albian knight any more than she had already, but it certainly seemed possible now.

"Indeed." Sir Maximilian nodded. So Emily hit him again, turned on her heel, and left him there.

The little black cat rubbed against her legs, whining, as Emily pounded on the wall where she thought Elizabeth's door was hidden. She didn't dare yell the Albian woman's name, afraid to give her away, but she refused to give up on trying to get her attention. She'd tried Michael's method of three sharp knocks, with no result, though she wasn't certain she was at the right spot along the wall.

Her pounding died away into silence, leaving Emily alone in an empty hallway. She picked up the cat and began considering how crazy she would have to be to ask it directly for help. Certainly it would have been helpful if its whole gang were there, eating or lounging in one specific spot.

A few yards to Emily's left, a section of wall slid open, letting a little gray light spill out into the dark hall. Shaking her head, she jogged to the door, letting the cat drop to run off into the shadowed corners of the castle.

Elizabeth was waiting just beyond the doorway, looking not at all surprised to see Emily instead of Michael.

"You'll want to look for the place where a whole column of bricks lines up along its left edge," said Elizabeth.

"Oh," Emily replied.

"Please, come in." Elizabeth gestured to the airy sitting room behind her. It only seemed airy, Emily reflected, an illusion of the white walls and wide windows. In fact, Elizabeth was trapped in here as surely as if it were a prison cell in the deepest, dankest dungeon.

"I have some bad news," Emily said as she stepped through the door. Elizabeth was standing by a small cart with a silver tea service on it. Emily wondered where the young woman had gotten tea, then decided that the answer was almost certainly Michael Fletcher and his obvious devotion to the mysterious young Albian royal.

"Bad news is best served with a treat," replied Elizabeth. Emily accepted the china teacup between finger and thumb, feeling like a giant holding a child's toy. Normally she loved being tall and tough, but Elizabeth's slender daintiness somehow made her feel clumsy. It was as though Elizabeth had such a deep well of inner power that her slight frame was an advertisement for the irrelevance of size when it came to strength. In anyone else it would have almost been insulting, but Elizabeth was a person of such genuine kindness that Emily couldn't bring herself to be offended.

Emily perched on the window seat as Elizabeth sat cross-legged in the rocking chair and pulled the bird blanket into her lap.

"Now then," said Elizabeth. "I know Michael is alive and whole, so what other bad news could you bring me?"

Emily let go of all the questions that one raised and plunged forward on her mission. "The Albian knights who are looking for you—they know you're here. Sir Maximilian told me. I guess Sir Richard figured it out before he died." She sat up straight. "I just realized—you didn't…"

Elizabeth shook her head, her long bone-colored hair swaying about her face. "No, poison isn't my style. In fact, I can answer both your concerns with one simple reminder: I can't leave my rooms. Remember?" She gestured gently around her. "These walls that keep me in also keep me safe. And the walls that keep me safe…"

"Also keep you in," finished Emily. "So you couldn't have left to go around poisoning without the Albians finding you."

Elizabeth nodded. "And they can't find me as long as I don't leave. Just so. Others have tried, Emily, believe me. Even the best spells of finding falter and fail against these walls. In my room I have nothing to fear."

Emily unwound somewhat, letting her shoulders drop as some of her tension drained away. "I'm glad. Max is hell-bent on finding you. That's the only reason the knights are even hanging around here." Elizabeth just stared at her, so Emily said, "I hit him. A few times, actually. It was great."

Elizabeth turned her head to hide a most unqueenly half-smile behind a curtain of hair. She stood and took Emily's empty teacup from her hand and replaced it quietly on the serving cart, then returned with a silver plate of finger sandwiches. Emily grabbed three, hesitated, almost put one back, then didn't.

Elizabeth replaced the plate, then sat on her piano bench and crossed her legs at the ankles. She gave Emily an appraising look. "There's more on your mind."

"Well…did you hear about Bronwyn?"

Elizabeth ducked her head sadly. "A tragedy. General Alder is…not well."

"You're not kidding," agreed Emily. "Of all the stupid…anyway, the problem is that I gave him our ticket out through the door in trade for not banishing Bronwyn. Which he did anyway. But the more I think about it, especially with Bronwyn gone, I think going through the door again is the right move. We just don't have the manpower to stand up against a proper assault."

Elizabeth nodded encouragingly.

"I mean, we wouldn't even have to go to Earth," Emily continued. "You could go to any of those worlds the dragon is invading and try to make an alliance. We'd have…options." She shrugged. "But not without that permission slip. And I gave it up for no reason. For nothing."

Elizabeth pursed her lips thoughtfully, her eyes somewhere else. "Do you think General Alder destroyed it?"

"Huh," said Emily, surprised. "No. No, I don't think so. It doesn't seem like him to throw away something so powerful. Even if he has no intention of using it."

"I agree," said Elizabeth. "So we wonder where it might have floated off to."

"Well, I don't think Alder would be carrying it around with him, either. He'd lock it away somewhere. Out of sight, out of mind, right? Is there, like, a safe in his bedroom or something?"

"Most likely," said Elizabeth, "but that's not where he would stow it."

"No?" Emily raised her eyebrows.

"No. He banished the dragon and kept its name. He had tapestries woven of his victory. He takes trophies."

"Which means there must be a trophy room somewhere," Emily said, her eyes lighting up. "But where? The castle is huge. And presumably he wouldn't leave it unguarded."

"Wait a moment," said Elizabeth. She opened the white door and passed into the room beyond. Emily waited, listening to the shuffling of papers and the creaking of what sounded like hinges.

Her curiosity getting the better of her, Emily stood and walked quietly to the door. Peering in she saw a huge bed with a plush, snowy white comforter and white gauze hanging from its four tall posts. Another large, closed window looked out on the sea, and two more doors led out, one to a bathroom and the other to a closet from where the sounds of searching emanated.

A rustling noise and a quiet groan came from the bed. The comforter was pushed back, revealing Michael Fletcher turning in his sleep. Emily took one short, sharp breath of surprise, then, her face flushing, hustled back to her seat by the bay window on what she desperately hoped were silent feet.

After another minute, Elizabeth came back into the sitting room, closing the door quietly behind her. She carried a large vellum map rolled up in one hand. Sitting next to Emily, she indicated that the fighter hold one edge of the map, then unrolled it fully until she held the other edge. A floor plan of the castle, level by level, stretched between them.

"There," said Elizabeth, "much better. Let's see..." Her finger traced the faded brown ink of the map, and she murmured the names of various rooms and sections of the castle as she passed over them.

"I don't see a trophy room," said Emily eventually.

"No," agreed Elizabeth. "But do you see this?" She pointed at the bottom left corner of the map, near Emily's hand. There, in a sub-sub-basement, a staircase ended in a small chamber from which only one door led. Beyond the door was a long, apparently empty hallway, and finally, a larger room labeled "Storage."

"That's a weird place for storage," said Emily, and Elizabeth nodded. "But what's with the hallway?"

"Ah," said Elizabeth with a smile. "That will be for all the traps."

Chapter 16

By this point in her life, Emily had a bit of experience in breaking and entering, but she still wanted to recruit the person who seemed more and more like an expert each time she learned anything about his life.

So it was that Emily and Jack stood in a small damp chamber at the very bottom of a worn stone staircase. It was chilly and smelled of mold, and only one door led out. It was closed.

"Do you think you can pick the lock?" asked Emily. She'd already asked him the same question on their way down, but it was easier to repeat herself than to bring up their awkward, failed conversation of the night before.

"Well, we'll just have to see," Jack said. "Or you could probably break it down with your little finger."

"I told you, that would be noisy." Emily shook her head. "This is a secret mission, remember? Can't just smash my way through everything."

"Okay," said Jack. He bit his lip. "Let's see what we're up against." He knelt before the door so his face was at the height of the lock. From a back pocket he pulled a rolled-up leather portfolio, which he flicked open on the ground in front of him. To Emily, it looked like a dentist's kit, full of thin, pointy metal tools with all sorts of odd angles to their heads.

Jack thought a moment, then selected a long, flat piece with a series of bumps along one edge. He inserted it slowly into the lock, working it forward and back as he did, until it was about six bumps deep.

There was a click, and the door swung open.

"Oh," said Jack.

"What?" Emily asked.

"Well, I wasn't really expecting that to work." He shrugged. "Just lucky, I guess."

"Maybe whoever built this thing isn't actually too worried about keeping their stuff safe," Emily suggested.

Jack stood, rolling up his leather case and brushing off his knees. "Somehow I doubt it. It's a bit too inviting, don't you think?"

The pitch-black hallway beyond didn't look particularly inviting to Emily, but she just nodded. "Remind me again why you can't come with me?"

"Ah," said Jack, looking at his shoes. "I'm afraid this is where my effectiveness ends. Reading maps, picking locks, sure. No problem. But once we get into the realm of death traps I'm out of my element."

"Which is what, exactly?" asked Emily despite herself. "You're obviously not a fighter. I don't think you're a Mental, no offense. Your dad, the Baron, is a magic-user, right? And you've always got that guitar with you, which is a style of magic. So can you magic us down the hallway?"

Jack opened his mouth as if to respond, then took a long breath instead. He gave Emily a piercing look that somehow melted into a shy smile.

"Not exactly," he said.

"Not exactly? Or not at all?" asked Emily.

The smile didn't waver. "Not at all," he admitted. "Dad got all the Gift. I just got these." He held up his hands and wiggled the extra finger on each.

"Got them? Got them where?" There was a strange, nervous feeling in Emily's stomach.

"You know how the Baron Wasteland kind of came out of nowhere?"

Emily nodded. "There isn't exactly a long, storied line of Barons or any-thing. My dad is the first. Before that, he was, um...I guess 'con man' would be the term for it."

"And a magic-user?"

"No, that was more of a midlife career change. We were on the run from—I can't remember, it was either the cops or someone's angry hus-band with a shotgun. Anyway, we headed out into the desert in Arizona to lay low, and after a day or two we found this abandoned trailer just sitting there in the middle of nowhere. So we turned it over, looking for water, canned food, that sort of thing. I found a trap door under a rug—turns out there was this whole underground complex tunneled into the dirt beneath the trailer. Including some very weird ritual...artifacts, I guess you'd call them."

"Like what?" asked Emily, fascinated.

"Well, I've done some research since it all happened, and they were definitely evil. Whatever that's worth. I don't know, it's hard to find much info about that stuff."

"You should talk to Ernest's dad," Emily suggested.

"Maybe I will. You know, two days from now." Jack smiled. "Any-way, my dad wanted to sell it all, but I started reading some of the books they had. Dad got pretty interested once I told him what was in there. He was always up for a get-rich-quick scheme...Long story short, we per-formed one of the rituals, or at least we did our best. Or I did. I don't really know how I pulled it off, but when all the howling and bleeding and indoor lightning was done, I had two extra fingers and my dad could raise the dead."

"He *what*?!" Emily sat heavily on the steps. "Nobody can do that, you know that, right?"

"Yeah," said Jack. "Again, not something that runs in the family, unfortunately. It's kind of ironic; we perform some evil black magic ritual and he ends up with the power to do more good than anyone in the world." He sighed and rolled his eyes to the ceiling. "Of course, my dad found a way to turn it into a con nonetheless."

"So you're not Gifted at all?" asked Emily.

"Nope."

"But the way you play that guitar…"

"Thanks." Jack smiled. "That's just practice. Although I guess the extra fingers kind of help."

Emily chewed that over for a while. "It can't be easy," she said at last.

"What?" asked Jack.

"Surviving in the Gifted world with no Gift. I mean, people do it. There's no guarantee anyone will be born Gifted, even the kid of two Gifted parents. But at least they grow up in it. To just be dumped into it and told to swim or drown…"

It was Jack's turn to be silent, and Emily let him take his time. Finally a flash of bitterness passed over his face. "Wouldn't be the first time." He clapped his hands. "Come on, we've got people counting on us and we're sitting here telling tales. Up, Emily! Once more unto the breach!"

"Does anybody else know?" asked Emily, standing.

"Ernest and Michael," said Jack with a nod. "And Bronwyn, I guess, though who knows what she knows anymore. Come on, get. I'll wait here. Don't die."

"I won't," said Emily. Jack stuck out his hand, and Emily shook it, then stepped through the waiting door.

It slammed shut behind her, leaving her in total darkness. She pulled a small flashlight from her pocket and clicked it on. Nothing happened. Looking at the face of the light, she could see the filament burning faintly in the bulb, but somehow none of its light escaped to illuminate the hallway. Emily stuck it back in her pocket, frustrated.

She drew a long breath, calling up the map Elizabeth had shown her before her mind's eye. Their best guess was that the hallway was about fifty yards long, ten feet wide, and a straight shot to the room marked as storage.

Counting her long-legged paces at a yard each, Emily started forward in a wary crouch. She had just reached ten paces when she felt a breeze brush her left cheek, like a faint sigh. She dropped to her stomach as something sliced over her head with a metallic whistle. A resounding *thunk* shook the corridor faintly—the blade, or whatever it was, hitting the right-hand wall. Or so she hoped.

Emily crawled a few feet forward then stood cautiously, her hands above her head. She found only open air, but couldn't help turning and feeling slowly back where she had dropped. Something nicked her finger, and she ran her hands over a large curved blade, still wicked sharp despite who knew how many years down here in the damp.

She let out the breath she'd been holding since she hit the floor and turned back towards the storage room, touching the walls on either side to make sure she was aligned straight with the hallway. A few more paces brought her safely away from the blade that had almost taken her head off.

Emily caught her breath. Her right leg had hung on something mid-step. It felt like a tripwire. Nothing immediately killed her, so she imagined she must have stopped herself before triggering whatever trap was attached to the wire; she was about to step back when she thought suddenly that relaxing the gentle pressure on the wire might be a bad idea.

Instead, she knelt awkwardly with her right leg stretched in front of her, keeping the pressure on the tripwire as even as she could. Nervous fingers reached out and found the top of the wire, stretching away from her leg in either direction. It was pushed about an inch forward at the middle, and felt close to breaking.

Emily touched the floor around her foot. It was paved with flat stone like most of the castle's corridors, but age and damp had combined to chew away the mortar between the stones, leaving little valleys running between the flags.

Slowly, Emily drew the little pocket flashlight out again. She turned it in her hand, judging its length and width. Then she felt around the floor just under the tripwire. There was a crack just to one side of her foot that seemed big enough…

Emily stuck the butt of the flashlight into the crack and twisted slowly, working it into the gap between flags. Old stone crumbled away as she wedged the light in. Once it was stable, she ran her fingers carefully up until she could feel the tripwire, about half an inch ahead of the light and just barely below its top.

She braced her thumb on the stone and pushed the top of the flashlight with a steady, gentle pressure. It leaned slowly forward, crumbling more stone at its base, until it touched the tripwire.

"Okay," Emily whispered. She pulled her leg back a fraction of an inch, feeling the tense wire follow it backwards. The wire caught on the flashlight, and she pulled her leg away fully. The flashlight tilted back a few degrees under her fingers, and Emily's heart stopped.

Then the light, wedged solidly between stones, resisted, and the wire caught again. Emily let half a minute pass in tense silence before she dared back away a few inches.

Nothing happened, and with a long breath, she stood and stepped over the tripwire.

The stone beneath Emily's foot clicked as it sank half an inch into the floor. She hissed in pain at a sharp sting in her stomach, and her questing fingers plucked out a small wooden dart. Her first thought was that it wasn't so bad; then she realized that the dart was almost certainly poisoned.

"Shit," she said loudly. Hesitating, she looked back over her shoulder, but of course the entire hallway was sunk in total darkness. She tossed the dart away and heard it clatter faintly on the stone floor, then continued forward.

The next twenty paces passed with agonizing slowness, but were mercifully uneventful. Emily guessed that she was within ten or fifteen yards of whatever waited at the end of the long hall, but she was starting to feel light-headed. It usually took quite a lot of poison to bother a fighter, as Emily knew from experience, but this hallway had presumably been built to keep out Gifted intruders as well as normal ones.

Her next step found open air. Trying to pull back, Emily overbalanced and fell on her rear on the lip of a pit, her feet dangling in space. Her head was spinning from the sudden drop.

After a minute her head cleared somewhat, and Emily sat pondering what to do. Eventually, she broke a small chunk off a paving stone beneath her and tossed it into the pit. She didn't hear it land.

She tossed another piece of stone forward, straining to hear it land on the floor on the other side of the pit. She was relieved to hear a faint clattering perhaps twenty feet ahead.

She stood, waited a moment for the dizziness to pass, then backed up a few paces, counting carefully as she went. Steeling herself, she took a running start, and just before she guessed she would put a foot down into nothing, she leapt.

The other side of the pit came quicker than she thought. The corner of the pit hit her in the chest, knocking the wind out of her, and she scrabbled to grab hold before she could fall into space. After a few panicked moments, she caught herself with both elbows on the edge of the pit.

This time the poison came up as a wave of nausea that Emily couldn't quite fight back. After a few minutes dangling gasping, she realized that the dizziness and sickness weren't going away this time. So she pulled herself up to the floor, and lay there curled up, taking deep breaths, until she felt she could at least stand.

She stumbled the rest of the way down the hall, focused completely on staying upright, praying that she'd met the last of the traps. Even if she heard something coming, Emily doubted she could dodge it in time.

Panic gripped her for a moment as she slammed into something cold and hard, then subsided somewhat when she realized it was the door at the end of the hall. Sweating, she leaned on the cool door for a moment, then felt around for a handle.

The door swung inward, almost dumping Emily on the floor as she threw up her hands to shield her sensitive eyes from sudden light. A lantern hung from the ceiling, throwing a warm glow that carried even into the hallway, clearly enchanted against whatever magical darkness had defeated her flashlight.

Once she could see, Emily was amazed by the room before her. As they'd guessed, it was a trophy room, full of fascinating objects labelled with little hand-written tags. She stumbled along a wall hung with weapons, reading names as they swam into view: "The Sword That Cuts Both Ways." "The Hammer That Carries Considerable Weight." "Occam's Razor."

A low wooden table at the back of the room was set with small objects, almost like a shrine. A twisted fang stood out beside a shred of gray skin. To the right of the skin, to Emily's considerable relief, the plastic card she'd come to find lay flat and dull. Her weak fingers needed a few tries, but eventually she picked it up from the table and pocketed it.

Emily staggered back to the door, then, contemplating the long hall of darkness before her, turned back and unhooked the lantern from where it hung. Holding it high, she stepped out into the hall. The first few yards were mercifully bare, up until the lip of the pit. She was surprised to see that this section of the hallway was actually a few feet higher than on the other side of the pit—no wonder she'd misjudged the distance and landed so badly.

A long board maybe a foot wide was attached by hinges to the right-hand wall above the pit. She flipped it down and discovered that it fit exactly across the opening, angled so it made a sloping path from the raised section of the hallway where she stood to the lower one on the other side of the pit. If she'd been well, she could have danced down it, but in her sickened state it seemed almost a more impossible challenge than the ten-foot jump had been.

So she turned around, got on her hands and knees, pulled both in tight, put the handle of the lantern between her teeth, and began to crawl backwards down the plank. It took a few tense minutes, but eventually she reached the blessed safety of the other side, where she lay in a ball as the hallway whirled around her.

Standing sounded impossible, so she kept crawling, the lantern hanging from her mouth. She crawled over the pressure plate, which clicked harmlessly, and saw that the tripwire she'd so carefully wedged with her flashlight was attached to two low wooden posts that clearly led nowhere. It had been a trick, a red herring to lead her to step on the pressure plate, and she'd swallowed it whole.

So she crawled over it, feeling it snap back into place as she dislodged her flashlight. She didn't have the strength to pick it up. At last she passed under the heavy blade, brown with rust or blood, and came panting to the door. She reached up from her spot on the floor, straining for the handle, and pulled it down, praying the door would swing open and Jack could pull her the rest of the way.

It was locked, at least from the inside.

"Of course it is," Emily whispered, and her weak, thready voice frightened her as much as the pressing dizziness and rising nausea. She wanted to lie down and sleep, or maybe die. She really, really wanted to throw up.

Instead, she grabbed the door handle again and pulled herself up into a sitting position, her back against the wall of the hallway.

"Jack, where are you?" she murmured. The hallway seemed to be rotating around her, twisting along its length, first clockwise and then counterclockwise. Her left hand still dangled from the handle of the door, and she hauled herself up to standing, blowing out a long, steadying breath as she did.

The door opened.

"Jack, thank God…" The sentence died on Emily's lips as the whirling images before her eyes resolved and steadied until she could make out the figure of Julian de Luna, a knife in his hand and death in his eyes.

CHAPTER 17

Julian lashed out with the knife, his face contorted in a snarl. Emily staggered back and bumped up against the open door, certain she would have fallen had it not been there. The young chef stumbled forward, propelled by the viciousness of his attack, and Emily pinned his knife hand under one arm as she caught him in a bear hug that brought both of them crashing to the stone floor.

There was a sharp crack as Julian's wrist broke between Emily's arm and her ribcage. He yelped in pain and surprise, but struggled against Emily's body weighing him down. It was all she could do just to stay on top of him; the poison was like fire in her veins, and black night was closing in all around her.

Julian got his head and shoulders up off the floor just as Emily brought her forehead down into his face, breaking his nose in a spray of blood. His head bounced off the stone and he stopped struggling.

Emily shoved herself off Julian's still body and collapsed against the wall. Her head was spinning and she was drenched in sweat, which mixed with Julian's blood to run down into her eyes, but the rough stone was cool against her back. Hidden in one corner of the small antechamber, Jack's body slumped among shadows. Unconscious or dead? There was no way to tell from here. The same question could be asked of Julian, Emily suddenly realized. He was very still.

She felt about dead herself, and as she passed long minutes watching the small room spin and wobble, Emily began to wonder if someone—Michael, maybe, having learned from Elizabeth where she'd gone—would eventually come down here looking for them and find three corpses and a cold, miserable mystery.

Jack stirred and opened his eyes. He tried to sit up, slumped back into his corner, then succeeded on the second try.

"Jack," said Emily, or she thought she did. It was hard to tell if the breath had made it any farther than her lips.

"Emily? Emily!" Jack stumbled over to her, giving Julian's body only a brief, understanding glance. "Are you okay? Did he hurt you?"

"Ha," Emily breathed. "Give me…give me some credit. There was poison, in there." She tried to wave a hand back down the hallway, but it didn't want to move.

"Do you need me to get Michael?" The warm light of the magic lantern made Jack's face an exaggerated mask of concern as he absently rubbed the back of his head.

"Probably a good idea," Emily agreed. Somehow Jack's presence, his care, was making living feel like a much better idea than it had seemed a minute ago.

"Probably not," said Julian from near the stairs. He was standing, if a bit wobbly, and holding the knife in his left hand. His right wrist was swollen and red, and his eyes moved a bit randomly in his head.

"Put it down, Julian," said Jack calmly. "It's over." To Emily's amazement, Julian dropped his knife and sat down heavily on the bottom step.

"I know," he said.

"Want to tell us what the hell you're doing?" asked Jack, picking up the knife.

"You didn't see it, Jack."

"See what?" Jack asked gently.

"I saw Alex get killed," said Julian, almost to himself. "In the great hall. I came back to do some cleaning and Alex was there, arguing with some guy in a spacesuit by the door. Alex turned around when he heard me coming up the stairs, and that's when he stabbed him. 'See you in a hundred days,' that's what he said when he did it. And then he laughed.

"Alex just looked so surprised…he touched the knife in his back, looked at the blood on his hand like he just couldn't believe it. I couldn't move. I was in the shadows in the stairwell and I guess the killer just couldn't see me. And then Alex turned around like he was going to fight, but instead he just fell. He got one hand on the murderer's helmet and then he hit the ground and he didn't move."

"Julian, I had no idea. Why didn't you tell us?" Jack was rigid, holding Julian's knife in a white-knuckled hand.

"I tried! But I was so ashamed. You Gifted, you don't understand what it's like. You're so much more than human, it's easy for you to be brave. How do you think it feels to be normal around you? It's like walking around with gods. You have no idea. It's so easy for you. And I knew what you'd all say: 'Julian, you let them kill Alexander and you just stood there.' So no, I didn't tell you. But I tried. I passed on the message, didn't I?"

"A hundred days," said Jack quietly. "You wrote that. Which explains why it was the wrong hand."

Julian nodded, his eyes downcast and shadowed. "But then I watched you all just do nothing. Fighting and arguing, trying to get help and failing over and over again. And meanwhile my mom's inn was dying. People stopped coming. And for all your greatness, you did nothing."

Jack opened his mouth as if to protest, then stayed silent.

"So eventually I realized it was hopeless. Whoever is on the other side of the door is going to come for us one way or another. The only question is how painful the transition will be. So what if I tried to smooth things along? We're all going to die anyway, if you idiots insist on fighting back."

"You killed Sir Richard," said Emily. Julian looked up, surprise showing beneath his hooded eyes.

"Yes, and I tried to kill you, too. Sorry about that. But I thought if I killed Sir Richard the knights would leave. And if I stopped you and your clever plans it might take the fight out of everyone else. And then you'd all just give up and let them take over without a fight."

"Do you really think your life will go back to normal if we let the dragon back onto Finalhaven?" asked Emily.

"Here's what I think," said Julian, his mouth twisting. "When gods fight, it's mortals like me and my mom that get stepped on. I don't care who I have to worship if I means we get left alone."

"Well, I've heard enough," said Jack. The knife flashed as he brought it up.

"Jack, wait," said Emily.

"He killed Sir Richard. He tried to kill you twice. And me, come to think of it. You don't think he deserves this?"

"One death is already too many. I've got a better idea," said Emily.

Julian was listless in Emily's hands as she dragged him across the short stretch of sand at the foot of the Castle Forlorn. The struggle up the stairs from the basement had helped Emily sweat out some of the poison, and the heavy summer sun was doing an even better job. Still, she was glad he wasn't struggling; she wasn't sure she was up for another fight.

Behind them, Jack held the knife steady in a white-knuckled hand. They'd had no debate, no discussion, but Emily knew Jack and she were thinking the same thing: the senior staff, under General Alder, could not be trusted. Every moment wasted was a chance for Julian to break free from Emily's grip, not as strong as he seemed to think, and bringing the cook before the senior staff meant both risking the secret of the permission slip and throwing Julian on Alder's unpredictable mercy.

They stopped at the shore, where a small silver bell hung from a wooden post. Jack tapped it once with the knife, and a quiet, clear chime rang across the water.

The sound seemed to shake something loose in Julian. "Please," he said quietly.

"It's too late for please," said Jack, pointing the knife back at Julian.

"I've lived on Finalhaven my entire life," said the cook. "What's going to happen if I forget?"

"I don't care," said Emily.

"I could forget everything," Julian continued. "Literally everything."

"I said I don't care," Emily replied. Ed Doughty's boat appeared over the horizon, moving with what seemed to be impossible slowness as the three waited under the broad blue sky. Julian still wasn't fighting back, but his white shirt was dark with sweat, and his arms were damp in Emily's grip.

They passed the long minutes in silence, then under the spell of the rising growl of the dinghy's motor, until at last it crunched up on the sand. Doughty came up to the bow with a coiled length of rope, but Jack waved him off as Emily marched Julian to meet the boat.

"What's going on?" asked Doughty, concern and confusion warring on his face.

"I need you to take Julian to the mainland, please," said Emily with immense self-control.

"Anywhere in particular?"

"I'm sure he can find his way," said Jack.

"Emily, please," said Julian. She lifted him bodily and dumped him in the back of the boat, making Doughty fight for balance as the dinghy rocked in the shallows.

"That's all, then. Thanks, Ed." Emily turned away, catching a last glimpse of Julian's face, pale with terror beneath his tan, eyes wide and staring. Staring back up at the Castle Forlorn, she heard the crunch as Jack helped Ed shove off.

"Emily!" Julian's frantic voice carried over the roar of the motor as Ed put the boat around. "Just don't tell—"

The voice stopped suddenly. Emily fell to her knees and threw up into the sand.

Emily and Jack passed through the massive gates of the Castle Forlorn as a knot of servants and other townsfolk pushed past them, headed in the other direction. Emily noticed Wentworth among them, headed for home, she supposed. She kept her eyes on the floor as he passed.

"It's funny," said Jack. "Back in the day, the common folk would rush to the castle for safety. Guess they never expected the threat to be coming from the other direction."

"We can still keep them safe," Emily replied. "Keep the mercenaries bottled up at the door, draw them off into the castle, don't let them across the sandbar."

"If you say so," said Jack.

At the foot of the great stairs leading up to the second floor, Ernest was leaning with his arms crossed, clearly waiting for them. He stood up straight as they approached.

"Let me guess," he said, "Julian was our little murderer. I'm only ashamed I didn't figure it out sooner. Mind if I ask you two to replay your deductive chain so I can double-check your work?"

"Well, he tried to kill me with a knife," said Emily.

"And then he admitted to all of it," Jack added.

Ernest nodded. "Solidly reasoned. I don't need to guess why you handled things yourselves, and I'd suggest we don't let the word around just yet, either. For Madame de Luna's sake if nothing else." He sighed. "It's a shame, really; he made quite a good crème brûlée. Anyway, Emily, need a bit of a chat with you."

"I think so," Emily agreed.

"You can't go back through the door," said Ernest. "They need you here."

Emily nodded. "I agree. It needs to be you."

"Wait—" said Jack.

"Exactly," Ernest agreed. "If this ridiculous plan of yours is going to work, whoever goes through needs to figure out where the gate is pointed, or better yet, how to reprogram it. And we all know I'm the most brilliant genius in this damned castle."

"Wait!" said Jack.

"Jack, I'm touched, really." Ernest reached out and squeezed his friend on the bicep. "But let's be honest. In a castle full of warriors, wizards, and whatever you are, I'm just a poet. Besides. I really need to repay you and Emily for that little unpleasantness with the crippling cowardice and drunkenness earlier."

Jack nodded and slapped Ernest on the shoulder, so that for a second they stood squared off, gripping each other's arms in what Emily figured was the closest thing to a hug two frightened young men raised by distant, narcissistic fathers would get.

Together, the three of them headed down the back hallway to the great hall. Picking their way around the barricades, they found the Blodring brothers standing a watchful guard at the door, while Poet-Captain Dhar sat cross-legged on the floor scribbling in a small notebook.

Dhar stood as they approached, putting himself between them and the door with a cautious care.

"And what can I do for you three?" he asked. "Actually, Emily, I'm glad to see you. You'll be on guard rotation in a few hours. Where've you been? You look a little pale."

Ernest started to say something, but Emily held up a hand, and he shut his mouth.

"Poet-Captain Dhar," she said. "I've been thinking about our conversation last night. I was wondering something, actually."

Dhar's eyes narrowed. "What's that?"

"As Poet-Captain, are you in General Alder's chain of command?"

Dhar raised an eyebrow. "Well, no, not strictly. He's in charge of the defense of the castle, but technically my post reports directly to the Marcher Lord."

Emily nodded. "I thought not. So the post itself, Poet-Captain. Based on what you told me about it, I—I think you fit the job pretty well."

"Thanks." Dhar smiled just a little.

"And I think you love this castle as much as, or more than, anybody. And I think you're willing to do anything to protect it."

"And I think," said Dhar, nodding slowly, "that you are asking me to stand aside and let you through this door."

"Not me, Ernest. But yes. Please. Poet-Captain Dhar, give us—give the Castle Forlorn—a fighting chance."

Dhar's lips thinned into a contemplative line. "How is Ernest supposed to get back out? General Alder took your card."

Emily dipped a hand into her pocket and pulled out the permission slip she'd recovered from Alder's trophy room. "He needs to do a better job of putting away his toys."

Dhar gave her an appreciative whistle. "It would mean disobeying a direct order from Alder."

"He's gone nuts, and you know it. Plus, he's not your boss."

Dhar glanced to his left and right, at the Blodring brothers, who had stood silent and rigid through the entire exchange. "What do you say, boys? Captain Queen reported to Alder, but the Queen's not here anymore."

"We were sworn to Captain Queen, and she to the General," said Uther. "The hierarchy is clear."

"I see," said Dhar. "But the Irregulars are a bit adrift. A leadership crisis, really. Ideally Captain Queen would have appointed a lieutenant to

231

lead in her stead, but this sort of thing is difficult to handle in such a flat chain of command. Well, are you two interested in joining up with the castle garrison? We could use a couple good fighters. It would mean leaving the Irregulars behind, of course. Can't serve two masters."

The Blodrings shared a glance, then Uther gave his younger brother a small nod.

"We accept," said Wulf.

"Very good," said Dhar. "Repeat after me. *I swear my sword to the defense of the Castle Forlorn.*"

"I swear my sword to the defense of the Castle Forlorn," the brothers echoed in their heavy Teutonic accents.

"*I forswear all other allegiances, and place the Castle above all else.*"

"I forswear all other allegiances, and place the Castle above all else."

"*The Castle is my home and its people are my family.*"

"The Castle is my home and its people are my family." Emily looked to her right, and was surprised to see Ernest quietly mouthing the words along with the Blodrings.

"Very good!" Dhar clapped his hands. "Uther Blodring, Wulf Blodring, I appoint you to the post of guardsmen in the garrison of the Castle Forlorn. Now I promote you both to the rank of Guard-Lieutenant, reportingly directly to me. Congratulations, you've earned it. Finally, I order you to do all you can to keep anyone from coming out of that door, but I say nothing about stopping foolhardy souls from going into it."

"If you lads are quite done, I'd like to get this over with," said Ernest.

"Right," nodded Dhar. "What's your plan? You need to get in, not get caught, get back out through the gate to somewhere else on Earth, is that right? And from there, organize the resistance?"

"That's about it," agreed Emily.

"And this is the same gate that we imagine our enemy is even now mustering on the other side of, for their all-out assault tomorrow."

"That's the one," said Jack. Wulf had moved over to his brother, with whom he was now having a whispered argument in German.

"So your plan for not getting immediately turned into a plasma scorch is…?" Dhar continued.

"Ernest, I would like to come with you, please," said Wulf. He turned to Dhar. "Captain, permission to accompany Ernest?"

"No, no," said Emily quickly, "there's only one permission slip. Only one person can get back out to wherever Ernest points the gate. If you try to go through without the card you'll get fried."

"Ernest will take care of me, I am sure," said Wulf. "He is very clever. Also, I am a Guard-Lieutenant in the garrison of the Castle Forlorn. I am sworn to its defense above all else, even my own life."

"That was the idea, yeah," said Dhar.

"Wulf, you don't have to do this," said Jack.

"I imagine I'll figure something out," said Ernest, walking to the door. He put his hand on the knob, tried it, and found that it turned easily. "What's the use of being a genius if you can't help your friends every once in a while?"

CHAPTER 18

Of the Irregulars, only Emily, Jack, and Michael were left. Uther announced with sober seriousness that he was present representing the castle guard as the four gathered in Ernest's room for one last party. It had nothing of the manic good cheer of Emily's first night in the Castle Forlorn and had a much more practical purpose: with the great hall under guard and the kitchen cold and empty, the best wine would be found in Ernest's room, and somebody had realized, or at least decided, that he would have wanted them to drink it.

The room itself was just down the hall from Emily's, more or less identical in shape and size. The bed was rumpled, clothes were strewn everywhere, and a pile of black notebooks tottered in one corner. The good wine was discovered in a wooden box under the bed, and Uther Blodring pulled the cork out with his fingers and took a long swig before passing the first bottle around so they could fill glasses they'd filched from the kitchen.

They settled themselves around the room: on the bed, on the floor. Jack perched on the single wooden chair, playing slow, quiet arpeggios over a droning bass note. They all drank in silence for a while.

"To absent friends," said Jack at last. He didn't have a glass to raise, but the others did, and they drank as he listed names. "To Queen Bronwyn, who we miss now more than ever. To Ernest Graves, the bravest idiot I ever met. To Wulf Blodring, so loyal it was crazy, or maybe just crazy enough to be loyal."

"And to Julian," said Michael quietly.

"Mike, he killed Sir Richard," said Jack. "Plus tried to kill me."

"So he wasn't all bad," replied Michael with a smile.

"Ah, dammit," Jack agreed. "He was one of us, even if he was a murdering piece of shit."

"For all we know, we'll see them all again," said Emily. Uther glanced up at her from his glass, then looked back in, seeing who knew what memories of his younger brother. They all drank to the sentiment, though.

"If I survive," said Uther slowly, "I'm going home to kill my father."

"I'm sorry, what?" said Jack. "Believe me, I know the feeling, but that seems a little extreme."

"No, no," said Uther, waving his free hand. "He is dying in his bed. It is a sickness, a terrible way. Better that he fights one last duel and dies with a sword in his hand. It is my duty, as his eldest son."

"Won't that make you man of the house?" asked Michael.

"Yes." Uther nodded. "Mama will need help, and it will be good to see Little Karl again."

"Little Karl!" Michael raised his glass.

"Not so little now, perhaps," said Uther, then lapsed back into his contemplative silence.

"Well, if I survive, I'll at least tell my dad to go to hell," said Jack after another empty minute.

"Forget my parents," said Michael. "If I survive, I'm going to live with someone I love. No matter where that is." Emily, thinking of the long-haired girl locked in two rooms forever, said nothing.

"How about you, Emily?" asked Uther. "Do you still wish to join the Sabre & Torch?"

Emily snorted a small laugh. "That seems like so long ago. You know, I was just supposed to find out what that symbol was? I only came all the way up here because I wanted to impress them. Oh, and because I got my dad into a huge mess of trouble at his job, and I guess I figured if

I unraveled the whole mystery I'd get some clue how to get him out of it again."

"Did you?" asked Jack.

"Nope," said Emily, and they all laughed. "I didn't really think that one through."

There was a knock at the door. Uther managed to shove it open with his foot without getting up from the floor, revealing Colonel Liu looking exhausted and harried.

"Where's Ernest? We need him." She took in the four Irregulars and the wine with obvious surprise.

"Um, about that," said Emily. She took a breath and plunged in. "He and Wulf went through the door to try to get help. It was my idea, so if General Alder—"

"General Alder is locked in the dungeon," said Liu.

"What?!" said Jack, hitting a sour, squeaking note on his guitar.

"I'm in command now," Colonel Liu continued. "General Alder was found unfit by unanimous decision of the senior staff. Which means—"

"Which means we're now without a Mental for tactical advice tomorrow," interrupted Michael.

"That's right," agreed Liu.

"In that case, I think I've had enough to drink," Michael said.

"We'll be there to support you, Colonel," said Uther, standing. "My tactics classes at Schwerteburg were quite thorough, and I'm sure Emily had similar lessons at Harkness. Dhar is no fool, either."

"Thank you, Uther." Colonel Liu gave him a nod. "I look forward to your input...tonight."

"Tonight?" said Emily numbly. The day had been so long, so full of tragedy, that it seemed impossible there could be more still to do.

Colonel Liu gave her a weary smile. "There's no way to know what time tomorrow the invasion force is coming through, so we're gathering at midnight. Come to think of it, my first order as commander of the defense of the Castle Forlorn is to send you all to bed. If you pretend it's nighttime you might be able to get a decent sleep."

The Irregulars stood and began to shuffle out into the hallway. Emily moved quietly next to Colonel Liu, who was watching Michael disappear around the corner, no doubt headed to Elizabeth's apartment.

"What is it, Emily?" asked Liu.

"Colonel, I'm sorry about Ernest and Wulf." Emily bit her lip. "But I really think it was the right thing to do."

Liu shook her head. "I just deposed my commanding officer. I have no idea what the right thing to do is anymore."

"There's something else," said Emily. "General Alder had a sort of trophy room down in the sub-basement. I had to go down there to get the permission slip before I sent Ernest through the door." Her stomach twinged at the memory of the poison she'd thrown up only a few hours ago. "There were weapons down there, too."

"What sort of weapons?" asked Liu, her eyes narrowing.

"I'm not sure," Emily admitted. "He had a lot of junk in there, I think. I...wasn't feeling too hot when I was in there."

"Best leave it alone," said Liu. "Apparently the General had a lot of secrets. I'd rather not dredge any more up. Get some sleep, Emily. That's an order."

That was all the invitation Emily needed. She moved slowly down the hall, feeling the day's incredible weight pressing down on her. Jack, who had been leaning against a wall, caught up with her and put a hand gently on her shoulder.

"What is it?" Emily asked quietly.

"You need to stay alive tomorrow," Jack said.

"So do you," Emily said, her brow furrowing.

"Believe me, I'm gonna try," replied Jack. "But this isn't really my scene. I'm normal. You've got a much better shot at survival."

"I can keep you safe," Emily said.

"You need to keep us *all* safe. Look, Bronwyn is gone, Alder's locked up, Dhar doesn't have command over the Irregulars, Colonel Liu is clearly terrified, Uther has half his mind on his family. When it comes to leadership, Em, you're it."

"Leadership?" said Emily. "That's not exactly my strength."

"I'm not saying you should be giving orders," said Jack.

"No, I'll be taking them," Emily said. "How many times have I screwed up in the last few weeks? Getting my dad in trouble at work, coming solo to the island, pissing off Alder and getting Bronwyn banished, sending Ernest through the door so we don't have a Mental. If I'd just done as I was told, we wouldn't be in this mess."

"I won't argue that you have a knack for getting into trouble," Jack said. "But I don't know, Em. I think it's a gift rather than a curse. Call it a...premonition from the twelve-fingered man. We have no idea what's coming tonight, not really. Just promise me you'll be yourself."

"Good night, Jack."

"It's like four in the afternoon."

"Good night."

But Emily didn't sleep. Instead her feet led her to the long hallway where four cats lay cleaning themselves among empty dishes. She found a seam in the wall made by a neat column of bricks and knocked three times, sharply.

The wall slid open, revealing Michael looking equal parts confused and sleepy.

"Hey," he said, and moved aside to let Emily in.

"Hey." She slipped past him into Elizabeth's apartment and watched as he shut the door. "I wanted your advice on something. Two somethings."

"Hello, Emily," said Elizabeth from the door to her bedroom. In a white nightgown, she was as unearthly and royal as ever, but her face showed obvious pleasure at seeing Emily.

Emily smiled back as she gathered her thoughts. "Okay, first. Trying to say goodbye to anyone who isn't on Finalhaven..."

"Would be a bad idea, yeah." Michael gave her a sympathetic look. "Trust me."

"But my dad—my friends from Harkness—I can't just *not*." It had been such a whirlwind since her arrival on the island, Emily had barely had a thought to spare for Chris, Andy, and Kayo. But now, with the deadline looming, she wanted more than anything to hear their voices one last time. The thought that they, and her dad, would never know where she'd gone, that she would just disappear without a trace, was too much to bear.

"It will make your hurt worse, Emily," said Elizabeth. Her voice was gentle but firm. "They will not understand, and it will make space between you."

Emily couldn't meet the queen's eyes, because she was right. "Okay then, second, what's up with the cats?"

"The cats?" Michael blinked, but Elizabeth's laugh was like a bell.

"Cats know more than they let on," she said. "Cats who dwell in thin places, even more so."

"Did you..." Emily cleared her throat. "Did you tell them to help me?"

"Cats do what they please," Elizabeth said, as though that answered everything.

"Okay," said Emily. "Well, uh, please thank them for me."

"It would mean more coming from you," Elizabeth said.

"Well," said Michael, "if that's everything—"

"It isn't," said Elizabeth.

"She said she had two questions."

"Is that everything?" asked the queen.

"No." Emily still couldn't meet her eyes, but now she couldn't look at Michael either.

"Everything okay?" the young magician asked.

"Yeah," Emily said. "I just…how did you two fall in love?"

"Are you asking about us?" said Michael. "Or are you really asking about a certain twelve-fingered guitarist?"

"Um, both?" Emily felt a flush creeping up her neck. It was ridiculous to think that she could stare down lindworms and dragons without blinking, but couldn't ask her friends for relationship advice. She made herself look up. "Yeah. Both."

"I noticed the cats," Michael said. "Always in that same spot in the hallway, either eating or waiting for food. So I started hanging out there too. Eventually I realized there was something different about the hall, a sort of magical…resonance? Anyway, the Marcher Lord cast a hell of a spell to hide Lizzie, but no magic is perfect."

"What did you do?"

Michael shrugged, his face alight with amusement. "I knocked."

"And I answered," said Elizabeth. "And we spoke for many hours over many months."

"So to answer your question," Michael said, "it took us a long time to fall in love. I introduced her to Alexander, then Ernest, then Jack." He looked away, out the window where the sea sparkled beneath the evening sun. "We had a good thing going, before Alex died."

"He kept Jack for last out of fear he might try to steal me away," said Elizabeth, with a very unqueenly smile.

"Did he?" Emily asked.

"No."

Michael cleared his throat. "After Alex died…I had to come tell Lizzie what happened: the murder, the message. And somehow that turned into me telling her how I felt."

"Tragic words softened by joyous ones," Elizabeth said.

"You should tell him how you feel," Michael said. "Now. In case…"

"It will make space between them," said Elizabeth softly.

"What?" Michael blinked.

"She's right," said Emily, her mind made up. "Now's not the time, not when we all need to be focused on the fight."

"He's a good guy," Michael said.

"I know." Emily shook her head. "But he's been through so much. I don't need him worrying about me, and I don't need to be worrying about him. I'll tell him after. If there *is* an after." She snorted. "Maybe."

O Days

At midnight, the entire fighting strength of the Castle Forlorn gathered in the great hall. Emily, the taller Sir Arthur, and his squire Daniel waited between the door and the first row of barricades along with Poet-Captain Dhar, who had command of their group. Emily was back in her gear from the sortie through the door, ballistic vest strapped tight and the comforting weight of the great hammer in her hands. Dhar was dressed similarly but held a short sword in each hand. The Albian knight and squire wore matching steel breastplates and helmets, in the old-fashioned style, and carried shields and longswords.

Looking back up over her shoulder, Emily saw the muzzles of half a dozen rifles poking over the top of the first palisade. These belonged to Dhar's guardsmen, non-Gifted men and women who Emily thought were probably the bravest people in the room despite being twenty feet up and behind six inches of solid wood.

Colonel Liu and Michael appeared together over the top of one of the front-line palisades, gesturing towards the door as they debated something that Emily couldn't hear. Liu called to Sir Maximilian, who stood with his squire Merry over the top of another barricade, lifted the face-plate of his helmet, then shook his head to her question.

Hidden among the palisades farther back in the hall were Uther, the other Sir Arthur with his own squire Flora, and Luke, the squire of dead Sir Richard. And, incredibly, Jack, who had insisted on fighting despite all Emily's arguments. He'd turned up a pistol somewhere and told her that even if the mercenaries could dodge bullets, he felt better with it than without.

100 days. It was a vague warning, Emily reflected, but at least they'd gotten one, thanks to the hubris of Captain Smiertkin as he murdered Alexander Cho. What had Cho been like? Everybody seemed to miss him quite a lot, though they didn't talk about him much.

They owed thanks to Julian, too, for being in the right place at the right time to see Cho's murder and overhear the mercenary captain's useless brag to his victim. Why he had to go the roundabout route of writing it in blood, Emily wasn't sure, but maybe even then his desperate plan to force a surrender by the defenders of the Castle Forlorn had been forming in his grieving, frightened mind.

Still, it was vague. Would they come now, at the start of the hundredth day? Hours from now, when the defenders were weary from hours of constant tension? Or maybe it was all a trick, and they wouldn't come at all—

The door slammed open.

"Fire!" screamed Colonel Liu, and the guardsmen's rifles banged as two mercenaries pressed through the door together, holding a large metal canister between them. Bullets whistled over Emily's head only to sizzle harmlessly on personal force fields that guarded the mercs—Tooms was one of them, she thought, but she didn't recognize the other. She recognized the body shields, though, cheap one-man models that kept them safe as long as they lasted, but also stopped them from fighting back...

"It's a bomb!" yelled Sir Maximilian from somewhere overhead.

As one, Emily, Dhar, Arthur, and Daniel pulled away from the door, opening space between them and the mercenaries' canister.

The shield surrounding the anonymous mercenary crackled and died, and he looked up in surprise just as a bullet shattered the faceplate of his helmet.

"Lilkin is down!" shouted Tooms as his companion crumpled to the floor. He dropped to one knee and began frantically working the controls of the metal canister. He could hardly been seen behind his force field, which sparked and sizzled purple and red.

"It's not—" shouted Emily, as Dhar yelled, "Front line, forward!"

But it was too late. Tooms gave a shout of triumph as the canister whined to life and threw up a faint red force wall, as tall as one of the palisades and twice as wide, with the mercenary and the door on one side and the front-line fighters on the other.

"Perimeter!" yelled Tooms, and the rest of Blood Squadron poured through the door as Emily and Daniel cut left and Arthur and Dhar cut right to get around the new force wall.

"Shit," Emily hissed as she left Daniel behind her in a flat-out sprint. From the corner of her eye she could see Captain Smiertkin, bloody handprint still on his faceplate, directing traffic as another full squadron came through the door, and then a third.

She made it around the side of the force wall and saw Dhar pacing her on the other side. Yelling, she put her head down and fixed her grip on her hammer as she charged.

They crashed into the flanks of Blood Squadron together; Uppagu, the tall, skinny alien, met Emily with his knives flashing. She rammed into him bodily and was met by his own personal shield, which crackled as she hit him.

Emily stepped back and began hammering at Uppagu, trying to bring down his shield. She could imagine him smiling behind the black glass of his helmet. What were they up to, dammit?

"Down!" yelled Captain Smiertkin, and suddenly the force wall disappeared. Uppagu side-stepped, letting Emily stumble past him, then joined the rest of Blood Squadron as they formed up with the other mercenaries and pushed past the front-line defenders, straight towards the palisades.

"Dammit!" Emily screamed. They'd been played perfectly, splitting around the line the mercenaries had established just to leave a nice, neat gap for them.

Furious, she threw her hammer at Uppagu, who was jogging backwards at the rear of the mercenary column, his rifle in his hands. He snapped off a shot at the hammer as it tumbled through the air—his shield had fallen at some point in that last few seconds—then collapsed backwards as it struck him square in the chest. His squad-mates shoved him away and let him fall as they pressed forward into the great hall.

The banging of the rifles was met with the sizzling hiss of plasma guns as the mercenaries on the outside of their formation fired back at the guardsmen. Emily heard their screams as she rushed to pick up her hammer, and the rifles stilled somewhat.

Uppagu was just pushing himself up onto his elbows as she grabbed up her weapon. Ahead of the mercenary column, Uther led the Albians in the second line to block the invaders from getting any further. Jack was nowhere to be seen, thank God. She drove the head of her hammer straight down into Uppagu's helmet, which split with a loud crack, and down to the floor. Blue liquid leaked out from the ruined gray mess beneath her weapon.

"Come on, let's split 'em up," Emily called. They fell into a wedge behind her, Dhar on her left, Arthur and Daniel on her right, and dashed among the palisades toward the back of the mercenary formation. They caught up just as Sir Maximilian and Merry leapt down from the barricades.

"We've got them surrounded!" said Sir Max.

"As long as Uther's line holds," panted Emily. A blue line of plasma fire burned over her head, bringing her attention back where it belonged. The mercenary column had been halted by the pincer movement and turned its plasma rifles away from the guardsmen still on the palisades, who couldn't shoot into the fray.

"Where's Michael?" Emily asked as they ducked behind a barricade to get out of the line of fire.

"Working on something up top," Sir Maximilian replied. "Don't look, you'll draw attention to him."

"Got it. You ready?"

"Ready," Max nodded.

Screaming, they charged, jinking left and right to draw off the plasma fire. They hit the invaders' line together. Emily's hammer crashed into one as Sir Maximilian, on her right, slammed into another with his shield and stabbed up from underneath. The mercenary gave a short scream, then threw down his rifle and frantically tried to unclip his faceplate. He got it halfway off before he collapsed onto the Albian knight, blood leaking from his open helmet.

"Merry, form up!" Max shouted, shoving the corpse away. "Form up, dammit! Where are you?"

Emily glanced over her shoulder and saw Merry's still form on the floor a few yards behind them, the hole in her chest still smoking.

"I'm here with you, Max," Emily said. The knight spared her a glance, and his lip was curled in a sneer.

"I don't need *you*, I need my squire."

They stumbled back together as the mercenaries pushed against them. Max turned a knife with his shield and slashed down, but cursed as his target dodged easily.

"Enhanced armor," Emily panted. "I told you." A blade came at her from somewhere; she caught it on the handle of her hammer. "I hate you but I don't want you dead."

Max opened his mouth to reply, but the mercenary at his throat had no intention of giving him a chance. As two glittering knives swept down into the opening Max had left, Emily steeled herself to watch a killing blow she couldn't possibly intercept.

The young knight was saved from death from a tall shape that crashed into all three of them, dropping them in a desperate tangle. Emily grabbed the mercenary by the throat and threw him away, revealing Jack halfway on top of Max. His white shirt was blossoming with blood.

"Stay out of this, you idiot!" cursed Max, shoving Jack back toward the palisades, where he stumbled and fell among the shadows.

"Scatter!" came Colonel Liu's voice, from above and behind. They did, leaping back away from the fray and ducking behind barricades. Over the noise of the fight Emily could hear something like a singing, humming sound, half whine and half roar. She looked back and up to see Michael turning his hands in a complex pattern as a black light rose and pulsed all around him in time to the singing.

The mercenaries paused too, catching their breath as the press against them momentarily let up. Then the singing became lightning and the roar became thunder as a storm broke above their column.

White arcs of electricity played over the personal force fields of the mercenaries, making a shrieking, sizzling noise so loud that Emily wasn't sure whether to cover her eyes against the light or her ears against the sound. Staggering, she felt Sir Maximilian grab her around the waist and drag her away from the electrical storm.

She only realized the light and noise had stopped when she heard someone yelling her name. It was Colonel Liu, still directing from atop one of the barricades.

"Emily! Sledge!"

"Here, Colonel!" Emily called back, looking up through blurry eyes to find the Lancer.

"They've broken through the second line," shouted Liu. Emily found her, standing in an open-legged firing stance with a rifle to her ear, taking potshots at mercenary targets between words. "Get to the town and ready the volunteers. We'll pin 'em here as long as we can. Go!"

Emily jumped, high enough to grab the walkway of the nearest palisade and pull herself onto it. From there, she leapt from barricade to barricade, headed for the door out of the great hall at top speed. Plasma bolts sizzled around her but couldn't quite touch her as she passed overhead of the melee.

She spared one glance down. The mercenary column was moving forward, slowed only by the harrying attacks of the defenders, who were fighting twice as fiercely now that the invaders' force shields had been shorted out by Michael's spell. She couldn't see Jack.

She made the door a dozen yards ahead of the mercenaries and dashed out, down the hall, through the foyer, and out of the castle. The sandbar was half covered, and the encroaching tide lapped at Emily's ankles as she sprinted towards town.

She was sweating when she reached the fountain. A gang of about a dozen townies waited there, spears in hand, with Madame de Luna at their head.

"They're coming," Emily panted, leaning her hammer against the fountain.

"We're ready," said Madame de Luna. Behind her, the various townsfolk nodded agreement or gripped their spears tighter.

"Is everybody else safe somewhere?" Emily asked.

Madame de Luna nodded. "The kids are in some caves on the southern beach, with most of the old folks. A few people who didn't fit there are in basements around town. They're as safe as they're gonna—"

The innkeeper caught her breath as a resonant boom sounded from behind Emily. She whirled to see rubble splashing into the ocean as the western side of the castle slumped into itself. Flames started out from the wreckage, spreading quickly in the dry summer heat.

"They bombed the castle!" Madame de Luna gasped.

247

"That was the great hall," Emily agreed. As they watched, the mercenaries spilled out of the open front door of the castle and began splashing across the sandbar at a sprint. They were chased close behind by the castle's defenders. Emily could just make out the flashing swords and armor of the Albian knights in the lead, then a mass of the other fighters, and finally a tangle of guardsmen running far behind their Gifted comrades.

"Spears ready!" Emily shouted, picking up her hammer. The townies behind her began to form up. "Make a wall up there, at the end of the road. Our job is to slow them down so the fighters can catch up. Everybody is responsible for the man on his left. Nobody fall back! Keep your spears up and they can't touch you!"

That last was a lie, Emily reflected as she shoved the volunteers into something resembling a spear wall, but it wasn't a bad thing for a bunch of terrified non-Gifted to hear. Time, that was all they needed, time for the real fighters to catch up. Then they could crush the mercs in another pincer.

She stepped out in front of the spear wall and walked a few paces up the road, then stood waiting for the invaders, leaning casually on her hammer.

"Come on, boys!" she called to nobody in particular.

They didn't even slow down for her. The mercenary column split around her, swallowing her up in a press of bodies. So she began swinging, laying all around her with the hammer, which sprayed blood as it whistled through the air.

"Fight me, dammit!" Emily screamed in frustration. They were ignoring her, ignoring her challenge, passing her by even as she knew she broke a few ribs and arms.

Turning, she saw the mercenaries quickly move to surround the line of spear-wielding volunteers, who suddenly seemed very small and sad arrayed against the well-trained mercs in their bloody, blackened combat armor. Emily was starting to feel small and sad herself.

The townie line collapsed naturally, changing to a lopsided circle bristling with spears that would do nothing against the plasma rifles the mercenaries were now unslinging. A glance back showed her that her comrades were just too far away, still coming down the long road from the castle.

"Smiertkin!" she shouted. A glassy helmet with Alexander Cho's bloody handprint still on it turned. "Fight me, you coward!"

Beneath his helmet, the mercenary captain laughed and turned away. He raised a hand, and a dozen mercenary rifles pointed at the helpless knot of townies.

"On my mark!" called Smiertkin. "Two! One!"

There was a sudden roar from the east, and thirty heads turned as one to see a mass of people charging up the white sand slope, Ernest Graves at their head. Behind them in the water bobbed a dozen boats of various shapes and sizes, including Ed Doughty's dinghy, its owner only a few paces behind Ernest and choking up on a baseball bat as he ran.

As she began to pick out faces in the crowd, Emily tried to find Wulf, but apparently he hadn't returned with Ernest. Then astonishment pushed the thought from her mind as she spotted Andrea Butcher wearing a ballistic vest and a huge grin, Kayo Jackson with purple fire playing around her twisting hands, and just coming up over the rise, a battered combat mech that Emily immediately recognized as Scout, Chris McLeod's favorite toy.

The reinforcements crashed into the eastern quarter of the mercenary firing squad just as the defenders from the Castle Forlorn arrived from the north. As the invaders broke apart to defend themselves, the now-forgotten townie volunteers began to stab out with their spears at the backs their tormentors presented.

Laughing, Emily joined the fray, shoving mercenaries aside with her hammer as she drove towards Captain Smiertkin. He stood a few paces apart, directing the melee with commands shouted into his headset, rifle slung across his chest and knives still sheathed.

Little round Bu leapt in front of her, blocking her way. The first blow from her hammer knocked him to the ground, the second broke his leg, and the backhand rattled his helmet for good measure. Now there was just empty space between her and the mercenary captain.

"Blood Squadron!" Smiertkin shouted as she approached. "Delta delta delta! Repeat, execute delta delta delta!"

Within the fray, three mercenaries echoed Captain Smiertkin's motions as he dropped to one knee and began weaving the complex patterns of a spell. Sudden fear choked Emily's throat.

Colors glimmered around the remaining members of Blood Squadron. Another set of personal force shields? No, this was different. It was magic, powerful magic, Emily realized as the hair stood up on the back of her neck and a tingle ran up her arms.

Smiertkin leapt into the battle, drawing his knives. He was blindingly fast, even to Emily's eye, and Poet-Captain Dhar's swords bounced off him as Smiertkin turned and slashed the fighter twice across the chest with motions that were almost imperceptible. Dhar crumbled.

Emily looked around in a panic. Led by the untouchable Bloods, the other mercenaries were rallying, shoving back against the castle's defenders.

"Kayo! Kayo!" Emily shouted over the din. Her friend was suddenly there at her side, but they had no time for happy reunions. "What the hell is this?"

Fear clouded Kayo's eyes. "Dragon magic," she said. "Guaranteed. Which means—"

"Which means there's a dragon nearby," Emily finished for her. "Shit. Shit!"

"Emily, what's going on?" asked Andrea, coming up behind them.

"Andy! No time. Keep these people safe. I'll..." Emily hesitated. What could she do against dragon magic? Against the dragon itself? What other weapon did she have, what card still up her sleeve?

Something in that mental choice of words triggered a memory in her head, from a moment that seemed to be a thousand years ago, although it was only the day before. What had Jack said? *It's a gift rather than a curse.*

"I'll be right back!"

CHAPTER 19

So Emily ran. She ran away from the fight, up the road, across the sandbar that was now more a suggestion amid ankle-deep pools, and through the front doors of the castle, one of which hung black and smoking from a single twisted hinge. The front hall was charred and stank of burnt flesh. Thick black smoke was everywhere, roiling down the front staircase and carrying a punishing heat with it.

Emily plunged through the clouds for the back stairs that led down, past the kitchen to the basement and the sub-basement beneath it. In the tiny room with a single door, she spent only a second casting around for the magic lamp before giving it up for lost and plunging into the long, pitch-black hallway that led to General Alder's trophy room.

Emily dove under the huge curved blade that still split the hall at neck height, felt the false tripwire snap where her ankle caught it, and leapt with arms outstretched as soon as her front foot felt empty air where the floor should have been. She hit the other side of the pit with her chest and scrambled up, then sprinted the last few steps and kicked open the door to the trophy room.

Feeling around along the left-hand wall, her fingers closed on the long handle of the hammer she'd seen before. What had the label said? She pulled it down, finding it surprisingly light and well-balanced.

After a few hasty test swings, though, she began to feel uncertain. If Kayo was right, the defenders of the Castle Forlorn were about to go up against a very old, very angry dragon. Was a hammer the right weapon for the job? Emily laughed as the weapon's name suddenly swam up in her memory: "The Hammer That Carries Considerable Weight." A huge weight and balance like the edge of a knife: it was the perfect symbol for the choice she was trying to make. Somehow she knew, instinctively, that the battle hinged on her decision in this moment.

She threw the hammer down, shaking the floor, and grabbed a sword off the wall.

Panting, Emily reached the front hall. She took a deep breath, then plunged into the thick black smoke that boiled around her. She was halfway to the open doors when a colossal crash from behind her sent her to her knees. Turning, she saw through the smoke and haze that the ceiling had collapsed, bringing the second-floor landing down into the entry hall.

Behind it came the dragon. Released from its glass sphere, it seemed impossibly huge as it swung its tattooed head to regard her with eyes flashing red. It opened its mouth to reveal row upon row of hooked fangs, and with a sound like a giant's sigh, steam vented from slits on its neck to drive away the black smoke, making a perfect frame for the terrible face for just a moment.

Emily was frozen on her knees, the sword dangling from her nerveless hand. The dragon stepped down from the wreckage of the second floor, moving toward her on six powerful legs. It drew a breath.

"Welcome home, you bastard!" someone shouted from near the half-collapsed staircase. The dragon's head swung in search of the antagonist, clearing smoke as it went. Emily saw it when the dragon did: a small, white-haired shape holding a longsword in both hands, wearing…a dress?

No—a nightgown. His bare legs pale, his wispy hair floating in the roiling air, there stood the Marcher Lord, his face turned up in defiance to the dragon whose home he ruled.

The dragon laughed.

"Come on then, if you're so big!" shouted the Marcher Lord. In the face of this insane bravery, Emily found her feet and hefted her own sword.

"Run, girl!" the Marcher Lord called without taking his eyes off the gray head that now hovered threateningly close to him, the gleaming eyes taking him in with interest. "Run! As your lord I command you!"

Emily was about to argue. Then in a motion so fast she couldn't believe it, the dragon darted forward and closed its jaws around the top half of the Marcher Lord. It shook its head like a dog, and pale, naked legs flew away as the dragon swallowed the rest.

"Yes, girl," it said, turning to her. "Run."

She ran, out the doors that she prayed were tight enough to slow the beast at her heels. The sandbar was gone, so she pushed through knee-deep water, swimming desperately across deep spots with the sword tucked beneath one arm. As she reached the other side, she glanced back to see the doors of the castle burst off as the dragon shoved through them and out.

She made it to the town square still dripping wet, where the melee was raging. A quick glance showed a mass of bodies all around the fountain and the four Blood Squadron mercenaries, still protected by dragon magic, in a fighting knot at the heart of the carnage.

"Emily! Where were you?" snapped Colonel Liu, grabbing her by the arm with one hand as she fended off a mercenary with a sword in the other.

"Dragon is coming," Emily gasped. She lifted her sword. "Magic. I hope!"

"No time to hope!" Liu retorted. She drove the mercenary back in a furious exchange of steel, and Emily, seeing her chance, drove her sword deep into the invader's stomach. He fell forward and to one side, and sheared in half on the blade that had pierced him.

"Damn, that's sharp!" said Emily.

A ground-shaking roar announced the coming of the dragon. For a moment, all fighting stopped as the combatants turned in a group to see the huge beast rearing up to its full height, which made the colossus Emily had seen in the castle seem puny.

Huge wings blocked the moon, casting them all in shadow even as the roar deafened them. Around her, Emily saw a few people stagger back from the dragon's fury, some of them even falling to the cobblestones of the town square.

The dragon's tail, as thick as a man and twice as long, lashed out, catching one of the townies and flinging him halfway across the square, where he landed with a crack and lay still.

Michael's voice rose up in a sudden crescendo of chanting. Emily saw him as he had been in the great hall, glowing with a rising black light as his hands formed impossible angles.

"Eager little wizard," the dragon boomed, laughing. It reached down a foreclaw, plucked up Michael from the square, and squeezed. He coughed rackingly as blood started out from long gashes in his sides. "Little magics are so delicious. Your body will give me strength for the killing."

The huge mouth opened with a snap, flinging drool that sizzled where it hit the ground. Michael squirmed feebly in the dragon's clutch. Emily tightened her grip on the sword and stepped forward, feeling very, very small.

The dragon's head swung towards her, smiling. "I told you to run." Emily heard Michael wheeze as the dragon crushed him tighter.

"Put him down!" she yelled.

"I don't think so," replied the dragon, and suddenly its free foreclaw lashed out and knocked Emily to the cobblestones. Her head bounced sharply and darkness edged in on her vision for a moment. She heard the sword clatter away somewhere.

Helplessly she watched as the dragon lifted Michael to its mouth, laughing.

There was a buzzing in her ears, so Emily shook her head, trying to clear it. But the buzzing grew louder, until it was a song. She thought Michael might be trying to cast another spell because the music sounded like him, but really it wasn't like him at all. It was higher, lonelier, and more complex, but also a thousand times more grand and regal than anything she'd heard from Michael. But his song was there, too, like a thrumming bass pedal below the harmony.

Even the dragon turned as Elizabeth Pendragon, thirtieth monarch and first queen of Albion, rose singing from the burning castle. As she came, the flames that licked red tongues from the windows and left black scars on the stone came with her, forming a burning wheel that turned behind her in the air. Then the scars of soot and ash themselves came, forming great black shadows in the bright fire. Elizabeth, in white, was untouched.

She came near, and Emily could see a red rose in her hand.

"Release him," said Elizabeth, and the dragon dropped Michael to the stones, where he lay still. As the gray beast beat its wings and rose to meet the queen, Emily ran to the young wizard. He was breathing, but just barely, and his blood ran in the gutters between cobbles as it leaked from his body.

The ground shook with a mighty crash, and Emily looked up to see Elizabeth driving the dragon bodily to the ground, with one hand on its throat. The firestorm that surrounded her had become huge wings of flame and smoke that dwarfed those of the dragon. The beast struggled and with a great roar, broke free of the Elizabeth's grip.

"To the queen!" screamed Sir Maximilian, and he ran past Emily, the sword she'd grabbed from the trophy room flashing red in his hand. "To the queen! For Pendragon! For Albion!"

Emily ran after him, though she had no weapon. The two Arthurs were nowhere to be seen, but the squires Luke, Daniel, and Flora were hard on her heels, their own swords blazing in the flames that lit up the night.

The dragon reared up and struck Elizabeth, who tumbled away in midair, lost in a swooping rush of flame. Clinging to the beast's neck was the armored form of Sir Maximilian. As the dragon tried to shake him off, it roared in rage, and the knight leapt. His clutching hands closed around one of its huge, twisted fangs, and somehow he managed to pull himself upright in the dragon's mouth.

It bit down, but Max braced himself, and Emily heard the metallic shriek of his armor twisting as it buckled in the dragon's teeth. He struggled there for a minute, then pulled his sword arm free of the gripping jaws and began to hack at the dragon's exposed throat. From his awkward position in its mouth, he could barely reach, but a few lashes of the sword struck true, and red blood started out from the cuts the supernaturally sharp blade left behind.

Then the dragon squeezed again, and Sir Maximilian was crushed to his knees. In his fight to keep the fangs from closing on him, he dropped the sword, which clattered to the stones just as Emily came up at the dragon's foot.

Without slowing her sprint, she grabbed it, and she leapt. The dragon was still struggling to bite fully through the knight caught between its jaws, and as it thrashed, it lifted its chin and showed a great gleaming length of throat.

Emily found a moment's footing on the dragon's writhing shoulder, and from there she leapt again, straight up. At the top of the jump she swung the sword, two-handed, as though she were swinging her hammer. She felt the briefest moment of resistance as she met the dragon's throat, and then the gray-scaled neck parted and the snarling head fell one way as Emily fell the other.

She hit the ground in a barely controlled roll that rattled her teeth and left her gasping on the ground yards away from the fight. Behind her, the dragon's head crashed to the cobblestones with a final tearing shriek of metal and fang. The colossal gray body took a few steps as blood sprayed from the thrashing neck, then the whole thing collapsed, shaking the square into stillness. The corpse's wings settled over it like a shroud.

Emily stood, shook away mazy thoughts, and ran to the severed head. In its death throes, the dragon had finally closed its jaws around Sir Maximilian, who lay looking up at the moon with a smile on his face. His blood dripped from between the jagged teeth that cut him nearly in half.

"Max! Max, hang on." Emily fell to her knees and took the knight's gauntleted hand. "It's going to be okay, just stay with me."

Max's hazy, swimming eyes found hers. "Sledge… skulking around?"

Emily laughed wheezily. "Just hang on, Max."

"No, listen. You have to understand…" He coughed rackingly, spattering blood around his lips. "Listen. If I had met her in the halls I would have…I would have killed her. Without a thought. But until then…" The knight trailed off as a grimace of pain racked his handsome face.

"Until then, she was your queen," Emily finished.

"She was my queen." Sir Maximilian coughed once, then died.

Emily stood up. The square was very quiet. Turning, she saw Elizabeth Pendragon, just a girl in a white dress, kneeling over Michael's body and holding the red rose. Past her, a few mercenaries stood looking helpless as Scout, Chris McLeod's combat mech, loomed over them threateningly. A few of the townies were now seeking each other out to whisper quiet words of disbelief, and then, slowly, begin the job of sorting out the wounded from the dead.

There was a clatter of metal as Captain Smiertkin threw down his rifle, then unhooked his helmet and threw that down as well. Colonel Liu stepped up to pick up the gun.

"I assume you surrender, Captain?" she asked with a scowl.

"Nobody left alive to pay us," replied the mercenary captain with a shrug. "Turn it in, boys!" He and Colonel Liu began collecting guns and other weapons from the assorted mercenaries, looking for all the world like they were on the same side other than the obvious disgust on Liu's face.

Poet-Captain Dhar, long twin gashes across his chest oozing blood, had gotten the volunteers organized, sending runners along with a few of his guardsmen to the caves where the children were sheltered. A handful were spreading out among the buildings, calling up those who had sheltered in basements and back rooms. The rest were already picking up the wounded and dead on makeshift stretchers and carrying them to the Twisted Wrist, which had its door flung open.

"Emily!" Chris ran up, peeling tactile control gloves off his hands but still wearing the rest of his control suit. Kayo and Andrea were close behind him. The four friends crashed together in a massive group hug that only split up when Madame de Luna approached, literally wringing her hands with anxiety.

"Emily," she began, then her voice failed. Emily turned away from her friends. The innkeeper was spattered with blood, with a black eye starting to show. The naked pain on her face, though, clearly came from within. Nevertheless, she made an effort to keep her voice steady as she asked, "Emily, have you—have you seen Julian?"

"He…" Emily paused, her mind racing, then plunged ahead. "He was killed when the bomb went off in the castle. I'm so, so sorry. He fought so bravely, but he was right there when they set it off."

"I see," said Madame de Luna in a surprisingly calm voice. She stood in silence for a minute, her eyes flickering back and forth as though watching the entire battle play out again. "You saw him? When the bomb went off?"

"Yes," said Emily, her heart pounding as though she were still in the fight. "I'm so sorry. But—but I'm sure he'd be so happy to know that the Wrist will be getting its clients back, now that this is all over. All he wanted was to keep you and Finalhaven safe."

"No, I think I'll be leaving," the inkeeper replied. "I could never cook like Julian could. See you around, Emily."

259

She turned and set off before Emily could reply, so the young fighter just stood and watched the woman go, her gray-streaked black hair swinging as she headed towards an empty future.

The next night, with the great hall collapsed and the Twisted Wrist turned into a makeshift triage center, the celebration, such as it was, was held in the town square. After everyone had slept and eaten a huge breakfast cooked by Wentworth, they'd dragged the dragon's huge corpse back to the castle to be dealt with later. The better part of the day had been spent picking through the rubble in the collapsed section of the castle, though serious repairs would have to wait. Meanwhile, Dhar and the castle guard had locked the surviving mercenaries in the dungeons; the mercs hadn't protested, and in fact seemed in fairly good spirits, joking and discussing what their next contract might be after they'd been ransomed.

After that, there was nothing left for the Irregulars, the guard, the Albians, and the townies to do but gather and share their colossal astonishment at surviving.

They filled Finalhaven town square, gathered around the fountain where they had stood fearfully clutching spears and swords and guns less than twenty-four hours earlier. Townies and guardsmen mingled with Irregulars and servants from the castle, and the three Albian squires were surrounded by local kids their age with worshipful stars in their eyes.

The first round was drunk in silence, in memory of Alexander Cho, Sir Richard, Captain Queen, Julian de Luna, Merry, and Sir Maximilian, as well as the handful of townsfolk who had been killed and Wulf Blodring, who had indeed not returned. Both Arthurs were among the injured, unconscious on stretchers in the Twisted Wrist, having fought fiercely in every step of the battle.

Incredibly, Michael was not only alive but seemed as though the dragon had barely scratched him. Emily hugged him fiercely as soon as he came into view, walking down the dusty road from the castle hand in hand with Elizabeth Pendragon. She smiled at Elizabeth too, but found herself shy about meeting the queen's eyes. Kayo, who had stuck by Emily's elbow all day, also seemed in awe of Elizabeth's display of power.

"Michael, you are a hell of a wizard," Emily said with sincerity.

"I'll say," put in Kayo from Emily's side. "I'm Kayo Jackson. You are…?"

"Taken," said Emily with a laugh and a sharp elbow in Kayo's ribs.

"Hey, can't blame me for trying," Kayo said with a shrug.

"And this is Her Majesty Queen Elizabeth the First of Albion," Emily continued. A stunned look crossed Kayo's face and she began a curtsey that became a sort of kneel, then stood up quickly when she realized she wasn't being knighted.

"Your honor," Kayo said.

Elizabeth laughed, and suddenly she was just a girl again, and Emily and Michael joined in, and then Kayo did too. Silently, Emily and Elizabeth hugged, and when they pulled apart, there were tears in Emily's eyes.

"What are you going to do?" she asked Elizabeth and Michael. "The protective spell must be broken. And call me crazy, but I'm pretty sure everyone saw you."

"We're going on the run," said Michael, taking Elizabeth's hand. "Once the Arthurs wake up, they'll be after her."

"So you're just gonna run forever?" asked Andrea, coming up with wine glasses for all of them.

"At least we'll be together," said Michael.

"And the fresh air will be nice," agreed Elizabeth.

"A queen in exile," said Andrea thoughtfully. "Huh. Hey, if you don't mind me asking, why are the squires being so, like, cool about this? Shouldn't they be trying to kill you, too?"

"They're young enough to know better," Elizabeth said. "I expect Daniel and Flora will fall in line when their knights take up the hunt again. As for Luke…it's all right, Luke, you can join us."

Emily looked in surprise, and indeed, Luke had been standing suspiciously nearby with his back turned, pretending as hard as he could that he wasn't eavesdropping.

"I, um…" Luke looked at his feet. "I just wanted to say something to Miss Sledge."

"Go ahead," said Emily gently.

"I'm sorry I ratted you out to the senior staff," Luke said quietly. "You were right about your plan."

"Well," said Emily, "I was lucky that Ernest and Wulf volunteered. They got the job done."

"That's another thing," said Luke. He still couldn't quite seem to meet her eyes. "I ran into Ernest when he was waiting for you in the great hall. I tried to get him not to do it."

"Oh, Luke." Emily shook her head. "Why?"

"Well, I thought I should go myself. You know, to make up for being a rat earlier. I don't know, it seemed like the right thing to do. I didn't know you were going to send Wulf, otherwise I would have volunteered for that instead."

Emily sighed. "I wasn't planning to. He insisted."

"Do you think he's okay? Wherever he is?"

"I honestly don't know. I haven't had a chance to talk to Ernest since he got back—"

"See?" Ernest's voice boomed jovially as the tall Mental drew up with Chris McLeod in his wake. "I told you they'd be talking about me!"

"God, how do you do that?" asked Michael with fake weariness. Ernest pulled him into a bear hug that the young wizard returned gratefully.

"It's lovely to see you, too," said Ernest. "Emily, just forgive Luke already. No harm done. And Luke, last I saw, Wulf was being dragged away by six guards, one of whom he'd just bitten quite savagely. So I expect he's alive. Somewhere."

"For the love of God, Ernest, will you please tell us what happened already?" Michael's fake exasperation was back, but he had a huge smile on his face. "I'm sick of asking and you've got a perfectly good audience now."

Ernest took a breath, then blew it out as his shoulders slumped. "Let us just say that your favorite poet is not intended for the adventuring life. If not for Wulf, I would have...well. Leaping ahead to the intellectually stimulating part, I only made it back out thanks to a most intelligent young man in Madawaska."

"Chris?" Emily said in surprise. She'd had time to hug her Mental friend, but not much more, and had yet to hear the story of how Ernest had recruited him to the defense of the Castle Forlorn.

Chris raised his missing eyebrow. "It just so happens that our lab was doing a wide-band gate frequency scan at the time Ernest was trying to punch his way back out through the Veil." With a glance at Andrea, he continued, "In other words, we had the radio on when Ernest was DJing."

"And Mr. McLeod very kindly unlocked the door for me, if I may mix metaphors," Ernest finished. "And not a moment too soon, thanks." He rubbed his shirt above his ribcage, where Emily guessed some secret injury lurked.

"The moment Ernest mentioned your name, Emily, we were able to put the pieces together pretty quickly." Chris smiled. "Did you know Ernest is Professor Graves's son? I had no idea...well, after we called Andy and Kayo we were able to stay pretty entertained on the drive down from Madawaska."

"Are you two still stuck together?" said Colonel Liu with a laugh, coming up with a mug of beer in her hand. "I swear, you put two Mentals together and it's like Velcro. You have to peel 'em apart by hand."

"A better metaphor might be superglue," advised Ernest.

"Or two electromagnets of opposite polarity," Chris put in.

"Enough! Enough!" Liu held up her hands in surrender.

"Colonel, is General Alder still in the dungeon?" Emily interrupted.

The Colonel sighed. "Yes, he survived. I'll be bringing him to the Lancers tomorrow." She shook her head. "The dragon's last revenge, to see his greatest enemy brought so low."

"Yeah, what was that whole thing about?" asked Michael. "Between Alder and the dragon."

"Well, it's complicated." Liu took a swig from her mug. "It seems that Alder never really defeated the dragon, *per se*. Rather, he tricked him into passing through a rip in the Veil. I think he figured that was the end of the old beast, but that rip must have lined up with the gate you found. So the dragon came out the other end into whatever political mess you saw a part of, and started to rebuild its power base."

"Commodore Dragon, huh?" said Ernest.

"Meanwhile," continued Liu, "Alder needed some sort of proof that he'd killed the thing, so he faked up the dragon's head that hangs in the Guild Hall."

"He made a fake dragon's head?" asked Kayo incredulously. "That tricked the Lancers?"

Liu shrugged. "Well, he was a genius. Anyway, I guess the victory, such as it was, went to his head. He...every Lancer has a personal crest, sort of a secret name within the society. General Alder took the dragon's name for his own crest. Sort of a way of showing off, showing dominance, I don't know."

"But dragon's names aren't just names," Kayo said.

"No," agreed Liu. "They're spells, sort of. Old magic."

"Taking a dragon's name as your own..." Kayo looked thoughtful and a little freaked out. "That would change you, I think. Corrupt you. And it would give the dragon control over you, in a way."

"What did you say your name was?" asked Colonel Liu. "And have you ever thought of joining the Lancers? We're about to have a leadership crisis."

264

Kayo laughed. "I'm due in Cascadia in the fall, but I'm up for a little consulting this summer."

Colonel Liu nodded. "Come with me to Boston. You can help me explain everything to the Lancers."

"What are you doing after that?" Emily asked Liu. "Are you going to stay with the Lancers?"

"Well, yes. I think so. But I also think I've earned a bit of a sabbatical. So...honestly, I'm going to try to find Bronwyn." Liu look away. "To apologize."

"Emily Sledge, how did I know I'd find you at the middle of this mess?" Emily jumped at the high, sweet voice behind her.

"Clea?" Emily turned, frowning. "What the hell are you doing here?"

Clea Coates, wearing the same sharp suit and perfect hair as always, waggled her soft fingers in greeting. "Hello, darling! Here on Commonwealth business, of course. Just making a quick report about whatever it is you got up to here." From her jacket pocket, Clea produced a notepad and an expensive-looking fountain pen covered with a swirling, flowery pattern. "Now, would you say the destruction in the castle is *a*, entirely your fault; *b*, mostly your fault; or *c*, primarily your fault?"

Emily's fists clenched and she took a step towards Clea, spitting as her mouth worked overtime to put out the most hurtful words it could. Suddenly she felt a strong hand on her shoulder, and a warm voice said, "Miss Coates, I understand you're from the prime minister's office. I'm Poet-Captain Dhar, leader of the castle guard, which puts me very approximately in charge of this circus. Why don't you come over here to this bench and take my report?"

Emily's rage collapsed as suddenly as it had come, and instead of punching Clea's head in, she found herself wrapping up Dhar in a tight hug. Tears were starting in her eyes.

"And you, Emily, should probably head over to the Twisted Wrist." Dhar smiled as he worked himself free of the hug.

Emily looked over her shoulder. Ernest and Chris were back in deep conversation, as were Kayo and Colonel Liu. Michael and Elizabeth had slipped away at some point during the conversation—getting a head start? Andrea seemed to be discussing the finer points of sword technique with Luke, who was looking at her with his mouth half open as she parried, thrust, and lunged with a glass of wine in each hand.

Only one thing seemed to be missing as her two worlds collided in a great shower of sparks: Jack.

She peeled herself off from the group without any of them noticing and made her way to the Twisted Wrist, which sat with its door closed and only a dim light in its windows. It looked sad and cold, as though the soul had been drained from it, leaving it a corpse where it had once been a living thing.

Quietly she pushed open the door, and stood at the top of the steps taking in the scene. The tables and chairs had all been pushed up against the walls, and stretchers stood in silent rows, filled with the injured. As she watched, one of the Arthurs moaned and stirred for a moment, then went still.

Walking slowly between the ranks of cots, Emily almost didn't hear Jack's quiet voice calling her name. She turned to see him lying on one elbow in a bed in a far shadowed corner of the tavern, looking even more pale than usual, but with a wide grin on his face.

She sat on the cot and watched as he propped himself up into a sitting position. As he moved, he planted a hand near her and without thinking, she put one of hers on top of it, curling her fingers around in a protective grip.

"I'm glad you're okay," she whispered.

"Me too," Jack murmured back.

They sat in silence for a while, hand in hand. Finally, Jack said, "I don't suppose you ever wanted to live in a castle?"

Emily snorted a gentle laugh. "You mean you won't be returning home to your lord father in Deseret?"

Jack gave a little shake of his head. "That was never my home. Dad never bothered to make it one."

"You know I'm not going to stay, right?" Emily said gently.

"You could lead the Irregulars," said Jack. "We'll need you."

"I think it's time either you or Ernest put aside your daddy issues and stepped up."

"Captain Jack?" He laughed. "I don't think so. But Captain Graves sounds good. Very romantic. He'll like that."

"He will," Emily agreed. "He'll do a good job. Dhar worships him, which will make things easy with the guard."

"True." Jack pursed his lips. "Now, when you say you're not going to stay. I get it. I do. If anybody knows the benefits of a vagabond's life, it's me."

"Jack…" Emily began, but he cut her off.

"Hang on. I'm not asking you to stay forever. Just one night. There's celebrating to do."

"Jack, you're in no condition to get out of bed," Emily said with mock seriousness.

"I never said anything about getting out of bed," Jack replied.

So she stayed.

AFTERWORD

5 DAYS AFTER

The door at the top of the stairs in the Guild Hall of the Most Excellent Brotherhood of Lancers, New World Chapter had been repaired quite nicely, Emily thought. The splintered wood had been glued back into place, sanded, and relacquered, and if there was a bit of a line where one of the ornate hinges had bent nearly in half, well, that was understandable.

She knocked and steeled herself for the worst. The worst opened the door in the form of Mr. Treat, looking as wiry and unamused as ever, until his tight face melted into open shock at the sight of Emily standing on the top step and staring him dead in the eye.

"I'm here to apologize," said Emily.

Treat looked her up and down with a raised eyebrow, then said, "Come in."

They sat on overstuffed chairs in the drawing room, where Emily noticed immediately that the gray dragon's head had been removed. There was nothing yet in its place, and the wall was somewhat discolored in the shape of the shield-like mount that had held it.

"Now, Miss Sledge, I believe you said something about an apology?" asked Treat tightly.

"Yes," Emily agreed. "I'm sorry for all the damage I did to your property. The door, all the chalk marks, your secret drawer. Was that everything?"

"I believe you also knocked over a mop bucket in one of the closets," said Treat.

"Right," said Emily, "sorry about that. But Mr. Treat, I'm not sorry for breaking in. General Alder was growing more and more sick and you guys thought you could just stash him away on a faraway island and be rid of him. That wasn't right, and it got people killed. It would have gotten everyone on Finalhaven killed if I hadn't broken in here, so I can't apologize for that."

As she'd spoken, Treat's face had gotten more and more twisted up in visible anger. Emily braced herself for what was about to spill out: a lecture, screaming, maybe another painful twist of her arm.

Instead, Treat blew out a long sigh, as though he'd been holding his breath for years and was finally allowed to breathe.

"Yes, you're absolutely right, Miss Sledge. Our treatment of Marshall Alder will be a black mark upon the Lancers for generations to come. And of course, we are grateful to you for putting an end to the Gray of the Island once and for all. I understand you did the fatal deed yourself."

"That's right," said Emily. She'd hated to give the sword back after the fight was over, but part of her was relieved to see it go. She'd been having a hard time not thinking of it as the sword that killed Sir Maximilian as well as the dragon.

"Have you ever considered a position as a dragonslayer?" asked Treat.

"Not really my scene, but thanks," Emily replied. "It's hard to be a dragonslayer when you're all out of dragons."

"Your point is well taken," agreed Treat somberly.

"I do have a request, though. A favor, for saving your honor and everything."

"Let me guess," said Treat. "Your father's job."

"Got it in one."

"Well, you'll be pleased to know that I never let him go in the first place."

"What, seriously?" Emily closed her mouth, which she had left hanging open.

"Who better than Robert to clean up all the damage you caused?"

That night, Emily met Durgan dun Raven at a bar called Gray's in Boston's Jamaica Plain neighborhood. She didn't know if dun Raven had picked the bar out of some deep-hidden sense of ironic humor, or whether the name was just a coincidence, but either way she was surprised to find that it was packed full of regular, non-Gifted folks and wholly lacking in the secret signs and strange decorating taste that usually marked places haunted by the Gifted.

Emily found him at the bar itself, taking up two stools and looking very strange in a T-shirt and jeans that did nothing to turn attention away from his massive frame and shaggy head. She squeezed in between him and a drunk young woman who had been trying to get his attention and muttered a nasty name under her breath as she slunk away.

"Sledge!" dun Raven shouted as he turned to take her in.

"Good to see you, too," said Emily with feeling.

"Here, drink this," said dun Raven, shoving a shot glass towards her.

"Am I allowed to?" Emily regarded the shot uncertainly. "This isn't a Gifted bar, right? I don't really understand all the laws of the mundane world but I don't think they even should have let me in here."

"Hmm," rumbled dun Raven. "Better not, then." He snatched up the shot and tossed it back. "Anyhow. Welcome to the Sabre & Torch."

"Really?" Emily sat up straight, feeling like an electric shock had just run up her spine.

"You completed your mission. Went above and beyond, even." Dun Raven began ticking points off on his massive fingers. "Showed no fear.

270

Aided your fellow man. Killed the last dragon known to exist. I'd say you qualify."

"Thank you!" said Emily. "I'm happy to accept. I guess I just expected more...ceremony, I don't know."

"Been spending too much time with Lancers," said dun Raven.

"They're not all bad, you know," Emily said.

"I know," the huge warrior agreed. "There are worse people to be in the shit with."

They sat in silence for a while, dun Raven drinking heavily with no apparent results and Emily just watching him and taking in the scene. It was strange to think that these people who surrounded her had no idea, no way of knowing, about what she'd just gone through. There was a good chance not a person in the bar aside from dun Raven would even believe her if she told them the story of the last few weeks.

But they seemed happy, for the most part. Some sat in pairs, others in laughing, shouting, groups, and the one man who sat alone had a newspaper for company. Happy enough for now, Emily supposed. And most of all: safe.

Looking at the crowd, Emily couldn't help but think of the friends she'd left behind on Finalhaven. In the short time she'd been there they'd spent so much time just like this, drinking and laughing. Those days were already starting to feel like a dream, intense but short. But that was how it was with friendships, wasn't it? They were your whole life for a while, until life rolled on and people moved away. Her friends from Harkness had come when she needed them, then scattered again. The Irregulars of the Castle Forlorn would surely be the same.

Wouldn't they?

"Sledge," said dun Raven suddenly. Emily looked back at him, up at the heavily scarred face that was splitting in a broken-toothed grin as he swept a gaze up and down the latest properly inducted member of the Sabre & Torch Society. "Time for your next mission."

ABOUT THE AUTHOR

Nathaniel Webb, aka Nat20, is an author, musician, and game designer. As a lead guitarist, he has toured and recorded with numerous acts including Grammy-nominated singers Beth Hart and Jana Mashonee and Colombian pop star Marre. His published writing includes the GameLit novel *Expedition: Summerlands*, various short stories and novellas, and adventures and supplements for the tabletop RPGs *Shadow of the Demon Lord* and *Godless*.

A graduate of Phillips Exeter Academy and Wesleyan University, Nathaniel lives in Portland, Maine with his wife and son under a massive pile of cats. He can be found @nat20w on Twitter and Facebook, where he mostly talks about games, writing, and obscure 80s progressive rock.